THE
SEPTEMBER
SOCIETY

**Center Point
Large Print**

Also by Charles Finch and available from
Center Point Large Print:

The Fleet Street Murders

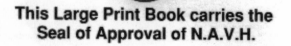

**This Large Print Book carries the
Seal of Approval of N.A.V.H.**

THE
SEPTEMBER
SOCIETY

Charles Finch

CENTER POINT LARGE PRINT
THORNDIKE, MAINE

This Center Point Large Print edition
is published in the year 2010 by arrangement with
St. Martin's Press

Copyright © 2008 by Charles Finch

All rights reserved.

The text of this Large Print edition is unabridged.
In other aspects, this book may vary
from the original edition.
Printed in the United States of America.
Set in 16-point Times New Roman type.

ISBN: 978-1-60285-666-0

Library of Congress Cataloging-in-Publication Data

Finch, Charles (Charles B.)
   The September Society / Charles Finch.
      p. cm.
   ISBN 978-1-60285-666-0 (library binding : alk. paper)
   1. Private investigators—England—Fiction.
      2. Missing persons—Investigation—Fiction. 3. College students—England—Fiction.
      4. Lincoln College (University of Oxford)—Fiction. 5. Large type books. I. Title.
   PS3606.I526S46 2010
   813'.6—dc22
2009041194

For Rosie, Julia, Henry, and Isabelle,
with a brother's deepest love

ACKNOWLEDGMENTS

I'm profoundly thankful to the people who made this book possible: Kate Lee, Charles Spicer, Michael Homler, Hector DeJean, Tara Cibelli, Larissa Silva, Sam Truitt, Louise Crelly, Harriet Bloomstein, James Dawson, John Hill, Richard McCabe, Stephen Finch, Charles Finch, Angela Finch, and, of course, Anne Truitt.

I'm also blessed with amazing friends: Rachel Blitzer, Matt McCarthy, John Phillips, Chris Compton, Dan Compton, Tom Jenkins, James Kelly, Nuala Trainor, Rob Crowe, Laurence Publicover, Sarah Tate, Kelly Jones, and the terrific Emily Popp.

My good friend Ben Reiter read an early draft of *The September Society* and improved it substantially with his suggestions.

I want to reserve special mention for my parents: for my father, who has given me much love and support, and my mother, who remembers all those trips to the library and who has always been my best friend.

PROLOGUE

The first murders were committed nineteen years before the second, on a dry and unremarkable day along the Sutlej Frontier in Punjab.

It was beastly hot weather, as Juniper remarked to Captain Lysander out on the veranda of the officers' mess, fit for little more than an odd gin and tonic, perhaps the lazy composition of a letter home. The flies, maddening creatures that had never learned to take no for an answer, crowded around the nets that blocked the porch, searching for a way in. "I would trade a hand to be back in London," Lysander said to Juniper after a long pause. "At least they have the decency to bar these flies from coming into the city there."

The battalion was on edge, because a recent retaliatory raid on a local village had turned bloody. Suspicion and rumor abounded. The officers, with a few exceptions, had long ceased to attend to their charges' morale. Though all the Englishmen in Punjab lived well, with villas and servants to themselves, every one of them at that uneasy moment would have made the trade Lysander proposed.

"Well," said Juniper. "I may go look around and have a bit of a shoot with Jim."

"Were you planning that?"

"Oh, yes."

"Where do you reckon you'll go?"

"That little patch of scrub east of here. Doubt we'll find anything worth a bullet. Maybe a darkie or two, looking for trouble."

Lysander smiled grimly. "Past that little grove of banyan trees, then?"

"Curious today, aren't you?"

In another place this might have sounded rude, but being white was a great equalizer in that country, and these men were too intimate to maintain entirely the ceremonies of respect and rank that defined the British.

"Always on the lookout for a decent bit of shooting, you know," responded Lysander, sipping his gin and tonic. He was a trim, forceful, savvy-looking man. "D'you know why they give us so much tonic, young pup?"

"No. Why?"

"Has quinine in it. Prevents malaria."

"I suppose I did know that, actually."

"They must've told you in training."

"Yes," said Juniper, nodding agreeably.

"Just past that grove of banyan trees, then?" There was a slight, casual persistence in Lysander's voice. "Ever shot anything edible there?"

"Not to speak of. There are a few birds, not much on the ground. It's poor sport."

"So's this whole country."

"Any more inspirational speech before I leave?"

"On your way."

Juniper stood up. "I'm sure I'll see you for cocktails."

But he wouldn't, and the other man knew it.

When Juniper had gone out of sight, Lysander leapt out of his chair and walked briskly up a small dirt path that led from the mess to his villa. The captain's batman, his assistant and a lance corporal, was on the porch, whittling an Indian charm to send back to his mother. He had been working on it for weeks.

"Best go do it now," Lysander said. "He's off with Juniper. Both of them, would you? They're hunting, out east, in that scrub."

"Yes, sir," said the batman, standing. Here rank still meant something.

"Do your best to make it look like an accident, obviously."

"Yes, sir."

Lysander paused. "By the way, that treasure?"

"Yes, sir?"

"There's talk of a society. Don't know what it's to be called yet, and it will be for officers alone."

"Sir?"

"But if you do right by us, we'll do right by you."

"Thank you, sir."

The batman ran off, and Lysander called to one

of the servants, a fair Indian lad, swathed in brilliant pink and pale blue that contrasted with the dull beige of the landscape and the military man's uniform. The boy with some sullenness came forward.

"That box," Lysander barked. "Bring it to me. And it's worth your life to open it before it gets here."

A moment later he was holding the box, and, when certain he was alone, he opened it to reveal a massive, pristine, and beautiful sapphire.

As he snapped the box shut and had it taken away, Juniper and his friend Jim emerged from the latter's house, guns broken over their arms, both wearing beige, broad-brimmed hats to keep the dying sun off of their necks and faces. They had a bantering style of conversation that sounded as if it had been picked up from a thousand other conversations before. It was clear how much closer they were than Juniper and Lysander.

"A farthing says you'll never eat what you shoot," Juniper said with a laugh.

"A farthing? I've played higher stakes than that with women."

"That serving girl of mine you like, then."

"What do I have to eat?"

"First thing either of us shoots."

"What if it's the dirt?"

"Bet's a bet."

"How much dirt would I have to eat?"

"Nice haunch of it."

"Farthing for the first meat, let's go back to that. Don't shoot anything too horrible."

"I'm insulted you'd suggest it."

It was a little more than a mile outside of camp, away from Lahore—and that city's dangers, which these two men knew all too well—that they found a decent patch of land. It had a few bushes and trees scattered around it. They didn't have a dog, but Juniper shot into the undergrowth and drove a few birds out into the open, where the two men had a clear look at them.

They observed the birds fluttering, partially obscured, soon to be dead. Ruminatively, Juniper said, "What do you miss most? About England?"

His interlocutor thought it over. "I wish I hadn't left it so badly with my family, you know. I miss them."

"I do, too."

"Only six months, I suppose."

Then both men heard a scratching emerge from the undergrowth that lay off to their side.

A shot. The fall of a body. Another shot. The fall of a body. A lone figure, Lysander's batman, rose from his hidden spot and ran off full bore back west. And then a long, long silence, in the empty land that stretched blank as far as the eye could see, in every direction, forty-five hundred miles away from Piccadilly Circus.

CHAPTER ONE

The only question left, he felt, was how to handle the matter—how it was to be done. Not if, for he had made his mind up entirely. Nor when; the moment would arise on its own.

But how?

Charles Lenox, noted amateur detective and scion of an ancient Sussex family, spent most of the morning of September 2, 1866, wandering around his study and pondering his few, daunting options. Normally imperturbable, he seemed during these long hours like a restless man. To begin he would sit heavily in one of the two armchairs by the low fire; then he would lean forward to tap the tobacco ash from his pipe into the embers; then he would stand up and walk across the room to shuffle the letters on his desk, or switch one book with another in the shelves along the wall, or straighten a picture that was to some imperceptible degree tilted; then he would return to his armchair, fill his pipe, and begin the entire dance again.

He was a lean man with a friendly face—even in the morning's preoccupation—hazel eyes, and a short brown beard. His carriage was upright, and as he paced he clasped his hands behind his

12

back. It gave him a pensive air, the kind he had during the most difficult moments of his cases. But there was no case at hand this morning.

All of this pacing and worrying and sitting and standing took place in a handsome white house on Hampden Lane, just off Grosvenor Square. Fifteen paces down the front hall and to the right was this large library, a rectangular, high-ceilinged room with a desk near the door, a fireplace and chairs at the end of the room, a row of tall windows along the front wall, and books everywhere else. It was where he spent the great majority of his time at home, both anxious and happy alike. He pondered his cases there, and on wet, foggy days like this one, he pondered the world—or the part of it that Hampden Lane occupied—through his trickling windowpanes.

At ten he rang for coffee and at a quarter past he rang to have it taken away, cold and untouched. Graham, his butler, looked concerned but said nothing as he came to and fro. By eleven, however, he could no longer prevent himself from intervening, and presented himself unbidden in the dark oak doorway of the room.

At that moment Lenox had just taken up residence at his desk, where he was looking across the street at the bookshop.

"May I get you anything else, sir?" Graham said.

"No, no," said Lenox distractedly, still peering through the rain-touched window.

"If I may venture to say so, sir, you seem anxious."

In many of the aristocratic Mayfair households surrounding Hampden Lane, such a statement would have seemed like the highest impertinence. Lenox and Graham had a long and complex history, though, and in the end were friends more than master and man. While Graham, a sandy-haired man with perfectly arranged clothes and a strong, utterly honest face, always spoke and behaved respectfully, he never hesitated to disagree with Lenox, often helped the detective in his work, and even, on rare occasions, spoke with the frankness he just had.

"Eh?" said Lenox, at last looking up. "Oh, no, Graham—no, thank you, I'm quite all right."

"Will you take your lunch here in the library, sir?"

"No," said Lenox. "Thanks, I'm having lunch in the City, actually. I shall be glad to get on the other side of these four walls."

"Indeed, sir," said Graham. He paused before adding, "I am in the hall if you require anything."

"Thank you," said Lenox.

Graham withdrew then, and Lenox sighed. Well! he thought to himself. If Graham had noticed, it had gone too far. He would have to stop worrying and go to lunch with his brother. Standing with a decisive air, Lenox patted the pockets of his jacket and went through the double doors of the library out into the hallway.

"Graham, will you call out the carriage, please? I think I'll leave now."

"Of course, sir."

"I'll be waiting at Chaffanbrass's while they rub down the horses."

"Yes, sir," Graham said as he began to walk downstairs. "It shouldn't be longer than a quarter of an hour."

In the front hall, Lenox took his overcoat down from its peg and pulled his umbrella out of its stand. Then he took a breath, ducked outside into the rain, and crossed the street, dodging several hansom cabs and a landau with no inconsiderable agility to get to the bookshop. He pulled open the door and saw the proprietor.

"Mr. Chaffanbrass," he said with a smile. "How do you do?"

"Mr. Lenox!" said Mr. Chaffanbrass, beaming at him from behind a small counter. "Happy anniversary!"

"Oh?"

"The fire!"

"Ah, of course."

As it happened, that very day, September 2, was the two hundredth anniversary of the Great Fire of 1666; what had started as a minor conflagration at the Pudding Lane bakery of Thomas Farriner, baker to Charles II, eventually consumed four-fifths of central London. By some miracle only a handful of people had died—the traditional count was reckoned at eight—but thirteen thousand buildings and nearly a hundred churches had vanished. Of the eighty thousand residents of the city, seventy thousand were left homeless. In a year that was already being heralded in some parts as the apocalypse because it contained the Number of the Beast, 666, few needed persuading in the first heady hours after the three-day blaze that the world was at an end.

"And yet," said Lenox, "my grandfather always said the fire did our city two great services."

"What do you mean?"

"For one thing, it allowed Wren to build his fifty churches, as well as St. Paul's Cathedral. The fire is the reason we live in such a beautiful city, Mr. Chaffanbrass."

"And the second reason?"

"Do you know how many people died of the plague in 1665?"

"How many?"

"About sixty-five thousand, and that despite two-thirds of Londoners leaving the city. The fire killed so many rats and fleas, leveled so many derelict buildings, that in the end it probably saved tens of thousands of lives."

Ruminatively, Mr. Chaffanbrass said, "Perhaps it's received a bad press, then."

"Perhaps," Lenox agreed. "Still, it would be better all around if it didn't happen again. Incidentally, has my copy of *Pickwick* come in yet?"

"It hasn't yet, I very much fear."

"Can't be helped," said Lenox.

"It will prove worth the wait, though! The finest red leather, with gold inlay!"

"And all the words inside?"

"Every last one!"

Ancient, homey, and comfortable, Calum's was one of the best bookshops around, small and a little dark with rows of crammed bookshelves along the walls. Mr. Chaffanbrass's squat counter stood in the middle of the room, just next to a freestanding oven that usually had a kettle on and a comfortable chair beside it. The owner himself was a very small, cheerful man, with red cheeks, tidy white hair, and a large belly. He wore perfectly round spectacles and a tweed suit, and the majority of his life was spent behind the counter and next to the warmth of the oven, reading. There was always a turned-down book on the arm of his chair.

"Anything else new?" asked Lenox.

"Nothing you haven't seen, no. Wait, though!" As Mr. Chaffanbrass skittered to the back of the store, Lenox looked idly through the books on the counter. Presently the gentleman came back with a small volume in his hand.

"What do you make of that, Mr. Lenox?" he said. "A new translation."

Lenox looked at the flyleaf. It was a thin, pebbled brown copy of *The Praise of Folly* by Erasmus, with an accompanying essay by one of the dons at Cambridge.

"Why not. May I take it?"

"Yes, of course. A poor bookseller I'd be if I said no," said Mr. Chaffanbrass, placing his hands on his stomach and chortling.

"Thanks. I'll be off, then."

"Wrapped?"

"No," said Lenox. "I need something to read straight away."

"As you please," said Mr. Chaffanbrass, taking a short stub of pencil from his breast pocket, opening a ledger, and making a small tick. "On your bill, then?"

"Graham will be around on the fifteenth."

"No doubt of it. I set my calendar by him!"

He said this with satisfaction and then shook Lenox's hand with great vigor, getting redder and redder and smiling furiously. After this brief ceremony he sat down again with a sigh and took his book up, groping with his other hand for a piece of toast on the stovetop. He would burn himself sooner or later. As far as Lenox could tell, the bookseller's diet consisted of dozens of pieces of toast a day, each followed by a cup of milky coffee. Not the regimen recommended by the best physicians, perhaps, but it suited him.

On the street again, wet smoke clouded the air. The drizzle continued. It had been a beautiful late summer until then, but perhaps they were in for a wet September, he thought. It would be too bad. He looked back across the street toward his brightly lit house and saw his carriage waiting, the horses occasionally stamping their feet and the driver huddled underneath a thick black coat to keep the rain off, with only a pipe protruding out of the coat's hood, its ember occasionally brightening to orange. Lenox dodged another cab and stepped into the carriage, and with a word to the driver he was on his way to meet his brother.

And while he was looking forward to lunch—and while he took pleasure in examining his new book—he could not rid himself of the question he had been asking himself for weeks, as well as that entire morning: How on God's green earth was he supposed to ask one of his oldest friends, Lady Jane Grey, to be his wife?

CHAPTER TWO

The sun rose mild the next morning, a rich, burnished gold that flooded the back of Parliament and the stone houses along the Thames, a light with pink at its edges. The air was cool, but warming. Along the windswept boulevards that ran by the river, lonely men on anonymous errands hurried past. On the currents, watermen poled their skiffs down each bank, collecting rubbish or ferrying supplies out to small ships. A single long barge, covered with coal, proceeded regally down the center of the river, demanding a wide berth. And under the shadow of Big Ben, on the river's western edge, Lenox gave a great final stroke of his oars, ran aground on the gravelly bank, and bent over his knees, panting.

Two or three mornings a week—providing he didn't have a case—he brought his single scull out to the river by Hammersmith and had a long pull back to his neighborhood, Mayfair, which stood behind Parliament. The person who liked this least was the driver of his carriage, who had to fit the scull to the roof and then wait for Lenox's slow return to fetch it again. But to Lenox himself it was a singular pleasure. He loved to row in the morning, his body warming itself with the world.

It was an old habit. At his school, Harrow, one of the beaks from his house, Druries (where Lord Byron had been, not to mention Lord Palmerston, who had died only a year before), had noticed Lenox's height and asked him to come row for the house team. After that he had rowed at Oxford, in the Balliol college eight (he had never been big enough to row for the Blues) and upon graduation had made himself a present of a single scull. It was battered and old-fashioned now, but he still loved it. The exercise kept him trim, and simply to be on the river was a great privilege.

Lenox took a last gulp of air and stepped out of the vessel. His driver was waiting with a cup of cold tea and a cloak—and when he had placed the latter on Lenox's shoulders, hoisted the scull over his head and moved slowly toward the carriage. Lenox sipped the tea gratefully, thirsty, and called out, "I'll walk home," to the driver. Then he climbed the stairs from the riverbank to the street, every muscle in his legs crying out for mercy, and with an exhausted happiness fill-ing his body started on the short trot home.

It was a little past seven in the morning, and Lady Jane was coming to have breakfast at eight. When he reached home, Lenox hurriedly bathed and dressed, checked to see what Ellie, the cook, was preparing, and with a quarter of an hour till his friend's arrival sat down to look over the morning post. There wasn't much in it, beyond a letter about Hadrian's Rome from one of his Italian correspondents, who wrote half in English and half in Latin, and who disagreed vociferously with Lenox about the social breadth of slavery. Lenox read the letter with some amusement and then tucked it into the book he had bought the day before to remind himself to respond to it.

There was also the card of a man named John Best, whom Lenox had never heard of.

"John Best?" he said to Graham.

"A young man, sir. He was here late yesterday evening."

"Don't know him."

Soon there was a tap at the door, and Lenox knew that Lady Jane had come. His heart fluttered a little, and he had that hollow, happy feeling of unspoken love. Checking his tie, he stood and made his way toward the hall, where Graham would be taking her things.

"Hullo!" he cried out cheerfully upon seeing her.

She turned from Graham, with whom she had been speaking. "Oh, Charles, hello! I'm delighted to see you."

"Likewise, of course. Have you been well?"

She was taking off her gloves, then removing her scarf, then handing over her jacket. "Yes, quite well. But I haven't seen you in ages, Charles."

"It's true," he said. "I'm forced to blame you."

Indeed, it was true. Though their usual routine brought them together every day, or near it, in the past few weeks she had been less available to him than at any time he could remember in the last fifteen years, and just when he most yearned for her presence. He hadn't yet broached the most mysterious point of all: that he had seen

her carriage emerge from the low, poor tene-
ments of the Seven Dials one afternoon the week
before.

"Come, it's only been a few days."

"Yes, but neighbors who are friends ought to
see each other every day."

She laughed. "You feel firmly about that?"

He frowned, pleasantly. "I do."

"Then I shall make more of an effort." She met
him halfway down the hall and gave him a light
kiss on the cheek. "I apologize, Charles."

Lady Jane Grey had been a young widow, her
husband, the heroic and much loved Lord Deere,
having died in battle only a few months after
their marriage. She was from one of the oldest
families in Sussex—older, in fact, than Lenox's—
and the two of them had grown up neighbors,
belonging to the two leading families of their
tucked-away cove of countryside. She was a
pretty and lovable but perhaps not a beautiful
woman, with wide, intelligent, peaceful eyes and
a smiling mouth that ran pink and red depend-
ing on the weather. She rarely dressed inside the
fashion, yet always managed to look fashionable,
and while there were those in London society
who condemned her curling, unostentatious hair
as dull, there were others who thought it her best
asset. Lenox, of course, stood with this latter
group.

In any case, her greatest charm wasn't in her

looks. It was in her character. Her mind was wide-ranging but never pretentious, and a loving sense of humor always lay beneath her speech. She sat at the apex of society in London, and in Sussex when she visited her brother, the Earl of Houghton, at home, but she wore the power that came with her friendships and connections lightly. Rarely was she mercurial in her affections. She had happy friendships awaiting her wherever she went.

Yet people whispered that a kind of sadness trailed her cheerful figure: solitary for so many years, childless, and a widow, after all. Lenox knew that loneliness played no significant role in her life, but he also wondered whether it sometimes came to her in brief, uncertain moments. Still, he never stepped an inch over their friendship's wide borderlines to discover whether his speculation might be correct. When he thought he detected sadness in her mien, he only aimed to be a better friend to her.

That was Lady Jane Grey; Charles Lenox's best friend, and the woman he loved better than anyone else in the world.

They walked arm in arm to the dining room—the room next to Lenox's study, straight down the front hall—where food and coffee were laid out at the far end of a long mahogany table with intricately carved legs and high-backed chairs all around it.

"Well, how have you been?" she asked as Lenox held her chair. "Solved anything recently? Seen much of Edmund?"

"I had lunch with him yesterday, actually. He's quite well. There's some upset with the Ordnance's finance at the moment, but he's working to clear it." Lenox sat across from her. "No cases, though. I wish one would come along."

"I could rob a bank, if you like."

"Would you? Thanks."

She laughed. "But perhaps it's nice to have a break, don't you think? Plan out a trip some-where"—Lenox was a great armchair explorer, though his elaborate plans were often side-tracked by real life—"and figure out what they ate breakfast off of in ancient Rome? Rest your mind, until your next case arrives?"

"You're right, of course. I ought not to com-plain."

"What *did* they eat off of, back then?"

"Plates, I should have said."

"Charles," she said in a tone of mock exaspera-tion.

He laughed. "I'll find out. Promise."

"I'll hold you to that promise." She took another corner of toast from the tray that lay between them and set it by her egg. "Do you know who I saw last night?"

"Who?"

"You won't like it."

"Ah," said Lenox grimly. "Barnard, then?"

"Yes."

George Barnard was the director of the National Mint, a former Member of Parliament, one of the richest men in London, and—Lenox was certain—one of the worst thieves in England's history. For the past several months he had been slowly untangling the web of protection Barnard had built around himself, dismantling the high fortifications of rank and reputation that obscured the truth. He had discovered a seam in the Hammer Gang—Barnard's henchmen—that he might exploit, and had traced back north a possible instance of the director's treachery. But it was long, slow work, and because he had to do it secretly took twice the time with half the results it would have if Barnard had been a common and well-known criminal.

"Was he in good form?" Lenox asked, grumpily pushing a fried mushroom around with his fork. Thinking about Barnard had even managed to dispel his quiet happiness at being alone with Lady Jane.

"Oh, yes, talking about some silver urn he had acquired for his collection."

Lenox snorted. "Collection."

"Don't make that noise," said Lady Jane, though tolerantly. "Have you found anything else out about him?"

"I'm waiting for Skaggs to return from Sheffield. I expect he'll have news."

"Remind me who Skaggs is?"

"The private investigator I use from time to time. He finds the pub an easier fit than I do. Useful chap. More coffee, Jane?"

"Yes, please," she said, and Lenox beckoned a maid to fetch it. In addition to her absence, here was another thing: She seemed—as she had in previous weeks—slightly preoccupied, careworn, and fretful over some secret anxiety. He did his best to cheer her, and wondered how he could discover what that anxiety was.

Their talk turned to the parties that were to occur that week, touched on politics, veered off toward a painter Jane had discovered, and then moved on to a mutual acquaintance of theirs, one Mr. Webb, who had been discovered cheating at the racetrack.

In all their long conversation, however, Lenox never said the only words he had hoped to before her arrival.

CHAPTER THREE

That night in the small hours, just past four o'clock, Lenox lay dreaming beneath the heavy covers of his bed when there was a knock at his door. At first it just nudged his consciousness, and he turned over, hugging the blankets close to his chin. At the second knock, however, he started out of his rest.

"Yes?" he called out.

"May I enter, sir?"

"What? Oh, yes, certainly, Graham. Come in."

Graham opened the door and came a few feet into the room.

"Just a social visit, then?" Lenox said with a smile.

"I'm afraid you have a guest, sir."

"Who is it?" he said, sitting upright and blinking his eyes awake. "Is anything the matter? Is it Jane?"

"No, sir," said Graham, and Lenox's shoulders relaxed an inch. "It is Lady Annabelle Payson."

Annabelle Payson? He had met her once or twice. She must have had a pressing reason to come, as it was well known that she detested London. At eighteen she had made a spectacularly unhappy marriage to James Payson, a captain

28

in the army and lad-about-town in the forties, who had moved her into his West End flat. They had had one son before he died off in the East (some said shot over a card table, though others said it was in battle), and now she lived entirely in the country with her brother.

"Has she said why she's come, Graham?"

"No, sir, though I might venture to say that her ladyship seems agitated."

"Very well," Lenox said with a sigh. "It's a bit of a bother. Do give her some tea, though, won't you? And I'd like a cup myself. I'll be down as soon as I can."

"Yes, sir."

"Decent of you to be so stoic about the interruption to your own rest, by the way."

"Not at all, sir," said Graham.

After the butler left, Lenox went to the west window of his bedroom, which stretched from his knees to the ceiling. Outside there was a dense fog, though he could make out a few figures on Hampden Lane, heads bowed, on late errands of mercy and menace. The sound of wet leaves dropping from the trees made its way to him. And a small smile crept onto his face. A cup of tea, and who knew what after that? Another case in play, and all the better that it came at this hour. These late ones were often the most interesting.

He appeared downstairs a while later, changed

from his striped blue and white pajamas into a gray suit.

"How do you do, Lady Annabelle?" he said.

He could have answered his own question: She was not at all well. A gaunt and frightened-looking woman, she wore a dark brown dress that bespoke her long widowhood. Once she had been pretty but no longer. She was several years older than Lenox, perhaps forty-five. He racked his brains for a memory of the terrible Payson. Handsome; awful temper; that mystery around his death. He had fought somewhere or other and picked up a violent red scar on his neck, Lenox remembered. It was the strangeness of his death more than anything else that stood out in his scant memory of the man.

"I'm terribly sorry to bother you, Mr. Lenox," she said, worriedly clutching at a long stone necklace she wore.

"No, no, don't be," he said. "I'm an early riser anyway."

"I should have waited until morning, I know, but sometimes a problem is so burdensome that one feels it cannot wait."

"Of course," he said. "You wouldn't have slept. What is the problem?"

"I need your acumen, Mr. Lenox."

"And my discretion?"

"I'm afraid I don't understand."

Lenox shrugged. "Well, if you've come to me I

suppose you haven't gone to the police."

"That's correct, Mr. Lenox, you're correct. You see, in the first place, I wouldn't want to go to the police. But in the second place, I think the police would have laughed. I know you won't laugh."

"Certainly not, no."

"You can't go to the police and simply say, 'There's a dead cat in my son's rooms at college,' can you. They'd think you mad."

"A dead cat?"

"Yes, Mr. Lenox; that's the root of all the problems." Again she reached for her necklace.

Wearily he thought, *Oh, no, not one of these.*

"You seem preoccupied, Lady Payson. Would you like a cup of tea?"

"Yes, please," she said as he motioned to Graham, "but Mr. Lenox, will you come to Oxford with me?"

"I suppose that depends," he said. "Is the problem a dead cat? Is that the only problem?"

She seemed slightly calmer. "It's certainly not the only problem."

"What is, then?"

"I've come because my son, George, has disappeared."

CHAPTER FOUR

In Warwickshire there were two families: the Lucys and the Wests.

The Lucys were the more famous of the two, for one thing because of the long-told, possibly apocryphal story that Shakespeare had been a tutor in the family of Sir Thomas Lucy and even poached his deer. But the Wests were richer. A West had played an important role in the crucial Battle of Edgehill during the Revolution, and now they lived in the north of the shire on land the King had granted to them after the Restoration, around the large towns of Nuneaton and Bedworth. It was far from the glory of Stratford and the beauty of the southern canals, but it was where the money lay.

Lady Annabelle was a West, and her brother, John, was the current patriarch of the family. John West was a kind, stolid, churchgoing, and thoroughly countryish man who loved his sister and hated London nearly as much as she did. He had tried to make up for her unpleasant marriage by making her widowhood comfortable, if not happy. As a result, she and Lenox were bumping along the road away from Hampden Lane in a beautiful six-horse carriage of the very best sort, with blue plush seats and a warm little fire in a steel grate at their feet. They hadn't spoken about the case yet. Once Lenox had heard that her son was missing, he had grabbed an overcoat and the small valise that Graham always left at the ready by the door for occasions like this, and been off. A packet of the cook's toasted tomato sandwiches served as a makeshift breakfast. As he opened them, the carriage was pulling away from London, moving quickly in those early hours that found the streets abandoned, and he said, "Now, will you please tell me the full details of the matter?"

"Yes, certainly. Where shall I begin? Today?"

"Tell me a bit about your son, if you would."

Tears came into Lady Annabelle's eyes. "George is a student at Lincoln College, where he is in his second year reading modern history. He is my only child, and I scarcely need to add that I value every breath he takes as much as my own life.

"The trip from my brother's house to Oxford takes only an hour, and though George is very busy with his work and his friends, I visit him whenever I can, sometimes as often as three times a week. I don't always see him, but sometimes I do, and occasionally I have lunch with the master there.

"But one meeting of ours is firm, and that is tea on Saturday in his rooms. Saturday was yesterday, as you know, and I set out earlier in the morning than I usually do, planning to spend an hour in the Christ Church Picture Gallery before I went to see him. But I was so excited when I arrived in Oxford that I went straight to Lincoln and asked the porter, who knows me by now, to let me into my son's rooms."

"His rooms?"

"George has a sitting room with a desk and a few chairs, and a smaller bedroom behind it, looking out onto the Front Quad."

"Are there also windows in the sitting room?"

"Yes, a short row."

"Go on, please."

Her hand reached for her necklace, which she clutched and worried. "I knocked on the door to his bedroom, which was shut. Then I looked in and saw it empty, so I sat in one of his chairs to wait with a book. At about noon I was very excited indeed, and stepped out of his room to go look in the quadrangle for his arrival. I saw him the second I walked out—and how I wish I had clung to him then, and not let him out of my sight! He was paler than usual and his hair was disheveled, but when I mentioned that he looked upset, he only said that he had been up late, working in the Bodleian.

"I asked him if he would like to go out then, and he said very rapidly that he would meet me at the tearoom down Ship Street where we sometimes go, opposite Jesus College. I started back to the doorway for my book, but he said, 'For God's sakes, go, I'll bring it!' and then kissed me on the cheek and told me he loved me."

There was silence for a moment, as she cried into her handkerchief.

"What a terrible mother I am! I went and waited in the tearoom, worrying slightly about how run-down George looked and drinking a cup of black coffee to steady myself. But the minutes dragged on until it had been nearly three-quarters of an hour since he had said he would be right down to meet me.

"I waited indecisively for another fifteen minutes before I paid and went back to the college. The porter—nice enough, though he seemed puzzled—let me into George's rooms again. My things were still lying as they had been by the chair, and nothing had changed in the room, though the fire in the hearth had guttered out. I knocked on the door to his bedroom—which was closed, though I had opened it earlier—and there was no answer. Then I plucked up my courage and opened the door."

"Was it closed tightly?"

"Yes."

"Is it a thick door? Might the wind have closed it?"

"No."

"Had the porter seen George leave college?"

"No—that was the first thing I asked him."

"Please, go on."

"It's a very spare room—just a bed and a chest of drawers. The bed was ruffled, but generally everything looked as usual. Except George wasn't there, and on the floor of his bedroom there was a white cat, stabbed straight through the neck with my late husband's letter opener—dead, needless to say." She shuddered at the thought.

"Did you recognize the cat?"

"I thought I might have. I know that George and his friends shared a cat."

"Shared it?"

"They each had it for a few days at a time, if you see what I mean. At any rate, I'm not sure."

"What did you do after you saw the cat?"

"I fainted. After a few minutes—perhaps even a few seconds—I woke up and nothing had changed. I felt very weak. The problem was that my brother is in Newcastle on business, or I would have gone straight home and told him everything. As it is I waited very miserably in the sitting room for about an hour, sipping at a glass of the brandy George keeps on hand. Then I checked back in the teashop to see if George had come in—they know him there—and he hadn't. By then I was at the end of my wits. I went home and sent a telegram to my brother, who wrote back that he would be at Lincoln by midday today—Sunday, that is. Then last night I had the idea to fetch you. Emily Foal speaks so highly of your skill."

"Yes, those emeralds. What time was it exactly when you last saw George?" said Lenox.

"Five minutes past twelve."

"Did you speak to his friends before you came to London?"

"No, I thought it best to seek you out right away."

""Did you consult with the porter or master?"

"No."

"What else do you know about this cat?"

"Nothing, really. I know that they've had him for a while now."

"Well, you've been awfully brave," said Lenox.

"I don't think it will be enough," she said.

"We shall see; I am certainly hopeful," he said.

"Are you?" This in a tone of despair.

"It seems telling to me that he saw you when he knew something was wrong—and didn't stop and run off with you."

"You're quite right," she said. "I suppose I hadn't thought of it that way. So you think he's alive, at the very least?"

"I hope and believe he is, yes, Lady Annabelle—but I shouldn't like to draw any conclusions until we arrive."

CHAPTER FIVE

They were ten miles outside of Oxford and Lady Payson had fallen asleep, perhaps unburdened to have told her story. Through the window on his side of the coach, Lenox was looking out at the farmland of Oxfordshire; herds of sheep grazed in the golden swales where dawn was swelling. They reminded him of the trips he had taken to and from Oxford during vacations from term.

For Lenox himself was an Oxonian. He had been at Balliol. It had been, oh, five years since he had returned to Broad Street and walked through the college's gate. This would be the first case to bring him back to Oxford, and even as he ran over Lady Payson's story from half a dozen angles in his mind, the carriage knocking down the road, he was thinking about having a pint at the Bear and going through the low arches into the Bodleian courtyard.

Before he had left London he had hastily written two notes. One was to Jane, telling her that he would be gone for a day or two. The other was to Thomas McConnell, who had by now settled into the firm role of medical examiner on Lenox's cases. To McConnell Lenox had written,

Not sure what there is for you to do (beyond examining a dead cat), but if you want to see a real university—McConnell had been at Cambridge—*come to Oxford at your convenience. You'll find me at the Bath Place Hotel above the Turf Tavern, or else they can direct you on.*

It was now morning, about eight o'clock, and they were a short way outside of Oxford. The carriage was approaching from the south; the Cherwell River wound in and out of view to their left. A number of long, shallow punts were covered and locked on the banks of the river, past their season until spring, and the famous willow trees had begun to scatter their leaves across the water. The yellowish light of morning appeared over the dreaming spires that Lenox knew so well—Tom Tower at Christ Church, the shining dome of the Radcliffe Camera, the ridged flutes rising from the towers of All Souls. It would only be a moment until Magdalen Bridge.

A dead cat! Well, but who knew.

Lady Payson stirred. "You've no idea how lovely it was to shut my eyes. Do please excuse me, though."

"I'm happy you could rest."

"Do you have children, Mr. Lenox? I don't think you do."

"No, I don't—not yet."

There was a haunted pause, and then she

steeled herself. "Where do you plan to stay?" she asked.

"I thought I might look in at the Turf, actually. I probably ought to stay somewhere else, but I can't help my sentimentality. I spent a number of undergraduate nights there, you see. And you? Shall you return to your brother's house?"

She laughed humorlessly. "I certainly couldn't leave Oxford. I'll be at the Randolph Hotel."

"Sound choice, from all I hear."

"My usual one. It opened just before George came up to Oxford."

The Randolph was the best hotel in Oxford, and despite being new looked like one of the ancient colleges, made as it was of the same golden stone, covered with the same red and green ivy. It faced the Ashmolean Museum (one of Lenox's favorite places in the world, full of beautiful paintings, Roman sculpture, and old, strange British treasures) on Beaumont Street.

Both Lenox and Lady Annabelle were silent. Oxford is a quiet and gentle river town, interrupted at its center by a cluster of buildings that happen to be among the most beautiful mankind has ever produced. They were reaching that center now, passing the botanical gardens and Queen's College into the very heart of town. Lenox took his satchel from the empty seat opposite and put it on his lap.

"Shall we meet in an hour, Lady Payson?"

She seemed more determined and imperial, less wholly fretful, than she had a few hours before in Hampden Lane. "May I ask why we should delay, Mr. Lenox?"

He smiled gently. "I'm afraid I need a few moments to collect myself, perhaps tackle a cup of tea and a bite of something."

"The Turf, as I understand it—never having been, myself—is on Holywell Street? Yes? Well, then, it's only a few steps from Lincoln. Shall we meet at the college gates in three-quarters of an hour?

Lenox nodded. "As you please," he said agreeably. It was a bother. Still, he didn't envy her the position she was in. "Oh—I say, you can let me out here, driver."

"Are you sure, Mr. Lenox?" asked Lady Annabelle.

"Oh, yes," he said. They were just by Hertford College. "I'll go in by the back way."

One could reach the Turf by Holywell, or else by a wending little cobblestone alley, probably not wider than an average man's shoulders. The alley was darkly lit, and even at this hour Lenox had to turn his back to the wall and make way for a thin stream of students. Many of them were wearing the undergraduate subfusc, in various states of dishevelment. Perhaps they had finished their second-year examinations the day before. Passing by the used brown kegs as he approached

41

the door, a smile he couldn't wipe away on his face, Lenox went inside.

It was a low-ceilinged place that dated to the 1300s. (Still leaving it a few hundred years shy of being the city's oldest continuous drinking establishment.) Once it had been a strong-cider bar, and then briefly a pub called the Spotted Cow, but even to the oldest gents at the stile it had always been and would always be the Turf, hidden away from all but those who really knew Oxford. The wood on the walls was darkened by smoke and time, though the beams holding the roof up were freshly painted white. There was a bar in the front room—above it was the famous first menu of the Turf, a wooden plank with DUCK OR GROUSE written on it—and another in the back room, just by a staircase leading to the rooms above. It was by the staircase that Lenox found himself confronted by a lad of perhaps twelve. He was plump with fiery red hair and a freckly face.

"Go on, sir," he said, rather rudely.

"Hello there—I was hoping I might have a room?"

"Full up, compliments."

"No rooms at all?"

"How about a beer instead?"

Lenox laughed. "I don't think so."

"Tom Tate, what d'you reckon you're doing!"

A strong, very short woman emerged from the

42

front bar, looking at the boy. Lenox smiled at her in recognition.

Her eyes focused on him after she had dealt the lad a cuff and told him to see to the tables in front. "Is that . . . is that Mr. Lenox, there?" she said. "Not Edmund, but Charles?"

"Too right, Mrs. Tate."

"Mr. Lenox!" She called back Tom, who was in high dudgeon with the world at having been cuffed, and told him to look out for Lenox's bag.

"You do have a room, then, Mrs. Tate?"

"Have a room! Bless you, of course we have a room!"

She led him up the staircase, behind her disgruntled employee and son. "Breakfast, then?" she said, looking back.

"That might do me well, thanks."

She led him down to the end of the hallway—to his old room. Clearing Tom out and promising that breakfast would arrive soon, she left, saying only, "Excellent to see you, Mr. Lenox! You must excuse me, we're busier than bees at the moment!" on her way out. Her brusqueness put Lenox in an affectionate mood; it meant nothing had changed.

It was a room small in proportions but comfortably arranged. There were two windows with a lovely view of New College, a large bed in one corner, a nicked and blackened desk that had seen many first letters to home, and by the window a round, rickety table with a comfortable armchair alongside it and a fireplace behind it in the corner. There would have been a better turned-out (and perhaps even more comfortable) room in one of the nice hotels on Beaumont Street or the High, but he wouldn't have been happy at either, knowing his room above the kitchen at the Turf was still available. He had spent so many nights here just before term started—that first, nervous night of his fresher year, in fact, waiting for his brother, Edmund, a third-year, to come fetch him for supper. Edmund—he would have understood. He would have stayed here too, as their father had, and his father, and his father.

A moment later the chastised Tom staggered in under a tray about as big as him. Lenox slipped him a sixpence and smiled conspiratorially. "Not a word to Mum, eh?" he said.

Then he slipped the window open to feel the breeze and poured himself a cup of coffee. There was a plate loaded down with toast, eggs, kippers, rashers, fried tomatoes, baked beans, and sausages on the tray, and he tucked into them with his mind on anything but a dead cat, smiling.

CHAPTER SIX

Lenox washed his face, changed his clothes, had a final gulp of coffee, and at the appointed time stood at the gates of Lincoln College.

Oxford was made up of about twenty constituent colleges. Each of these had its own traditions, its own library, its own chapel, its own dining hall, its own professors, and its own buildings (though most of the colleges were in the same Gothic style, which gave Oxford its medieval look). United, along with the structures that belonged to Oxford as a university, like the Bodleian Library and the Sheldonian Theater, one of Wren's most beautiful buildings, they formed Oxford. Against Cambridge every student from every college was an Oxonian, but within the university there were these other minor allegiances, though there was a great deal of exchange and friendship across their fluid boundaries.

Lincoln was a middling sort of college, full of young men more amiable and athletic than scholarly, young men who would rather drink at the pub than debate at the Union. Both it and its students were well liked around the university. The first rank of colleges—Christ Church, Balliol,

Merton—could be less cheerful places, especially when class reared its head too high. Lincoln's merriness was enduring.

It was also beautiful, folded into a side lane between Oxford's two main thoroughfares, Broad Street and the High. It was made from the same quarry of yellowish, ancient stone as the other colleges that dated to the fourteenth and fifteenth centuries. In fact, it had been founded in 1427 by the Bishop of Lincoln, and it was often said that it looked more like the colleges of that era had than any other place standing, because it was still only three stories high, cozy rather than grand, a home and a haven rather than an impersonal palace. Nobody was allowed to walk on the quad, of course, and its brilliant color, even at this time of the year, was the result of only about twenty men in four and a half centuries treading on it— each generation's lawn mower, who in his turn was as famous a character in the college as the junior dean or the head porter.

One of the most notable members of the college had been John Wesley, the religious reformer, who with his brother had held the first meetings of the infamous Holy Club in college rooms. This had all occurred in the 1720s and '30s, long ago, but even then religious zealotry couldn't weigh Lincolnites down—they had made a joke of Wesley, naming him and his followers Methodists because of their dull, methodical ways. It was a light-hearted college. Its alumni were famously devoted to it, the mark of the best places in Oxford, places like Lincoln and the Turf.

Lady Payson arrived a few minutes late. "Do you think he's alive?" she said without preamble.

"I certainly hope he is, and I certainly think there's a good chance," said Lenox.

"You don't know George, Mr. Lenox. Nothing would have made him miss our lunch except a crisis—and no explanation, no note! Some sons might be capable of that, but not George. Only real trouble could have made him leave me like that."

"At any rate, I shall try my best to find him. That is what I can promise you. Would you rather I went in alone? Or will you come?"

"I'll come," she said stoutly.

"Just as you please, though I must ask you not to touch anything. Unless you have already?"

"No, I left everything as it was. Why?"

"It may be important to see what George left behind—whether he left in haste or deliberately, for instance, whether there's any sign of forced access to a window or door."

"I see. No, I shan't touch anything. I only sat in the chair by the window when I was here before. That may be slightly disturbed, but otherwise the rooms are as George left them."

Lady Payson nodded to the porter on duty, and she and Lenox walked along the stone path that circled the lawn, toward an entrance at the rear of the Front Quad.

"Does anybody at the college know of anything amiss?" he asked.

"I don't think so."

"Best to keep it that way, perhaps. What do the porters think of your coming and going?"

"I told them I was visiting, and asked if I could have leave to enter the college freely. They said I could, on the word of the master."

"And you haven't spoken to any of his friends?"

"No."

"Have you ever met any of them?"

"Only very briefly."

They reached a slim stone stairwell in which the morning light angled through the mullioned windows on each landing. On the third and top floor, Lady Payson pointed to a door. Lenox took the lead.

The sitting room looked as familiar as the back of his hand, and immediately Lenox took a liking to the young man who inhabited it. There was a grate just by the door, full of ready coals (a sensible proposition—no use fumbling in the coal with wet hands as you got in), and by it there was a single armchair, maroon and stuffed, accompanied by a medium-sized circular table on which there were several books and a battered sort of walking stick. Walking boots, heavy with mud, sat on their sides in the chair.

In case of a guest there was a small table and two chairs by the window, which looked out over the Front Quad and had a view of the Radcliffe Camera, the domed library at the center of Oxford. On it were the remains of a breakfast that the scout had yet to remove—from two days before, it would seem, as Lady Annabelle confirmed that it had been a day old the day before. Lenox wondered about this and made a quick note of it on a pad that he whisked from the inner pocket of his jacket.

There was a bookcase, stacked with old newspapers and bric-a-brac, along with a few volumes on Tudor history. The center of the room was covered by a thick, ornate rug, which Lady Payson explained her late husband had sent back from India. Stooping to examine it, Lenox saw several small artifacts of the missing man's life: a frayed piece of string about two feet long of the sort you might bind a package with, half of a pulpy fried tomato, which was too far from the breakfast table to have been dropped, a fountain pen, and lastly a card, which said on the front THE SEPTEMBER SOCIETY. Lenox turned it and was surprised to discover on the back two pen lines, one pink, one black, forming an X.

The September Society—hadn't been an Oxford club in his day. What was interesting about the items on the rug was that they were all scattered within a few inches of each other, while the rest of the rug was spotless. He stood up. Why this spot? It had but a poor angle on the window: too far from the fire for warmth, and too far from the desk (opposite the bookcase was a desk, which was tidy—in contrast with the mess on the carpet) for glancing over papers. Its only distinguishing mark was that it was in a kind of no-man's-land in the room.

He examined the rest of the room and found only one thing that he thought enough of to add to his notebook: a messy line of ash from a pipe, on the floor just beneath the window.

"Was your son much of a smoker?" he asked Lady Payson, who was lingering in the doorway.

"No, not that I know of. He didn't smoke when he came home."

"I don't see a pipe in this room, at any rate. He might have carried it on his person—but why not tap the ash outside the window, within arm's length, rather than on the floor just by it?"

"I confess I don't know, Mr. Lenox. Have you any clue of what happened yet?"

"Clues—but no clue yet. Still, we shall see. I think I may proceed to the bedroom now, Lady Payson. Would you like to sit in the armchair? I could light a fire."

"No, no," she said. "I'll come in."

Just then, however, there was a clattering on the stairs behind them, and they both turned. A voice said, "Really, I quite assure you that I am expected—really," while the voice of a porter said, "But sir, we can call up—no problems on that account." The first voice said, "Ah, but it's a matter of urgency." Then there was a brief silence—the coin of the empire changing hands, perhaps?—and the first voice came to the door, found it open, and walked in.

"A dead cat?" the voice said. "Has your grade of case declined?"

Lenox smiled, and said, "Why, hullo, McConnell. How good of you to come."

CHAPTER SEVEN

The bedroom was narrow and dark, with only a diamond-shaped window letting any light in. Like the sitting room it was plain, and like the sitting room it was untouched by the scout—the bed unmade, books strewn on the floor by an armchair that stood under the window, and clothes on the floor by the wardrobe. Still, the room retained the amiable hominess that was recogniz-able in the sitting room. Lenox liked George Payson, no mistaking it.

Lady Payson was sitting by the grate, which McConnell had lit.

"Much too chilly in here," he had said. "No evidence in it, is there?"

Now he and Lenox were walking gingerly through the room. Its only remarkable point was the dead cat lying in the center of it.

"Will you tell me what I ought to know?" McConnell said.

The doctor hadn't looked better in years; not since before he began to drink. He was a tall, handsome Scot, with wry and caring eyes. A talented surgeon, he had let his practice lapse after making a brilliant marriage to a young, charming, beautiful, rich, and high-strung woman called Toto. The marriage had been a rocky one, however, at some points even on the verge of divorce. The sorrow of those first years had driven McConnell to drink. Recently, though, as the doctor had unbended and Toto had grown, things had been better. The secrets of a marriage are impenetrable, but the secrets of a man are not: McConnell was happier, especially when he worked with Lenox. Toto was, too. Both were older and sadder, but they had made it to the other side. Or so their friends ardently hoped. McConnell still had the sunken eyes of the flask, yet there was some jolliness in his face that Lenox could only ascribe to the partial reconciliation with Toto.

Lenox briefly explained the outline of the case. "Hope I haven't called you here for naught," he said.

"I daresay the cat will be as interesting as anything else that comes my way this week. Animal, vegetable, mineral, you know—I'm not a real doctor any longer, I'll take them all."

He smiled as he said this, though Lenox detected in the smile a customarily wan aspect.

The cat itself was white and glossy, well taken care of, without any markings at first glance. It was stabbed once through the neck. Turning on a lamp, Lenox leaned down to verify that the weapon was indeed a letter opener. It was of the old-fashioned kind, he saw, broad and silver, inscribed with a cursive *P*. McConnell stooped down with Lenox and ran his hand through the cat's fur.

"Only the one wound," he said. "Odd, that."

"Why?"

McConnell stroked his chin. "Have you ever tried to stab a cat?"

"Oh, dozens of times."

He laughed. "But really, cats aren't docile, you know. They squirm and dash about. I love dogs, myself—a good Scottish terrier."

"In a murderous mood, you mean?"

"Don't joke, there's a good fellow."

"You're right, though, it would have been diffi-cult."

"Even for a strong man—it wouldn't matter. There would be more than one mark, as the person tried to hit the right spot. In fact, there would probably be seven or eight lighter ones, I'd guess. Here there's a single deep one."

"So either two people did it," said Lenox, "or the cat was drugged."

"I'll find out for you."

"Let's lift it."

McConnell gingerly worked the letter opener out (it was plunged straight through to the floor) and dropped it into the pocket of a cloth bag he had brought. Rigor mortis had set in, and the body was stiff. He picked the cat up and dropped it into the main pouch of the bag.

"What's this?" said Lenox.

In the blood on the floor was a damp red note, which had been stabbed through at its center by the letter opener. He picked it up and examined it. One corner was untouched by blood, and he saw a blue edging on it. Writing paper. It was folded in half, and he opened it.

"It says . . . it says, 'x12/43 21 31 25/x2.'" Lenox looked at McConnell, puzzled. "Any meaning you can gather?"

"That's your area." The doctor held out a little bag, and Lenox, after making sure there were no markings anywhere else on it, placed it inside.

"What kind of code could it be?" Lenox muttered. "I wonder."

He walked across the room, stooping here and there to look. He found little of interest, and nothing so singular as the collection of objects on the Indian rug. Still, he left with one thing: On

54

the bedside table was an empty dance card for a ball that had apparently taken place the night before at Jesus College, with a note on the reverse that said, *Yes, sir, that will be fine,* and was signed Roland Light. According to Lady Annabelle, this was the hallway's scout, who cleaned the rooms, lit the fires, and made meals. Otherwise, their inspection yielded nothing.

"Bit of lunch?" McConnell whispered.

"I shall have to look after Lady Annabelle."

"See what she means to do."

"Yes, all right," said Lenox.

She was sitting by the coals, warming her hands. There was a dazed look in her eyes.

"Shall I ever see my son again?" She felt for her necklace.

"I certainly hope you shall, Lady Payson."

She turned to him. "Can I trust you?" she said. "Are you a good enough detective?"

"Fair enough, yes. If you would like to go to the police, I recommend it wholeheartedly."

"Oh, the police," she said with a wave of her hand.

"At any rate, I think the best thing now would be rest. Perhaps you should withdraw to your brother's house."

"Perhaps," she said tiredly. "What do you mean to do?"

"This afternoon I shall interview whomever I'm able to find. This evening I'll consider all

55

that I've learned. Tomorrow morning, I think, I shall return to London. I have plenty to work on."

"Leave Oxford!"

"Only for a day, possibly two, Lady Payson. And I will not leave without an ally in place here."

"Who?"

"I cannot answer that, I'm afraid."

Gradually it was settled that she would leave, and with a great deal of trouble Lenox managed to send her off in her handsome, dejected carriage, with a promise of keeping in close touch.

McConnell was waiting in the courtyard of Lincoln eating an apple, his cloth bag at his side.

"Saw her off?" he said.

"Yes," said Lenox thoughtfully. "Poor woman."

"She barely seems to be holding on."

They set off up the High and turned onto Cornmarket Street, then into St. Giles. A little ways up St. Giles at number 12, Lenox led McConnell into the familiar doors of the Lamb and Flag—one of his favorite pubs in Oxford, companion to the Turf in that respect. (Inevitably a tour of Oxford becomes a tour of its pubs.) It was an old coaching inn, the kind that had been so important to British travel in the eighteenth century but had only just straggled into modern times, where horses could be fed and stabled, groups could meet and stay the night before traveling north, and there was always a pint and something good to eat available, no matter how late or wet it was. It was still the best place to order a cab or fly in Oxford. St. John's College had always owned it, since 1695. There was a distinguished look about it—a place where kings had slept and beggars had drunk, all within the six or eight dim rooms, odd shaped and illogical, crammed under their ancient black beams.

Lenox and McConnell sat at a table overlooking a broad field by St. John's, talking easily. They had been working together more and more frequently in the past few years, and an intimacy had sprung up between them. For half an hour they lingered over a pint of beer before McConnell decided to order lunch.

"What do you reckon is safe?" he asked when they looked over the menu.

"Oh—I've eaten all of it in my time," said Lenox.

He didn't have anything now, however, having eaten a large breakfast. McConnell ordered the round steak with a fried egg and mashed potatoes, and both of them ordered pints of autumn ale. The fat, red bartender brought it all out, along with a cold chicken sandwich and a bottle of beer that Lenox meant to save for later.

As the two men talked and drank, the detective recalled his undergraduate days in these rooms; but his happiness and nostalgia were tinged with anxiety over George Payson, whom he knew he would like.

CHAPTER EIGHT

On some unrecorded day in the 1090s, perhaps a little earlier, perhaps a little later—the Battle of Hastings still in memory, at any rate, and the Domesday Book not more than a decade old—an anonymous cleric and one or two students gathered by appointment in a small room (was it at an inn? in a church?), and the University of Oxford was born. Soon students from the University of Paris staged a minor revolt and joined those unremembered pioneers, and Oxford began to flourish. It was the first university in England and one of the few in Europe; before a century had passed it was the greatest institution of higher learning in the world. It had an astonishing number of books, for one thing—hundreds. Thanks to these books and the men who taught from them, generations of clergymen began to share, in their far-flung parishes, an Oxford education, an Oxford way of thinking and teaching. Thus was created a world of ideas, a world of the mind, which collapsed the difference between Devon and Yorkshire, which for the first time aligned the beliefs of the people all over England—and indeed, Europe.

Then on some equally uncertain day in the

1200s, one of the constituent colleges of Oxford began, perhaps Merton College, perhaps University College, probably at first just a house where students could rent a room and have a meal; and then slowly, as the years washed over them, the colleges consolidated, joined by other colleges, until sometime in the 1400s when Oxford truly began to look and feel like Oxford.

There was something that age bestowed, Lenox thought. A depth and richness to the afternoon light in the windows; a kind of holiness even in the buildings that weren't religious. When you became a student at Oxford you realized both your own mortality, in the flow of this near-millennium of students, and also the small particle of immortality that attaches to you when you begin to belong to an immortal place.

Lenox strode across the cobblestones of the forecourt of Balliol College, the site of his undergraduate days, gazing at the high windows he had once known so well. There was a smile upon his face, that mostly happy but slightly sad smile people have when they go back to a place they have loved. This had been a place of wonder for him, cut loose as he was from childhood and the halls of Lenox House, with new friends and new studies. Even the few streets of central Oxford had seemed huge to him, lined with a bewildering number of shops stretching the quarter mile from St. Giles to St. Aldate's, from

St. John's College to Christ Church.

He was older now and felt it. Nearly forty. Unmarried still. Caught up with some of his dreams, fallen behind in others. He had thought since he was a boy that he would enter Parliament, and it had never happened. He had wanted a son. That was what he had found: The things one assumed would happen sometimes never did. It was a lesson his undergraduate self wouldn't have understood.

For an hour or so Lenox sat in the Balliol court-yard and thought about the case; one result of this brown study was the increased seriousness he now saw that it merited. The distracted manner in which George Payson had greeted his mother the morning before had tended rather to mitigate the case's depth than add to it; Lenox remembered that all students had private lives that they guarded from all but their friends, and thought that if he had seen his mother even an hour early in his day he also would have been distracted. Too close a rub against his independence. With the step back, now Lenox saw that the strange, almost intentional dishevelment of Payson's room, along with the presence of the white cat, which since he had seen it in the flesh had grown more eerie than comical, could hardly be anything but grave.

As he stood up and left, he was more puzzled —but had a better grasp, too, of what he was puzzled about.

Although now he had to shift into a different mood.

Being a detective requires many skills, and just then he was an actor, attempting a kind of genial frivolity: He was leaning up against the gilt steel front gate of Lincoln, where he had just come from Balliol, and pretending that he was George Payson's carefree visiting uncle. He swung his cane and hummed a tune, looked around curiously, and all the while waited for the right person to come out of the gate—a student who wouldn't mind a few prying questions. As he waited he read the *Times*.

The stories in the paper were comfortably familiar. There was a long article condemning the new speed limits that had been introduced that summer, of two miles per hour in towns and four miles per hour in the countryside. An infringement on people's daily lives, the editor argued. There was an update on the search for John Surratt, who had fled to Canada and then across the Atlantic after being implicated in Abraham Lincoln's death. (Like many other Englishmen, Lenox had a deep admiration of the president and had closely followed the American Civil War. He thanked God it was over. The death counts listed in the papers alone could throw him into a horrible mood for days.) The Austro-Prussian War was just over as well, making it a good year for lovers of peace. Then there were the reports of the first months of marriage of Princess Helena, Victoria's third daughter, who had been wed that summer to . . . Lenox peered at the paper to sound out the name for himself . . . to Prince Christian of Schleswig-Holstein-Sonderburg-Augustenburg. Gracious. And most thrilling to Lenox, who had his age's deep love of the new and revolutionary, the Atlantic Cable was nearly complete. As he understood it—and he would be the first to admit that he didn't quite—the cable would allow people to telegraph between Europe and America! What would my grandfather have said, thought Lenox? Brave new world . . .

All the while he had his eye on the slow trickle of students coming in and out of the college. He passed the first one up, a tall, censorious-looking fellow in glasses. The second wouldn't do either, a terrified first-year from the looks of him. The third shot out of the gate as fast as he could and didn't give Lenox a chance to approach. The fourth student, though, evidently a temperate second-year, judging from the flower in his buttonhole, looked hale and likely. Lenox threw out a studied word, relishing his role.

"Oh—I say there, would you mind stopping a moment? I'm Charles Payson—awfully sorry to trouble you." He shook hands with the student, who looked bewildered but nodded politely, as if strange men introduced themselves to him at random moments throughout every day.

"I thought I might bother you. You see, my nephew is here in Lincoln—George Payson—and I thought I'd pop in on him while I was passing through Oxford, you know, but I can't track him down."

"Ah," said the young man, who had brightened at Payson's name.

"You couldn't tell me the name of a friend of his, could you? It'd be a favor."

"I shouldn't want to give out information that might . . . well, I don't know what it might do."

"No, quite understandable," said Lenox. He looked up at the sky. "You know, I was at Lincoln too. Great place, isn't it?" He sounded even to himself like a bluff clubman up from London, the role he had decided he would play. "Games and youth, I mean. Full of promise. Well, please, be on your way. Sorry again to stop you."

The young man said, "Oh—I suppose it can't hurt. His uncle, you say? Father's brother, I guess?"

Lenox nodded.

"Well, they're a real trio—Payson, Bill Dabney, and Tom Stamp. Dabney and Stamp live in three rooms toward the front of the Grove Quad—by Deep Hall, you may remember, through that old stone stairway."

Lenox hadn't the faintest idea of where the place was in Lincoln, but nodded cheerfully. "Beautiful there, ain't it?" he said, inwardly thinking that perhaps he should have been on the stage. He had already formulated a military history for himself if the conversation somehow wound its way there.

"It is. Good luck finding Payson. Nice chap, your nephew."

"Cheers," said Lenox and shook the boy's hand.

Lenox walked into the college whistling a low tune and contemplating which story he would tell the porter to gain entrance to the college. Luckily, however, the porter's head was turned toward a student requesting his mail, and Lenox was able to walk into the Front Quad without any trouble. The Grove Quad—a piece of luck—was marked clearly, through the back corridors of the front square, and he followed it with the young second-year's instructions in mind.

In the Grove Quad there was bright green ivy on the walls and covering even the doors, but he found the right one without too much difficulty and walked up the stairwell. He knocked on the first door he saw. The bleary-eyed student who opened it appeared to have come straight from bed.

"Dabney and Stamp?" Lenox asked.

"Next floor up and to the left," said the young man and unceremoniously closed the door.

Climbing the stairs, Lenox found the spot easily enough. The door was ajar. He knocked, and a fair-haired young man came forward. The room behind him was a bit of a mess, and from the look of the desk where he had been studying, it was work, not sleep, that made this one bleary-eyed. Still, he seemed pleasant.

"Bill Dabney?" Lenox asked.

"No, I'm Tom Stamp," he said. "May I ask who you are?"

"Charles Lenox." They shook hands. "I'm here because I was hoping to have a word with you and your roommate about George Payson."

"Are you a relation? Something of that sort?"

"No, I'm a detective."

Tom Stamp blanched. "A detective. Has George gone missing?"

"Why do you ask?" said Lenox sharply.

"Because I haven't seen Bill or George, either of them, for days. I'm getting pretty damn worried."

"Have you contacted the police?"

"Not yet."

"Why not?"

"I don't know. I have collections—exams, you know—tomorrow morning, and I hadn't really thought about the lads until a few hours ago. I thought I'd run over to the dean's office in a little while if they weren't back."

"Did you see anything out of the ordinary in Dabney's room? Any signs that he had left in a rush or even of a struggle?"

"Nothing like that, no. Hang on a sec, though—

I did find this." He motioned for Lenox to follow him into the room and then found a book and took a slip of paper out of it, which he handed over. "Make anything of it?" he said.

Lenox narrowed his eyes thoughtfully. The artifact with which Tom Stamp had presented him seemed to confirm the conclusions he had reached after thinking the case over at Balliol. It was a plain card inscribed with the words THE SEPTEMBER SOCIETY.

CHAPTER NINE

They're your two closest friends at Oxford?" Lenox said.

"Easily. We do everything together."

"How did you meet?"

"As first-years we went down to the Sheldonian together, all the freshers, to matriculate. Did you have matriculation in your day? Everyone puts on hats and gowns and dinner jackets, and then the chancellor reads off some Latin and you promise not to burn any books in the library, and all of it combined means I suppose that you're an Oxonian for life. After that everyone goes to have a pint at the White Horse Tavern, just across the way, and out of our class Bill, George, and I ended up last there, still nursing our beers and having cigarettes. After that we just fell in naturally together."

They were sitting on a bench in the Grove Quad. It was about five o'clock by now and the day had gotten rather gray, a few drops of rain scattering across the ivy. Stamp was having a cigarette.

He was a jovial-looking lad, under the middle height but with good, strong features. He had on a suit but no tie. Perhaps the most distinctive thing about him was the crop of fair hair that was continually falling in his face.

"What were they like separately?"

"Hard to think of them that way. I suppose Dabney is moodier, often worried about his work. Rather a more sturdy, Midlands type of fellow than Payson or me. But good fun most of the time, and absolutely dead loyal. Dark hair, very smart.

"Payson is generally jollier company than either of us. He loves to go to balls in London—I think he may have had a girl down there—and sometimes said Oxford was too small for him. Bright red hair." Lenox noted this down. "Glasses when he reads, not otherwise. Not as smart as Dabney, but then again, neither am I."

"What are the two of you reading?"

"Oh, right. Should have mentioned." He stubbed out the cigarette. "I'm on modern history. Expect I shall go into politics. My father is in it, you know."

Lenox resisted the urge to ask how. "And Dabney?"

"Dabney, strict classics. As I said, the brightest of us. I could barely muddle through ten lines of Virgil at Winchester. Always most looked forward to rugger and that sort of thing."

"Aren't you a bit small?" Lenox asked.

Stamp laughed. "A bit. Helps you slide in between people. So I told myself. I hadn't a chance when I came here, but you know how it is at school, with games between the houses. They always want more people, and everyone gets a chance."

"What about Payson?" Lenox already knew, but wanted confirmation.

"Do you mean . . . ?"

"What was he reading?"

"Oh—right, of course. Modern history, too, just as I am. One of the reasons he and I were perhaps a trifle closer than either of us with old Dabney. Spent all of our days together with the tutor here, a crazy sort of fellow, wears the exact same clothes every day."

Lenox laughed. "Different copies of the same? Or the same?"

Stamp laughed, too. "Ah—the very question. We debated it our entire first year, until at last Payson landed on a scheme to figure it out. Always a laugh, George is. What he did was, he pretended to trip as he came in the door, and had to grab Standish's—Standish is our tutor—Standish's shoulder. Well, he had dipped his finger in green ink. Not a lot. Just a dab, enough to make a mark. It's a sort of checkered coat, so it came off pretty well. We couldn't keep a straight face the entire lesson and had to keep pretending that some rot about the Nine Years War was what made us laugh."

"What happened the next day?" Lenox asked.

"Same exact jacket." Stamp broke into peals of laughter. "Lord, I certainly hope they're okay, you know. Both of them."

"About George. Wouldn't he have had the same exam as you tomorrow? Wouldn't you have noticed him gone?"

"No—it was a makeup exam, you see. I was rather poorly last Trinity term. They let me defer exams until the beginning of this Michaelmas term. Hell of a way to do things. I've nearly broken myself in half over it. Anyway, I haven't seen old Standish or our other tutor, Jenkyns, as much as I should have done. Payson, too."

"May I see your rooms more closely?" Lenox asked. "I should like a chance to look over Dabney's things as I have Payson's."

"Certainly," said Stamp.

As they were walking up the stairs, Lenox asked, "What made you notice the card—the one that mentioned the September Society?"

"Only that I hadn't heard of it and was surprised that Dabs would go in for anything I didn't know about. And then it hadn't been there before, I'm sure of that."

"Can you think of anyone that William Dabney and George Payson have in common?"

"Me, I suppose. I'm the most obvious connection between them." He lit another cigarette. "Lord, it makes them seem almost dead, you saying William instead of Bill. Too formal."

"Anyone else who connects the two of them?"

"Oh, yes, sorry. Well. I suppose there's Professor Hatch. He's their advisor—just luck of the draw, we all have them. He often throws small parties at his house, a big place just past the King's Arms on Holywell. The parties go to all hours. There was one Thursday, in fact. I was glad then that Hatch wasn't my advisor, or I wouldn't have done a moment of work that evening. They took that cat of theirs and let it wander around, which they often do. Sometimes they brought London girls, though not on Thursday. Anyway, they're both rather favorites of his."

"About that cat—was it white?"

"Yes, exactly. Longshanks, they called him, like Edward I—because they insisted that he was taller than the average cat. I couldn't see it, and we got into frightful arguments about the average cat's height." Stamp laughed fondly. "They had him from the dean's wife."

"Is there anybody else to connect them?"

"I don't think so. Oh—I suppose there's Andy Scratch. He's a decent fellow, though rather of a different crowd. A year older than us. The three of them serve on the social committee together. You can usually find him playing cards with the bartender down at the Mitre on Turl Street in the evening. Sandy-haired chap."

"Scratch or the bartender?"

"Scratch."

They had arrived at the rooms.

"Why did you live with Dabney?" asked Lenox. "If you were closer with Payson?"

"Oh—I suppose I put that too strongly. We're all about equally friendly. All three of us requested a triple room, but only Dabney and I were put together. Between you and me, I reckon it was George's mother who intervened, because he got practically the best digs in college."

"Oh yes?"

"I'd trade. Although it's a bit lonely for him. He spends a good deal of time over here, or at the Mitre. More sociable. Payson's a sociable lad. The sort who would have been friends with the cricket captain at school even though he didn't play cricket himself. Popular, I mean to say."

Lenox smiled. It was a good description.

The room offered relatively little useful evidence. There was the usual assortment of books and tennis rackets and shoes lying about, and a fair amount of paper covered with Latin translations and other incidental coursework. On the back of one of these pages, the name George Payson was written several times in script.

"Any clue why this is here?"

Stamp shrugged. "Probably George was bored and practiced his signature. I sometimes doodle during lectures. Same thing."

"Yes," said Lenox.

There was also a fair collection of matchboxes. "A smoker?" Lenox asked.

"No. Perhaps he collected them."

"Yes, they're all from clubs and bars."

"I remember now—he got quite touchy if I nicked one."

"Odd."

"Well, Dabs can be moody, as I told you."

A few other things—none of them really interesting. Odds and ends. Lenox couldn't make much out about the lad from the detritus of his life.

"Where did you find the card—the September Society card?" he asked.

"Lying on top of all his books," Stamp said. He was in the process of taking another match from one of Dabney's matchbooks to light a cigarette. "Only about an hour before you came. I misplaced a biography of Cromwell. Hope it stays misplaced, actually. That's why I was digging through here."

Lenox finished looking at the room, making a thorough job of it. Outside it was dark.

"Thank you for your help."

"Don't mention it. You will find them, won't you?"

"Where are you from?"

Stamp pushed his hair away. "Why, London. Do you ask for a reason?"

"If I were you I might consider returning home this weekend."

"Why?"

"Both of your best friends are missing. I only suggest caution, not anxiety. But caution, certainly. This is a deep business."

Stamp looked surprised. "Rum, that. Perhaps I will," he said. "Rum," he repeated to himself.

He showed Lenox downstairs and out into the courtyard. At his last glimpse Lenox saw anxiety dawning on the young man's face, despite the counsel against it that he had just received.

CHAPTER TEN

Are you going to consult the police?" McConnell asked, lifting his glass of beer.

"I shouldn't think so. Not yet, anyhow. It's been a day and a half and there's no conclusive evidence of foul play. For all we know they may be on a trip into London. Though I doubt it."

It was about seven in the evening, and the violet twilight had given way to darkness outside. For a passing moment, Lenox gave in to a deep wave of exhaustion. It had been a long, long day already.

"Sure," said McConnell. "Kill your cat, go on a binge in Park Lane. Common enough."

The doctor was wearing a gray wool suit of the sort that every don at Oxford seems to live in. There was a plaid handkerchief in his pocket, an allusion to his Scottish lineage. He was still a handsome man, fit and red-cheeked, accustomed to the outdoors, though the weariness of his eyes made him look older than he was.

At the moment he was smiling, however. "A dead cat, Lenox. Really. No wonder I became a doctor."

"Your whole career has been building toward this moment, has it?"

"No doubt of it."

They were at the Bear, the oldest public house in Oxford. McConnell had wanted to go somewhere nicer, but Lenox put his foot down. He so rarely came back to Oxford that when he did he liked to revisit the spots of his student life. The Bear, its three tiny, dim rooms, arched over with old wooden beams, its rickety tables and delicious food, was one of the happiest places in the world to him. As it had been for students like him since the thirteenth century, 1242, if he recalled correctly.

Lenox was having a chop in gravy and garlic potatoes, as he had every Thursday night of his third year when his friends gathered from the libraries to commiserate over the gloom of year-end examinations. McConnell was pushing around a bowl of cottage pie, but sticking mostly to beer.

"Where do you think you'll travel next, Charles?" he asked between sips.

"Hard to say. I have my eye on Morocco, though."

There was a twinkle in McConnell's eye. "Morocco! I never heard of a less civilized place."

"Oh, the French are down there, and I would love to see Tangier. It's meant to be beautiful."

(If Lenox had gone on all the trips he planned, he would have been one of the great travelers of his age; inevitably, a case blocked his carefully laid plans. Still, he loved nothing more in the world than to pore over his maps and travel guides, to meet with his travel agent, to correspond with foreign consulates and plot elaborate routes through territories both known and unknown. Recently it had been Morocco; before that Persia; before that the French coast near Villefranche. His friends loved to josh him about his grandiosity of vision, rarely fulfilled—

though there had once been a remarkable trip to Russia, nearly a decade before—but it was all good-natured, of course.)

"Is it?" said the doctor, his eyes still laughing.

"Yes! One can hire a group of tour guides, mountain men. It's very occasionally dangerous, but I have a friend from the Travelers' Club who might go with me."

They talked about Morocco for a little while longer; then Lenox took advantage of the lightness of their conversation to slide in a dangerous question. "Is everything all right these days, Thomas?" he said nonchalantly.

It went against every instinct in Lenox to put such a question to his friend, but Lady Jane had been worried about Toto (McConnell's young, beautiful, tempestuous wife was Jane's cousin) and had asked Lenox to see what he could find out. Her instincts tended to be correct—at any rate, better than his—and it was possible that McConnell's happy appearance that morning might only have been because of the prospect of a new case, or a momentary renewal of his spirits. Who knew?

"No, no, quite all right," said McConnell.

"Oh, good," said Lenox. "Please excuse—I mean to say, it was out of bounds . . ."

There was a moment's silence. McConnell's open, friendly face was downcast now. "To be honest, actually, Toto and I have been rowing a

76

bit. Nothing serious at all, mind you!"

"I'm sorry," said Lenox. And he was.

"Well, too much of that. Would you like to hear what I've found out about the dashed cat?"

"Certainly," said Lenox.

"The animal was poisoned, as we originally conjectured; not enough poison to kill it, but enough to put it out for a good long time."

"As you originally conjectured, not me. But pray go on."

"It was poisoned about an hour before it died. That fact points to premeditation, clearly. Well-taken-care-of animal—expensively bred, I should say, though really I'm more expert when it comes to dogs."

"Any indication about the weapon?"

"Ah, yes—a letter opener, with the letter *P* engraved on it, as we both saw. Dates back about twenty years—it has a manufacturer's mark from the 1840s."

"Did you ever know James Payson?"

"The lad's father? No. What was he like?"

"Terrible temper . . . had an awful scar on his throat. An unpleasant chap. At any rate, what else did you find?"

"The remaining question is, of course, why did someone want to send the young fellow this kind of message?"

"Do you think so? I see it rather differently."

"Oh yes?"

"I think Payson himself killed the cat. Longshanks, they called him."

"No, really? Why on earth would he have done that?"

"A better question would be, why would the people hunting him down have done it? It immediately makes his disappearance suspect, doesn't it? I think if I kidnapped somebody, I would want to make everything he left behind seem as normal as possible."

"Something in that."

"And then consider that there was that cryptic note underneath the cat. Maybe he felt he couldn't leave a note in plain sight, so he had to kill the cat to conceal it. Difficult to focus on finding a letter when there's a dead cat in the middle of the floor."

McConnell laughed wryly. "Yes, I grant you that. But why not write a more explicit note?"

"Perhaps he felt that even with the dead cat there, he couldn't risk it. Did he know Bill Dabney was in danger? Perhaps. Or perhaps he feared for his mother's safety, Stamp's safety. Any of a dozen reasons."

McConnell frowned. "But here's my trump card, Lenox—the cat had been fed poison an hour before it died. If Payson were in a rush, he couldn't have afforded an hour."

"I would make the same argument about our criminal, or criminals—they would be less inclined to linger in their victim's room than anybody, wouldn't they? In a college with round-the-clock security, where anybody unusual would instantly stand out? As for Payson, I should say that he saw the danger coming early. That would explain his detached and anxious behavior with his mother, with whom he was usually on such good terms. Or alternately, perhaps he found the cat poisoned and decided to put it to use, the poor thing."

"What on earth do you think it means?"

"There you take me into deeper waters. It's difficult to gauge whether the cat was merely used to conceal a message, or whether it was in itself a message—to us."

There was a pause while McConnell seemed to consider something. At last he laid his fork and knife down and said, "You know, it really is good of you to use the word 'us,' Charles." It had plainly been difficult for him to say.

"Pure self-interest," said Lenox. "I'd drop you in a second if you weren't so useful."

Both men laughed. They resumed eating, and the conversation moved into other areas; while Lenox still enjoyed it, he saw the spark of involvement dying away that had lit McConnell's face while they talked about this poor, absurd cat. Soon the Scotsman laid down his fork and knife altogether, his eyes fell slightly, and he pulled a flask from his side pocket.

A short while later McConnell had gone back to his hotel to turn in, and Lenox had started toward the Mitre (his fourth pub of the day, he thought with a smile) to find Andy Scratch.

He was a big, hale young man with a friendly face. Lenox found him, as predicted, playing cards with the man behind the bar, who was small and strong-looking—an ex-jockey or bantam-weight boxer, perhaps. A little pile of peanuts that marked their debts to each other sat between the two men.

"Could I have a word?" Lenox asked Scratch.

"Certainly. What are you drinking?"

"Oh—a half of bitter, please. Thanks."

Scratch nodded at the bartender. "Do you mind, Bob?" The bartender went down to the tap, and the lad said, "How can I help you?"

"It's about George Payson and Bill Dabney. They're missing."

"Dabs and George? Never! I saw them in hall only two evenings ago!"

Hall at Oxford, no matter the college, was always a pleasure; it was what everyone who had been there thought of first when Oxford came up. Students sat at the lower tables, eating, drinking, and mostly laughing, while the fellows gazed on sternly from the high table. There was a long-winded Latin grace, always a great deal of wine, and the nostalgic sparkle of candlelight and crystal. At Balliol, Lenox had sat with the same people for three years, many of them to this day his dearest friends. There was one tradition of hall that was universal in Oxford and Cambridge: pennying. If one could surreptitiously bounce or drop a queen's-head penny into a tablemate's wineglass, the glass's owner would have to drink its entire contents in one go to "save the Queen from drowning." As a result, much of supper was spent with one's hand covering one's wine-glass . . .

Lenox again outlined the situation. The young man was amiable enough, and the half pint went quickly, but he wasn't able to offer much help. Lenox asked him to keep an eye out for his friends and thanked him for the drink.

As the detective was parting, though, he said, "By the way, do you know what the September Society is?"

"Of course I do," said the young man. "My father was a military man himself."

CHAPTER ELEVEN

Lenox sat at the Turf Tavern, sipping a pint of stout. He was in a small window seat near the bar that had once been famous for belonging to Jack Farrior, the noted professor of maths at Merton. Every morning at eleven, old Farrior came to the Turf to work on his great theorem of prime numbers, which he said would build on Gauss's work. He knew he had done enough for the day when there were six empty glasses on the table—he asked the bartender to leave them there so that he could tell. Wrestling with the great mathematical problems of the day and unable to count to six without assistance, as Edmund had always joked.

Farrior had once caught Lenox and his friend Christopher Compton invading Merton to steal the fellows' Christmas pudding. The pudding took a month to make and spent most of that time buried underground in a patch of earth on Christ Church Meadow, to absorb the earth's dampness. Stealing it was Lenox's third-year practical joke. The two lads had glided silently down the river on a stolen punt to come toward the meadow from its other end, disembarked, and begun digging. Things were going perfectly until Farrior stumbled upon them. It was an incriminating scene. They were both covered with dirt and had shovels in their hands and dark clothes on.

He stared for a moment. "What's two plus five?" he had said, chewing on the end of his pipe.

"Seven," Compton had said. "Last I checked."

"How about three plus four?"

"Also seven, I should say."

With a twinkle in his eyes, Farrior had said, "I

myself hate Christmas pudding. Have since I was a boy. Tastes of ashes." Then he had walked away, leaving Lenox and his friend in fits of laughter as they finished the job. It was still part of Balliol lore, passed down to each incoming class along with the theft of the Wadham chandelier and the transfer of several deer from Magdalen's deer park to the Brasenose courtyard.

There was such a multitude of memories and associations here! He loved this little, many-roomed tavern, its low ceilings and smell of barley, its black casks of ale, its glass decanters of brandy. It was part of his love for Oxford.

Upstairs to his room in a moment. First he wanted a few more seconds to think.

Before him was a book he had borrowed from Andy Scratch, called *The Heroes of Punjab*. It told the story of the Anglo-Sikh wars, which were by now about twenty years in the past. One chapter briefly mentioned that the September Society had been created after the war by the surviving lead officers of the forces there during the period. The Society maintained close bonds, according to the book.

The question was: Why did a society of former military officers want anything to do with George Payson and Bill Dabney? What on earth connected them? Or was it a false lead? Swallowing the last of his beer, he decided he needed to look into Bill Dabney a bit more. In good time.

For now, to bed. It was only half past ten, but he was completely and entirely exhausted. Still, it was a tiredness tinged with satisfaction, the end product of a long, good day of work.

Lenox woke up later than usual the next morning, Monday, with the rays of the sun striping his sheets. He pulled the bell by his desk and stood up to put on his robe and slippers. In about ten minutes there was a sharp knock on the door, and young Thomas Tate came in with a tray that once again must have weighed about what he did. Lenox gave him another sixpence and thanked him with a smile, before fixing himself a quick cup of tea. Always important to have that first gulp so that one could feel human again.

He ate at the table by the windows that peered into New College. It was a pretty, clear day, when yellow leaves hung thick on the branches and a breath of wind scattered another dozen to the ground. The sun was watery but bright, and the sky a pale, early blue. Perhaps because Oxford had so little to do with factories and trains, or perhaps because it was in a valley, shielded by its depth, there was rarely the blinding fog of London here. It refreshed Lenox. In twenty years it might not be any longer, but for now Oxford was still the country, with meadows at the end of every street and many roads made only of dirt. Cleaner air, and birds still giving morning voice to their songs.

The September Society. Could it be an accident? One thing was a relief to him: If the boys had been either of them murdered, even if their bodies had been thrown in the Thames, something would have come out by now. Lenox had instructed Graham to wire up any accounts of unidentified bodies, and the only report that had come was of an elderly man discovered in Covent Garden, stabbed to death without identification on his person. Nothing had been reported closer to Oxford.

He ate a last bit of toast and poached egg, took a last swallow of tea, and looked at his watch. Quarter to nine. He just had time to interview Professor Hatch before catching the 11:50 to Paddington.

Hatch's house, which was located only a few steps away at 13 Holywell Street, was an old, narrow stone place with four windows facing the street and a green front door. It was painted white, and to match the door there was a green roof. Rather nice for a professor.

A maid answered the door and led Lenox into a front drawing room that was small and close, filled with science journals spilling off of bookcases. Very little light made its way through the blinds.

The professor took quite a long time to come down, and after a while Lenox realized that he might have woken the man. When at last he came into the room he was a surprisingly tall and hearty chap, indeed strong, though with sallow skin and black circles underneath his eyes. He had a mustache and wore an impeccable dark suit.

"John Hatch," he said.

Lenox introduced himself, and the two men shook hands.

"How may I help you?" Hatch said.

"Nobody has seen Bill Dabney or George Payson in two days, and I'm trying to find them."

Hatch looked genuinely puzzled, if not all that concerned. "I'm afraid I'm not the most likely man to have seen them," he said. "Though I'm sorry to hear of it. Have you checked around much?"

"Yes, a bit. Oxford is such a small town that it seems probable that a friend or a classmate would have caught sight of one of them. When did you last see them?"

Hatch considered the question. "Both about a fortnight ago. I had a small gathering here at my house for the students I advise, as I often do. Bill and George usually came."

Lenox made a note on his pad. "Any idea where they may have gone?"

"None at all, unless they went home."

"No."

"Then I don't, I'm sorry to say. London? Your guess is as good as mine."

"What are they like, the two boys?"

"Both bright. Above middling, anyway, though I really couldn't say with any expertise. Medicine is my field, not classics or history. Dabney was more introverted than Payson. Both the sort of gentlemen to be popular in a place like Oxford. Payson was at Westminster like myself, so we had that in common. I don't know what else to say."

"Have you heard of the September Society?"

"Can't say that I have, no."

"Have you noticed Dabney and Payson pulling apart from the other students at all?"

"Not the sort of thing I'd be likely to notice. I'm not in college much, except for hall, and then I sit with my colleagues at high table."

"Did you know they kept a cat?"

"Did they?"

"It was found dead."

"That seems odd."

"Decidedly."

"I could use the body in class, if you like."

"No, that's all right."

"Well, it's the same to me."

"Was either of them at all in trouble, that you knew of? Financially? Did they break rules?"

"Just in normal amounts. Financially, I couldn't say. Not really my place, is it?"

"Some might say it was."

"No," Hatch said firmly. "Not quite done."

"You speak as if you were more friend than advisor to them."

"I admit that, to be sure. Oxford's a dull place, Mr. Lenox. I don't mind a *coupe* of champagne or a glass of beer here and there. I miss London something devilish. And the lads and I have more in common than I do with the dons."

There was a strange kind of unease in the air. Lenox couldn't put his finger on it.

"You don't know anything about Dabney's background, then?" he said.

Hatch raised his eyebrows in contemplation. "Certainly not much. I know he's from north of here, somewhere in the Midlands, I believe. I know that he shares digs with Thomas Stamp, rather a friend of the two boys."

"You haven't met Dabney's parents?"

"No. The master will have, Banbury."

"Payson's?"

"Oh, yes, his mother. Father's dead, I heard."

"How did his mother strike you?"

"A little bit rattled by life, perhaps? Introspective, I would call it."

Lenox nodded. "Is there anything else you can think of? Anything relevant?"

"No, not particularly. Sorry."

"Oh—by the way, when did you start giving your parties?"

"I've been here many years. Began with them straight away."

"I see. Thanks again."

Lenox showed himself out. A decidedly strange

man, he thought to himself. Why had he stayed in Oxford for eight years if he didn't like it? Walking briskly past Trinity College, Lenox also thought how unusual it was for somebody innocent to lie twice in twenty minutes to a complete stranger. For one thing, Stamp had mentioned that Dabney and Payson took the cat to Hatch's parties and let it wander around his house. For another, he and Scratch had both said that the last party was four nights before, on Thursday, not eight or nine, and certainly not a fortnight.

CHAPTER TWELVE

Before he left, Lenox stopped by Lincoln College again. Hall was still open for breakfast, and there were loose groups of students framed in the windows, eating, studying, and lingering until classes began.

He took a walk around the Grove Quad and the Fellows' Garden, thinking. Each of the lads would miss a tutorial today; they hadn't been at meals for some time; their friends, beyond Stamp, would begin to mark their absence. The police would have to be involved, he thought. He would write them from London.

He went to Stamp's room and knocked on the door.

"Had your collections?" Lenox asked him.

"Yes," said Stamp, pushing his blond hair away from his face as he constantly did. "Brutal. We had a question on Cromwell's protectorate that you wouldn't believe. I couldn't even understand it, much less answer it. Some bother about predestination and right rule and I don't know what."

"It's over, at any rate."

"Yes. I wish this matter with Dabs and Payson weren't going on, or I could have a drink to celebrate."

"Has anything further come to you? Perhaps a conversation with one of them? Or a trip they had talked about?"

"The only thing I thought of after you left yesterday was that Dabney sometimes talked of getting digs in London after we leave Oxford, the three of us. It couldn't possibly be related, but he did talk it over a good deal."

"Were they spontaneous?"

"Not exceptionally, and I would be surprised if they had done something off the cuff without me."

"What do you think of your head porter here? Reliable fellow?"

"Red?"

"Is that his name?"

"Well, we call him that. His real name is Kelly. He's Irish, though."

"Ah."

"I don't know if I've heard anyone call him his real name in my life, other than the junior dean or the chaplain or some dour chap like that. The lads' mothers."

"Is he reliable?"

"I should say so, yes. Pretty steady with us, doesn't make trouble if you're a moment or two past lock-in. All of the porters around the college belonged to one company in some regiment of the army—can't remember which, maybe the Royal Pioneer Corps?—and we got more or less lucky. Nice chaps. The worst is at Queen's, down the lane. They have the Scots Guards. Absolute dragons, they say. It's a pretty miserable lot over there anyway. The students, I mean."

"Have you thought about my advice? A spell at home?"

"I've thought about little else. More about that than Oliver Cromwell, unfortunately. Or Charles II and the Restoration or Dryden as court poet or anything like that."

"I'm sorry to hear it."

"Well, it's not ideal, but I do appreciate it. I think I'll go to see my aunt in London for five days—until my next tute. They're good about letting you use the British Library there, if you run into the right librarians. My aunt doesn't have a world-class collection of modern histories, unfortunately."

Lenox laughed. "I'm glad to hear you'll be safe

down there," he said. "I'm leaving in an hour if you'd like to share the train."

"Nice of you, but I'll go this afternoon. Have to send a few hours' warning."

Lenox handed Stamp a card. "Please come see me if you like, or if you think of anything. I live round St. James's Park."

"I say, that's decent of you. I shall."

They said good-bye, and Lenox went up to George Payson's room again.

It had been tidied since yesterday, books straightened, old tea removed, boots cleaned, so Lenox went back downstairs to find the head porter.

He was a man of middling size wearing a black suit and a pair of thin silver spectacles that were just perched on his nose. When he spoke there was no trace of his country of origin, and his hair was in fact black, not red. Some long-graduated student's idea of an Irish joke.

"Mr. Kelly?" Lenox said.

"You've found me—but call me Red."

"I'm Charles Lenox."

"Ah, Mr. Lenox. How do you do?"

"Not badly, thanks. May I ask a housekeeping question?"

"Certainly."

"Did you know that the scout had cleaned George Payson's room since yesterday?"

"Yes, as usual."

"He hadn't for two or three days prior."

"True enough—at the student's special request. But it had been two days since we cleaned it."

"Is it common for students to request that the scout not clean their rooms?"

"Not uncommon, if they're studying for an exam and have their papers and things as they like. Or if they've lost something."

"Did Payson ask you or his scout?"

"His scout. I would have discouraged the lad."

"Why did you ask for it to be cleaned today?"

"As I say, I discourage it as a policy. A porter's second concern is always cleanliness in the college."

"His first?"

"Security."

Lenox thought it best not to point out the irony of this. "To be sure. How did you discover that the room was untouched?"

"From the scout himself. I get weekly reports, and it so happens this morning was his."

"Any ideas about Payson's whereabouts?"

"I should say on a trip to London. He didn't report it, but again that's not entirely uncommon. We try not to send students down for relatively minor infractions like that any longer."

"Wise policy. Different than my day."

"Times change."

"Can you think of any other places where Payson might have gone?"

93

"I'm afraid I can't, no."

"Thank you, Mr. Kelly."

"Call me Red, as I say," he said.

"Well, in that case, thank you, Red."

"Pleased."

Lenox wandered down Broad Street, its bookstores and cafés busy with students from the nearest colleges—Trinity, Wadham, Jesus, and Lenox's own, Balliol—and thought over the case.

When he boarded the train he was still thinking, and as it began to move he asked himself: Could it be a coincidence that Payson had left the odd assortment of objects on his floor and then asked to have his room left alone?

More important, he thought as he gazed out over the low, misty fields south of Oxford, set back from the Thames: Could it be a coincidence that all of the objects—the pen, the long, frayed string, and, of course, the tomato—were the color red?

CHAPTER THIRTEEN

He arrived at Paddington just in time to have a late lunch at the Marlborough Club, where he ran into several people he knew. After speaking with them he sat in the long front hall, whose windows looked out over the street from just a few feet above it, and wrote a letter to the Oxford police, stating the case as he saw it.

In his heart he felt guilty for leaving Oxford, and this letter helped defray that guilt. He wasn't proud of his return to London, however brief he made it, but he felt that he had to see Lady Jane.

A September breeze blew mildly down the streets, which were sparkling and slippery after a morning rain. Lenox sent a message to Graham asking for the carriage to come round. It gave him time to sit in the club and smoke a pipe waiting for it. In fact, if he were honest with himself, he didn't truly *want* to go back to Hampden Lane straight away.

His friend Lord Cabot had taken the afternoon away from the House of Lords, and the two men sat talking about politics, Cabot excitedly disagreeing with Lenox's every word, leaning forward, both hands on top of his cane, which he occasionally stamped if he was making what he thought to be an especially salient point.

He left for home a little while later, peering thoughtfully through the window of his carriage. Funny how he disliked to leave London even for a day, even to go to a place he loved as much as Oxford. Was it because of Jane, he asked himself? Because he was an old bachelor, set in his ways? The only place he could truly stand to visit was Lenox House, and that because Edmund lived there and Lenox himself had spent the first years of his life there.

In the past month he had given longer attention to himself, to his own virtues and flaws, than at any time in his entire life. By nature he was introspective, analytical, second-guessing, but now he forced himself toward self-evaluation. Lady Jane deserved that, before he put their friendship in peril with such a dangerous question.

What had he discovered? Well, he thought, he was too ingrained in his ways, too much a bachelor with his clubs, friends, and habits. He liked his eggs poached a certain way, to rise at a certain time, to take certain walks every evening, to make certain social rounds. He liked to read the papers in the morning and again in the evening—it consumed an alarming amount of time. He could occasionally be cross when his patterns were disrupted. His and Graham's strange, useful friendship might not accommodate a third party well.

He didn't think that he had any major flaws, no particular vices, but all of these small things perhaps added up to one: He was growing increasingly resistant to change. It was a quality he truly disliked in others. There were two sides to that coin; either it was all the more reason to change his life, to make a radical gesture (though that was secondary to his real, enduring love), or else it would be ungentlemanly to impose his foibles on the person he most admired and loved in the world.

What were his virtues? He was honest. He was happy and cheerful. He had little trouble admitting that to himself. For the sake of inquiry he also overcame his dislike of self-congratulation by admitting that he was generous. His generosity fell short of Jane's, but he was generous—that is, not only with money but with time and tolerance, generous toward people's bad impulses. They were well matched in that respect.

Was he ambitious enough? Was he a dilettante? Didn't Lady Jane deserve to be the partner, the equal companion and helpmeet, of a Prime Minister or a bishop? His life was something of a disappointment to him in this way; he had hoped to be Prime Minister when he was young. He had assumed it would come to him. Instead he had gotten sidetracked and into this field— which was in no way shameful, and which he held his head high when discussing, but upon which the world bestowed very little prestige.

All of this flashed across his mind, swerving this way and that, sometimes even before words attached to the idea, sometimes more deliberatively.

By the time he arrived home he was nervous. Lack of courage, he thought, add that to the list of flaws. Faint heart never won fair lady. He decided to knock on her door.

Just as he stepped out of his coach, however, he saw a tall, slim man, about his own age, leaving Lady Jane's house. His heart turned over—nobody he recognized. This was the peril of propinquity. Of course, Jane did go out more than he. (Not social enough, add that to the list.) He quickly changed course for his own door, though he stopped on the step to watch the man hail a cab. He was in a long gray morning coat. No beard, but a few side-whiskers. He had no watch chain, which Lenox found odd.

Then he felt ashamed of himself and went inside, determined to put the man out of his mind.

Later that afternoon, getting toward five, he asked Graham to take an invitation for tea next door.

"An invitation?" said Graham, plainly disconcerted. Usually the two friends dropped in on each other.

"She may have other plans today. I'm not sure, I was away."

Graham said nothing more, but nodded and took the note.

In about five minutes Lady Jane came into the library. "An invitation? Is the Queen visiting?"

They both laughed. He was struck at her beauty, the sort of simple beauty he admired most, perhaps because that was his taste or perhaps because he associated it with her. It was the beauty of the good and the considerate.

"How do you do?" he asked, rising and smiling.

"Quite well, quite well—not a dull moment. There was that little party you missed at Toto's last night. She nearly fainted because McConnell came in late with a dead cat in a bag. She has you to blame for that, hasn't she?"

"I'm afraid so."

She was her usual cheerful self, brimming with good humor, but once again Lenox detected in her some slightly careworn aspect.

"At any rate, they had a row of furious whispers, and all that saved the day was Edward Leicester arriving and tripping over the threshold, to everyone's amusement."

She was busy taking off her gloves, smoothing her gray skirt out, checking that her hair was still in place—all the minor offices Lenox was so accustomed to seeing her complete and yet were so estranged from his daily life, from the solitude of bachelorhood.

"Yes," he said, "I'm afraid McConnell and Toto are rather backsliding. Fighting, I guess. It's the absolute devil. We had a talk together, and he seemed like his old despondent self, I'm sorry to say."

She nodded wisely and unhappily. "Toto is restless too. I should have spotted it earlier. Perhaps I'll take her on a trip to Bath so they can have some time separately. They married when she was too young, as I've said to you a thousand times. She had the maturity to love, but not to be married."

"Yes."

"Oh, but here I am prattling on like a girl. Ridiculous. How are you, more importantly, Charles?"

The look of affection in her eyes when she said this wrecked him. But all he said was, "Oh, very well, thank you. A puzzling case in Oxford. Two lads missing, no sign or reason why."

"How odd."

"It is, actually. There's something more than usual at the bottom of it, I think, but I can't say what it is because I don't know." He paused in thought and then shook himself out of it. "But tell me something of life here. I'm out of touch."

She laughed. "After two days?"

She told him about the dinner party the night before, then about the rumors circulating that there would be a change in Parliament, and so they talked on in their usual fashion, laughing and conspiring, old jokes passing between them. A dozen times the fateful words rose to Lenox's lips, and a dozen times he left them unspoken.

Then, as she rose to go, there was a frantic knock on the door, and McConnell rushed in.

"Oh, hullo, Jane," he said. "Sorry to barge in, but I have urgent news—for you, Charles."

"What is it?" both Lenox and Lady Jane asked at once.

"I've had a telegram from my friend Radley."

"Radley?"

"Up at Oxford. He's a don there. It seems the police have found a body."

CHAPTER FOURTEEN

Lenox would never forgive himself for returning to London. Of all the selfish acts in his life, was there any worse than this? Had he lost his mind?

Sitting on the train, watching the dim and ashen light of evening spread over the countryside, its darkness his own, he asked these questions again and again in his mind. For once there was no solace in the prospect of finding the killer. For once no comfort rallied to dethrone his self-doubt.

"Whose body?" he had asked McConnell back in London.

"It was Payson's, I believe. My friend sent the telegram off hastily, though, so it might well be a false alarm."

"I'm certain it's not. I've been unfathomably stupid. Found where?"

"Christ Church Meadow, just behind—is it Merton?"

"That's right," Lenox said. "I say, could I see that telegram?"

McConnell handed it over. It read:

THOMAS BODY FOUND STOP CH CH MEADOW STOP PAYSON STOP DASHED SORRY RADLEY STOP

It had been sent from the post office opposite Pembroke.

"Radley?" said Lady Jane.

"A friend of mine from the Royal Society. Awfully good chap. Not at all alarmist, I shouldn't say. I went round to his rooms for a visit while you were with Lady Annabelle and told him about the case."

There was a long moment of stunned silence in the room. Then Lady Jane had done something Lenox was already grateful for, even in the dark pessimism of the train ride. She had said, "Well, Charles, you had better pack your bag and go."

It didn't seem like much, but it was one of those small instances when a friend's decisiveness means the world. She had bothered over his coat, his hat, his suitcase, tut-tutting, asking Graham for an article he had overlooked, while McConnell whipped back home to get his things. Then, when Lenox had tried to thank her, she had said, "No time for that—off with you, and we'll speak soon," and hustled him out to the waiting hansom.

Now McConnell was in the seat across the compartment, having a sip from his flask and reading over Lenox's notes.

"Rum business," he said, sealing the flask. He smiled weakly at his own pun.

"I'm to blame," Lenox answered dully. "I made two errors. I shouldn't have left Oxford, and I shouldn't have delayed in contacting the police."

"Perhaps the first, but not the second," McConnell answered. "Lady Annabelle asked you to keep it from the police."

"Lady Annabelle's not a detective, Thomas."

"And you're not the boy's mother."

Lenox shrugged, ignoring the kindly look in his friend's face, and they passed the rest of the trip in silence.

When they arrived in Oxford, they took a cab straight to Lincoln. There was general alarm on the Front Quad, students ringed around the lawn in small groups, and the dons standing above them on the steps leading to the chapel. Everywhere were worried faces and anxious voices.

Lenox spotted Stamp, who was as pale as a ghost. "They're saying it was Payson, poor chap. Somebody garroted him. I shipped my train."

"I'm so sorry," Lenox said.

"It's not your fault, of course," said the young man, brushing the hair away from his face.

"What do you plan to do?"

103

"Unless I'm needed, I'm leaving in ten minutes—I've hired a coach. No use messing about any longer. What a fearful thing to happen!"

They bade each other a quick good-bye. As Stamp wandered away, shaking hands with a few of his classmates, the head porter came over to Lenox and McConnell. He was more collected, subdued, somber, but with an unmistakable efficiency in his demeanor.

"No fault of your own, Mr. Lenox," he said.

"How did they know it was Payson?"

"It was him, though they didn't confirm so for some time. The body was badly mauled, and there was a terrible amount of blood. The hair on his head was cut close, nearly shaved—as a disguise, we all suppose. But once he was clean somebody identified him, I think Professor Hatch, perhaps, or Master Banbury. It's all settled now. Confirmed by his clothes, his papers, his billfold, his eyeglasses, his brand of cigarettes. The family is on its way." He sighed. "Awful business, of course. At Lincoln!"

McConnell shook his head sympathetically. "A horrifying sort of death, strangulation. It takes looking your victim in the face."

Lenox nodded. He saw four bobbies at the other end of the quad and after shaking Kelly's hand walked toward them.

"Hello," he said when he reached them. "I'm Charles Lenox."

The one who appeared to be in charge said, "May we help you?"

"I've been looking into this matter in the past few days."

"Ah, that one," said the same man. As he turned away, he said, "Might'uv told us before just now. Might'uv helped."

"Well, I'd like to help now, if I may."

The man looked at him scornfully. "Come by the station, then," he said. "Ask for Goodson, he's in charge of this investigation. But don't think of looking at the crime scene."

As the bobby walked away, McConnell said, "Don't be too hard on yourself, Charles."

Lenox grimaced. "Look—we'll just have to figure it all out, that's all."

"Damn right," said McConnell tersely.

"Can you devise a way to have a look at the body?"

"May be hard."

"If you can think of a way to do it—make friends with the coroner, offer to assist him, anything—give it a chance, would you?"

"That's the spirit. Off I go. I'll be at the Randolph Hotel tomorrow morning if you'd like to have breakfast. Say eight? All right. And really, don't be too angry with yourself. You were only gone eight hours."

The two men parted, while Lenox debated with himself what his next move should be and thought the case over.

He would have to start with Professor Hatch and the head porter. Somehow neither seemed to him like the type to murder a man in cold blood, but then again neither seemed entirely guileless. For now, he would go back to the hotel and think over what he already knew, searching for the line of clues that would lead him irrevocably toward the truth. Surveying the quad one last time, he turned on his heel and went out of the gate, into the sudden and startling quietness of Turl Street.

CHAPTER FIFTEEN

The Turf Tavern was bright and loud with merriment, full of students in the back bar sipping pints of ale and the local gents sitting in the front bar with their strong cider. Lenox remembered that division between the old townsmen and the young university ones, the two sets united by an unspoken love for Sally, who had been the serving girl then. Lenox's friend George Caule had always stopped into the front room to have a drink with old Hedges, who had once run the tuckshop. Their friendship had sprung up eerily: over a ghost.

The story was that Caule had been studying alone at the Turf in Trinity term of their first year. He was maths, was Caule, and had the legendarily terrifying Mead as his don at Balliol. Lenox strained to remember what had occurred. Had he been—yes, that was right, he had been smoking a cigarette to wake himself up when at last he dozed off, the last person in the deserted room. Just as he had dropped the cigarette onto the tinder pile by his feet, a girl of perhaps ten had brushed by him, nudging him just enough on the arm to wake him up. He had quickly stamped out the fire and then left for the night, realizing he was too tired to study any longer.

Caule described the little girl so well—how she had blond pigtails, a dainty little dress, and a pearl and obsidian necklace, how she carried a tray of mustard jars. When he had returned the next day to thank the girl's parents, though, nobody could identify her, and he discovered that the mustard jars had been long collected by that late hour.

Unbeaten, Caule had asked around. Only Hedges had recognized the description.

"Small girl, pigtails, blond, ten, mustard jars?" Hedges had asked in his uniquely concise speech, gruff-voiced and cautious. "To be certain. Polly Millwall. She was a year younger than me. Daughter of the last chap who owned the Turf. She died in the fire that killed them all, perhaps forty years ago. Then Edmonds bought the place."

"Oh, I'm afraid you've misunderstood," Caule had said. "I've—"

He broke off when Hedges pointed upward, to an exact portrait of the girl who had nudged him awake, just when he was in danger of starting the fire in the tinder pile and burning the Turf to the ground.

Lenox sighed. How the years passed! Caule was still one of his closest friends—and still swore by the story—but lived up all the way up at Stettleton Hall in Lancashire, a genial, rather broken-down place. He hadn't been south to London in two years. As Lenox went inside, past the portrait of the blond girl that still took pride of place over the bar, he wondered for the hundredth time whether Caule had been so tired that delusion had set in or whether maybe, just maybe, something inexplicable had happened.

"Back already, Mr. Lenox?"

"I'm afraid so, Mrs. Tate. Could I have a room?"

"Why, of course," she said. "Anything to eat?"

"That's all right, thanks. I suppose I only need some sleep."

She looked at him sympathetically. "All right," she said. "You know where the room is. Here's the key."

Tramping up the staircase again, Lenox felt none of the same thrill of return. The room now seemed bare and comfortless, too small, the memories it held inconsequential. As he sat in the hard, narrow chair by the window, he was full of the deepest self-recrimination he had ever felt. The starless sky refused to return his gaze, absorbing the darkness of his thoughts: She would never consent to marry him, and quite rightly. What was he? A small-time detective, pretending he was better than those who did the same job for their bread and butter.

He sat by the window for half an hour and then stood up with a sigh and went to the bureau to unpack his suitcase. He did so listlessly, doing a job so untidy that Graham would have cringed to see it, and wondered if he could remember that other old ghost story about the Turf. Yes, of course he could. He would never forget it.

Lenox had been quite close with his grandfather, his mother's father, the 3rd Marquess of Lansdowne, and often visited him at Bowood House, the Lansdowne family seat in Wiltshire. This was long past the days when the marquess had been the Member of Parliament for Cambridge University and served as chancellor of the exchequer. By then he spent most of his time in his large library, compiling his memoirs and reading. He was a tall, wrinkled, mischievous old man with snow white hair and an endless succession of stories.

One of them was about the dirt hauling lane behind the Turf, where the local farms' animals tracked on their way across the city to the butcher's. A boy, Samuel, was returning from the butcher, having dropped off a flock of sheep there, when by the back door of the Turf two menacing gents had appeared, drunk and restive.

"What do ye want?" Samuel had shouted at them preemptively. Lenox could hear his grandfather imitating the voice.

"You have yer butcher money there, isn't it?" said one of the men, and a moment later both had started walking toward him.

At that instant, a massive black dog, something like a Great Dane, had materialized (the boy swore) out of thin air and started growling at the two men, standing between them and the boy. The men had leapt back into the Turf's doorway, cursing the dog and the boy alike, and let them pass safely. Then the boy had run all the way through the city, past the dim colleges and murmuring pubs, until he reached the fields on the other side of town, by the river. The dog had run with him all the way, but there he stopped, immovable.

"What?" Samuel had said. All the dog did was nuzzle the fence they stood by and stamp on the ground over and over. "What?" the boy asked again, and the dog had put his nose to the same spot. So Samuel had marked it with a stick by the side of the road, and as soon as that was done the dog had vanished, again (the boy swore) into thin air.

The next morning, after he had safely deposited the money with the farmer, the boy had gone back to the spot by the fence and dug a hole. About three feet down he found a dog's bones. In the rib cage was a small box, and in the box were forty gold pieces. A few years later, at the age of sixteen, Samuel had used them to buy the Turf Tavern.

The old myths. There was some small relief in the memory of them, in the memory of his grandfather. But it passed, and Lenox went to bed that evening caught in a world of his own ghosts, his own dead, thinking of the newest in their number—poor George Payson, who didn't even have the blessing of sorrow anymore.

CHAPTER SIXTEEN

Enough. That was Lenox's first thought when he woke up in the morning. Would it serve the dead to indulge in any further self-recrimination? Of course it wouldn't. Solving the case was the only thing he could do of any consequence. When he had made this decision the room seemed like a brighter place, and after he had called down for a pot of coffee Lenox sat at the small table and wrote out a list of information in his notebook.

He wrote:

Clues in the Death of George Payson

1) The cat and its peculiar death.
2) x12/43 21 31 25/x2
3) Letter opener, initial P.
4) Frayed string; pen; tomato; all red,
   in unlikely spot.
5) Disrupted line of ash by the window.
6) September Society card, black and pink
   X on reverse. (Unlikely to doodle in
   two colors . . .)
7) Muddied walking boots (on the chair)
   and walking stick. (GP the type to take
   long walks?)
8) Hatch's two lies.

Having written this out, he sat and thought for a few more moments, tapping his pen on the table, then stood up to change into his morning suit. He was due to meet McConnell soon, and didn't want to be late. The eight clues rattled around in his mind the entire time he dressed.

McConnell was sitting at a table by the window at the Randolph Hotel that overlooked the Ashmolean. When Lenox came into the room, the doctor stood up and met him, subtly searching his face for the sorrow that had been there the night before. All at once Lenox, disconcerted, realized that it must have been the look McConnell constantly received, the reason his eyes were so often cast aside when he sipped from his flask.

"Well, you look a thousand times better, old chap," said the doctor.

"Nothing like hard work to lift your spirits, you know. I've had a conversation with myself—abominably long-winded one, too—and decided to solve the case."

"There's the spirit of Agincourt," said McConnell with a laugh. "A Lenox on the front lines there, I bet."

"Twinging the arrows around, that's right." Lenox laughed too. "But look here, what happened last night?"

"Ah—about that, why don't we gulp something down, and then I'd like to take you over to see someone."

"Who's that?"

"Better to leave it."

"That's awfully mysterious."

"Not especially," said McConnell with a smile, "but I want to have a bite of breakfast, and I know you'll be dragging me off before the fish course if you begin thinking about the case."

They ate their eggs and rashers quickly, washing them down with tea and talking only about McConnell's next cataloging expedition north—the doctor had a particular hope of finding an unclassified and possibly apocryphal sea otter rumored to live in the Fjords—and when they had laid down their forks and knives both men lit cigarettes.

"Go on, then," Lenox said. "Release me from the suspense."

"They'll let you look at the crime scene in the meadow."

"Thomas! How on earth did they consent to that?"

"By pure chance I knew the coroner assigned to the body, a chap named Alfred Morris. Rather grim fellow, you know, but we studied at St. Bart's Hospital together. I asked if I might help, and he said I could willingly enough."

"Why?"

"Probably wanted to make certain that he didn't bungle the thing, second set of eyes and all that. They don't have many murders up here. At any rate, I can tell you about the body later." After saying this McConnell stubbed out his cigarette, stood up, and motioned for the check. "Just put it on room 312, would you?" he said to the waiter. "What's more important for the moment is that after Morris and I looked over the body, we went to meet Inspector Goodson, and I talked him around to letting you in on the work. Dropped a few names—the Marbury case, Soames, that small job you did for Buckingham Palace—and in the end he was quite pleased to have you in town."

The two men had left and were walking along

Magdalen Street now, south toward Merton and Christ Church.

"I don't know how to thank you," said Lenox. "I'd be nowhere if you hadn't come up. You're invaluable, Thomas."

Presently they came to the slender path that ran inside of Merton (one of the most beautiful of all the colleges, in Lenox's opinion, more beautiful by far than the ostentation of Christ Church) between the imposing beauty of the chapel, cut through with the strangely evanescent light of its stained glass windows, and the old Mob Quad, the small quadrangle responsible for the shape of Oxford to come—for all universities to come, in fact, the oldest structure of the ancient university. Merton was one of the most interesting colleges at Oxford historically, as well as probably the oldest; it was the only one not to side with the Royalists in the Civil War, and among its early alumni was Sir Thomas Bodley, the namesake of the Bodleian. Lenox relished seeing it again, though too soon the narrow perspective of the path had opened out into the fields of Christ Church Meadow. About two hundred yards away from the rear of Merton was a still-bustling crime scene.

"This looks to be it," said McConnell, "and there's Goodson."

The Oxford inspector spotted Lenox and McConnell just as they spotted him.

"Mr. Lenox," he said, putting out his hand, "I'm afraid you caught my sergeant at a bad moment yesterday evening. Glad to have you here."

He was a medium-sized man, brown-haired and freckled, with a look of intensity in his face. There was also honesty there, and in his green eyes a hint of amiability.

"Not at all. It's a damnable business from top to bottom."

"If you come this way, you can have a look around." Goodson motioned for a constable to lift the rope and beckoned Lenox and McConnell inside. "The body was here, sprawled on its back with its arms behind its head. There were foot-prints all around the area, unfortunately. People tramping around here all day, I'm afraid, and leaving every conceivable kind of shoe mark."

"Clever of the killer, that," said Lenox. "A good place to leave the body—or indeed to kill someone—if you have very little time, because it's completely empty at night and yet still bears the signs of an active thoroughfare."

"Precisely."

"Where do you think they came in from, the murdered man and his murderer?"

"Came in from?"

"Where did they enter the park, I mean?"

The meadow was triangular and bound by Christ Church, Merton, and the two rivers. Away from the city of Oxford toward the south end of the

park, there was a lower meadow, which sometimes flooded, and past which there were mostly
fields.

"We haven't considered that," said Goodson.

"Down at the south end, I'd reckon," said
Lenox. "To come from any other direction would
have meant either passing porters, students,
and dons or else scaling a high fence. But it
would have been easy enough to come in over the
rivers, and the fields in that direction are empty,
aren't they?"

"I suppose that's right," said Goodson dubi-
ously. "You mean they were hiding out just past
the rivers there?"

"Exactly. Before yesterday the lads were probably south of here, by the least crowded part of
the meadow, but still not that far from Oxford."

It dawned on Goodson how significant this
was, and in unison the three men strode south.
When they got there they found the ground less
worked over by pedestrians. Goodson beckoned
to the crime scene, and two constables came over
to see him. There were a few walking bridges
over the rivers.

"Look on these bridges here for any marks of
struggle—"

"Blood," said Lenox.

"Blood, yes," Goodson said.

"I would also recommend sending people
south of the city, even farther than here," said

Lenox, "to check in the small hotels and the pubs, the little shops, that sort of thing."

"I will," said Goodson, noting it down.

As they walked back, Lenox said, "We should all realize the intelligence it took the murderer to disobey his instincts and return to a *more* populated area to kill George Payson. Of course, the killer's first thought would have been to go somewhere remote—but it would have taken time, first of all, to find somewhere so remote that a body would remain hidden for long. He didn't have time to be that careful."

McConnell said, "I don't believe it negates your point, Charles, but it's worth mention that George Payson was dead before he came to lie here. We also learned from the body that he had been sleeping rough, outdoors, at best in barns or lean-tos. Only his face and hands had been recently cleaned."

"That makes sense." Lenox puzzled it over. "I suppose you'd better tell me all about the body, McConnell. But first, let's look at the place where he was found. We can't properly call it the scene of the crime, unfortunately."

CHAPTER SEVENTEEN

Anybody who has ever studied at Oxford loves Christ Church Meadow. With water to one side and the tall, beautiful college spires to the other, it is quintessentially English, almost like a picture by Constable in which water, grass, and a building so old it seems like part of nature itself all breathe against each other. To Lenox, it was most beautiful in the long golden light of spring-time, when its green expanse seemed limitless and the soft water sounds of rowers and punters floated on the air, while in the distance cattle grazed in the lower water meadow. The line of boathouses down at one end was a happy place, too, for a day spent punting with friends along the Cherwell, drinking champagne (or champs, as they called it at Oxford) and eating cold chicken, was as close to heaven as this earth could get. A day of punting could erase weeks of dark Bodleian nights from the memory.

But Lenox pushed these memories aside now and concentrated on the site where George Payson's body had been fifteen hours before.

There were five or six policemen around the roped-off area, as well as another dozen curious passersby. The men from the force were spending their time either classifying footprints or keeping people back from the site. To Goodson's credit, they had left the scene in good working order, and the imprint of the body was still visible. Lenox noticed that it was slightly deeper toward the middle.

"The person who dropped George Payson's body must have been carrying him like this"—Lenox demonstrated—"just the way you carry a bride across the threshold, if you see what I mean, and then simply dropped him."

"I figured as much," said Goodson rather testily.

"Oh, certainly," said Lenox. "This has all been done in a first-rate way—a sight better than some I could name from London might have done. I was only straightening the thing out in my own head. That means, then, that the person's footprints are probably just ten inches to the left of the body—ah, a dense patch, I see," he said, responding to Goodson's pointing out the spot. "I really have to congratulate your thoroughness. The only other point to gather here, then, is that Payson must have been newly dead, garroted only a few moments before the killer dropped him here."

"Why?" Goodson asked.

"Because the arms were splayed out above the head," said Lenox, pointing to where the arms had left indentations in the soil. "They were still loose. The killer wouldn't have carried him with his arms like that. Too unwieldy, too easily noticeable. He left the body as it fell. McConnell, how long would rigor mortis have taken to set in?"

"It can take anywhere from five minutes to two hours, but in this case, given how the body has loosened again, probably on the shorter side—call it fifteen minutes."

"There you have it, Inspector," said Lenox.

"What do you mean?"

"Even if the killer had some means of transport, the scene of the murder can't have been far off at all. And this park is only accessible by foot, which cuts down the distance even further."

"Ah," said Goodson, writing on his pad. "So the fight could only have taken place within a fifteen-minute walk of this spot."

"Call it a four-minute walk, actually—perhaps a six-minute perimeter south of here, figuring that one walks much less quickly when carrying so much weight."

"All right—I'll tell the lads."

"Just a moment," Lenox said. "What about objects near the body?"

"At the station. Here, Ramsey, take these gentleman to the station when they're ready to go and show them the box of things we found. All right, Mr. Lenox, Mr. McConnell." With a nod Goodson walked off to give the men by the river to the south their instructions, stopping on the way to bark at the crowd that had gathered until they dispersed.

Ramsey came over. "On your signal, then," he said.

Lenox nodded. "Give it ten minutes, if that's all right?"

"Just as you say."

When they were alone, McConnell said, "What do you reckon?"

"Well, above all I'm grateful to you for finding a way for us to see this place. My other two thoughts are that we're dealing with someone remarkably clever and that if there's no sign of Dabney anytime soon it looks a bit black against him. Now what about the body?"

"We've covered some of the details these past few minutes. There's not much else to tell. He was garroted, but he put up a damn good fight. I'd say the murderer will have some wounds to show for it. It was a standard stud chain garrote."

"What's that?"

"A long leather loop with a metal chain on the end."

"How easy do you reckon it is to acquire one of those? I most often see scarves or fishing line as garrotes. Piano wire once."

"Quite easy. It was a stud chain, the kind used to whip horses. You can find one in any stable."

Lenox thought for a moment, then said, "Go on."

"There were two other singular circumstances that Morris and I discovered. One, the body was bloody and badly mauled around the face and torso."

"Unrecognizably so?"

"No, perhaps not, but badly. It's strange, given how short a time the body was exposed to the elements."

"Animal wounds?"

"That's hard to say."

"What was the other singular circumstance?"

"How closely shorn his hair was."

"Disguise, I would have thought."

"On his head, to be sure—but the hair was shorn from all over his body, you know, not just his head."

"That's passing strange."

"We thought so, too."

The doctor and the detective discussed George Payson's corpse for another moment and then made their way to look at the objects found around the body with Constable Ramsey.

At the station the constable brought out a small cardboard box, filled with a random and, truth be told, somewhat unsatisfactory collection of odds and ends, most of which had probably been simply dropped in the park and never cleared away. There was a white feather, a receipt for a new hat to be picked up in a day's time, several candy wrappers, a child's mitten, a muddy and blank sheet of small paper, and a pin that was, Lenox saw with a thrill undercut by doubtfulness, the color red.

"Disappointing lot," he said to Ramsey.

"It is, yes. 'Spector Goodson was 'opin to find a bit more. If that's all, sir?"

"Yes, yes, thanks."

As they left the police station and walked up Cornmarket Street, McConnell pulled Lenox into a doorway.

"One more thing, old man," he said. "I kept it aside for you."

"What is it?"

"We found Payson's university identification in his pockets, cigarettes, some money, a pair of eyeglasses—and this." He handed Lenox a scrap of paper. "I thought it might be important."

"You were right," Lenox said in a low, startled voice. There was a long pause during which he cycled rapidly through the list of clues he had made.

"What do you make of it?"

"For one thing it proves, I think, that we have a third companion in the search for the murderer: Payson himself is helping us."

He looked at the scrap of paper again: a flimsy card, blank except for the words THE SEPTEMBER SOCIETY, which were written in red ink.

CHAPTER EIGHTEEN

Lenox sat drinking a cup of coffee in the back room at the Turf, wondering whether Goodson had made any progress. Likely they had at least found something that would help establish that Payson had been staying in the fields to the south of Oxford—but, he thought with a sigh, where would that get them? Unless Dabney had left behind a witnessed and notarized description of what had happened, there would probably be little to gather from the site where they had stayed.

Then, just as he found himself sinking into pessimism again, Lenox saw something delightful hovering by the bar, looking respectfully toward him. It was a welcome sight: Graham.

"Graham! Good Lord!"

"I hope I haven't startled you, sir?"

"A bit, yes. Rather like seeing Banquo's ghost in gray spats. Why are you here, anyway? Not that it's not jolly to have you, of course."

"I took the liberty, sir, of catching the morning train. I thought I might be of some assistance."

(Graham often helped Lenox with his cases, possessing as he did an uncanny ability to discover information that seemed lost or buried, and understanding intuitively what mattered and did not. It was another example of their unusual friendship, so different than any other in London.)

"Dead right," said Lenox warmly. "I've never needed it more. What of home?"

"Sir?"

"Everything calm there, I mean?"

"Ah—yes, sir. I've brought your post as well."

"Thank you very much, Graham. I really am glad to have you here."

"There's not much in it, sir, though you've had another visit from John Best."

"Whose card I had the other morning?"

"Yes, sir."

"Who the devil is he?"

"I cannot say, sir."

"Odd."

"Yes, sir. I trust the case is progressing?"

"It's hard to tell. Hopefully."

"Yes, sir."

Lenox thought for a moment. "I say, Graham, why don't you check us into the Randolph over on Magdalen Street?"

"Sir?"

"I've been staying here, but it would be appalling of me to impose my nostalgia on you. I doubt you'd see the charm in the place if you hadn't been dropped here before every term."

"I shall attend to it straight away, sir."

"Mrs. Tate?" Lenox called out, and the Turf's

proprietor popped her head around the corner. "Mrs. Tate, do you mind awfully if I leave for the Randolph?"

"Is everything all right, Mr. Lenox?" she said.

"Oh—perfect, of course. It's only that my valet here has come up, too, and I think it would rather stretch your hospitality to find a bed for him."

She gave an understanding nod. "It won't be too long before we see you again, though, will it?"

"Oh, definitely not," said Lenox. "It had been too long since I last visited Oxford."

"Certainly had, sir. Ah—a customer!"

When she was gone, Lenox said, "Can I talk something over with you, Graham?"

"Of course, sir."

"Have a seat here. Anything to eat?"

"No, thank you, sir."

"Good enough. The problem is this fellow Hatch, the professor at Lincoln. He's got his back up about me, I'm sure, because I went around and asked him about the two lads. I think he may be at the bottom of all this somehow, whether he's the primary mover or not."

"Indeed, sir?"

Lenox briefly recapitulated his conversation with Hatch, emphasizing the two lies the professor had told. "He's at 13 Holywell Street, just around the corner. Queer fellow, you know."

"How so, sir?"

"From what I can gather, he's better friends

with the students than with the other dons, acts somewhat debauched, in fact, as a student might. My impression was that he was unhappy, if that makes sense. I only say so because I've found that unhappiness can disguise a multitude of sins."

"Yes, sir."

"So I'd like you to get round him, Graham. See if you can discover anything about his relationship with George Payson and Bill Dabney, and see as well what he gets up to—what his daily life is like, whether he would have had the chance to kill somebody in the dead of night, for instance, or whether his servants keep a pretty close watch over him. And of course what he was doing yesterday evening."

"I shall endeavor to learn all I can of his activities and character, sir."

"Good of you, Graham, thanks. That's exactly what I'm after."

"Not at all, sir."

"Good as well to see a friendly face, now that I'm over the shock of it."

"I apologize again, sir," said Graham with a low laugh.

Lenox waved a hand. "Oh, not at all. This is a baddish problem, and I admit I felt defeated after McConnell got that wire about Payson. Time for all good men to rally round, I mean."

"Of course, sir."

"Good enough, then, and you'll check on the

Randolph? I'm going to go up to the Bodleian."

"Yes, sir. With your consent, sir, I shall send a note up to you at the library confirming that the rooms have been secured."

"Perfect. I should be there for a few hours, at any rate, and then I'm sure I'll see McConnell and Inspector Goodson."

"Very good, sir."

"Excellent."

After Graham had gone, Lenox read the *Times*. News of Payson's death had made the front page of the paper, underneath a somber headline that read MURDER AT LINCOLN. Lenox pictured all of the proud old Lincoln alumni in the far-flung provinces of the empire reading the news and feeling as shaken as he would have if the case had happened at Balliol. There were only a few things Lenox took special pride in, but as he read the *Times* he realized that Oxford was one of them, and told himself that if he couldn't solve this case he might as well retire.

CHAPTER NINETEEN

It was late in the afternoon, perhaps four o'clock, and Lenox was in the Bodleian Library's Upper Reading Room, leaning back in his chair and rubbing his tired eyes with his knuckles. He had been there for two hours and received very little recompense for his assiduousness, but had hopes that the next hour would bring greater success.

The Bodleian above anything else made Oxford what it was to the university's alumni. If there were diverse college allegiances, club allegiances, and sporting allegiances that fractured Oxford, what unified the undergraduates was the Bod, lying in all of its beauty at the center of life in the city. There was something incommunicably grand about it, something difficult to understand unless you had spent your evenings there or walked past it on the way to celebrate the boat race, a magic that came from ignoring it a thousand times a day and then noticing its overwhelming beauty when you came out of a tiny alley and it caught you unexpectedly. A library—it didn't sound like much, but it was what made Oxford itself. The greatest library in the world.

At the heart of it was the Old Schools Quad, a hushed cobblestone square. Its high carved walls gave it the feeling of a tower. Along the walls were the low, dark doors where the original schools had been, each bearing a Latin description of what was taught inside—philosophy became *Schola Moralis Philosophiae*, music became *Schola Musicae*—in high black and gold lettering above the doorways. Painted on the doors in blue was Oxford's motto, *Dominus*

Illuminatio Mea, the Lord is my light. Walking past students in their black gowns and white ties that afternoon, treading the quiet stone steps worn away by time and traffic, the beautiful, intricately worked stone walls reaching up on high toward a statue of James the First, the famous dreaming spires reaching heavenward—confronted with all of it, Lenox had been lost for words, lost even for thoughts.

He looked up at the graceful stained glass window of Duke Humfrey's Library, which housed the most extensive collection of rare books in the world; he looked in through the broad doors of the Divinity School, the oldest surviving university building in the world, its famously intricate Gothic vaulted stone ceiling serenely accepting the worship of a few scattered sightseers; he looked through the narrow walkway that led out to Oxford's most famous building, the circular library called the Radcliffe Camera; and as his eyes traveled over these familiar sights his main feeling was that he had come home. These buildings, the Clarendon, Sheldonian, Bodleian, these were the first home that belonged solely to him, to his adult self. Now, in the twilight of early fall, he felt almost breathless in the face of all the memories they held, all the promise spent, all the students like him who had turned out one way or another, whatever their first dreams had been when they arrived.

The appearance of the librarian jerked him out of his reverie.

"Doing all right, Mr. Lenox?"

"Quite well, thanks, Mr. Folsom. What are those?" he asked, nodding toward the papers in the other man's hands.

"Ah—a few more we found on the September Society."

"I'm awfully obliged."

"Oh, and here's a note that came up for you from one of the pages at Jesus College."

The note, to Lenox's surprise, was from a woman named Rosie Little, asking him to come visit her the next morning at Jesus—the place, he noted, where Payson had been to the dance on Saturday evening. He wrote back to her saying that he would come, and then turned to the papers.

Lenox had ascertained a few bare facts about this Society that kept popping up, but only a very few, and the work was slow going. He was trawling through old newspapers that the library had cross-referenced and through the books of club and society histories, as well as the histories of eastern military action by the British Empire. In this hodgepodge of sources he had found nine references to the September Society, three of them entirely incidental, five ancillary, and one that was more intriguing. The three incidental mentions all came in the middle of long lists of organizations, groups with a representative at a conference, for example, or groups that had all donated to a single cause.

Of the five ancillary mentions, two were interesting to Lenox. The first reported that select members of the September Society had been received by Queen Victoria. It was in a copy of the *Times* about ten years old. The second was about the same event, but was slightly more specific and had appeared about a week later in the *Spectator.* Its chief usefulness to Lenox was that it gave the number of members of the Society (roughly thirty, awfully small) and a more detailed account of the club's formation by a group of officers who had served together in eastern India and all received high military decorations.

This added information to the most interesting of the sources, a book called *A History of the Pall Mall*, about ten years old, which had an appendix entitled "Club and Society Profiles." The entry on the September Society was instructive.

Opposite the War Office in Carlton Gardens is a building occupied by the Biblius Club (*ref. p. 502*) on the lower floor and the September Society in the upper two. The Sept. Society was founded in 1848 by Maj. Sir Theophilus Butler and Maj. Peter Wilson, and is open to veterans of the military action in India who served between 1847 and 1849, attained the rank of captain or higher, and have received approval from the admissions committee. The Society's mission statement reads: "For the promotion of the values and memory of the heroes of Punjab and their families." The floors contain a dining room, a library emphasizing military history, upper and lower lounges, billiards room, and card room. Two servants are in full-time employ, and the Society shares a kitchen and cook with the Biblius. The Society is closed to the public without exception. It has limited reciprocal privileges with the 40s Club in Devon, a club with a similar membership but open to all officers who served in the East during the 1840s. Prospective members may apply to Capt. John Lysander, 116 Green Park Terrace, W1.

This gave Lenox three names to research and a building to focus on. He also knew that someone in his web of friends would belong to the Biblius, an elite and prideful sort of club which accepted members regardless of background who had exceptionally fine collections of incunabula. Lady Jane would know it. Her family had a famous library of early books.

Swallowing the thought of his old friend, Lenox picked up the papers that Mr. Folsom had just brought. On top of the pile was an unpublished collection called *Seals, Crests, and Coats of Arms of Some British Organizations, Being an Attempt to Classify Their Genealogies and Histories*. It was by somebody named H. Probisher Protherham whom Lenox thanked his lucky stars he didn't know. A man who could write a treatise on crests was a man capable of anything, was Lenox's feeling. Give him open rein at a dinner party and there was no level of tediousness he might not achieve.

He languidly flipped to the *S* section of the papers and perked up a bit when he saw that the seal of the September Society had been included. It was a rather ornate thing. Below it H. Probisher Protherham had written:

The September Society. Design: Butler. Approved 1849. Argent, a wildcat over ermine chevron, passant Sable. Motto: *Nil Conscire Sibi*. "Of Clear Conscience."

Lenox sat back in his chair, thinking. Could it be? He read it over again and then copied the entire entry down in his notebook, also marking down the shelf number and the book's title and author. He glanced through the index to make sure there was only one reference to the September Society and then read the description over one more time for good measure.

So, he thought. Another cat.

CHAPTER TWENTY

How do you do, Mr. Kelly?"

"Quite well, thank you, Mr. Lenox, but as I said before, please call me Red."

"That's right, the students call you that, don't they?"

"They do, sir, though not because of this." With a laugh, the head porter tugged at his shock of black hair. "Because I'm Irish, you see."

"I remember we used to give our head porter a bit of chaff in my day, too. Sign of affection, I expect."

"I hope so, sir. Was there anything I could help you with?"

"As a matter of fact there is, Red. I was hoping to talk to you about the day Bill Dabney and George Payson disappeared."

"I can't, sir, not after poor Payson's body showed up in the middle of Christ Church Meadow. Dreadful, dreadful blow, that."

"In that case I have a note here from Inspector Goodson asking you to answer my questions."

Kelly looked over the note Lenox had handed him and then nodded. "Fair enough," he said, "though I don't reckon I'll be much help."

"Why is that?"

"I didn't see much of Master Payson that day, sir."

"But you saw his mother."

"Aye, at a little before midday."

"Were you accustomed to seeing her?"

"Certainly, sir."

"She visited quite often, then?"

"Aye, sir."

"And did you see the meeting between George Payson and his mother out here in the Front Quad, by any chance?"

"Can't say I did, sir, no."

"When was the last time you saw George Payson?"

"I did see him when he came out, sir, after he saw his mother and promised to meet her."

"Ah!"

"He didn't look at me, though. And that was the last time."

"He followed his mother out?"

"She went out down Ship Street, sir, and then he went out five minutes later."

Ship Street (once known as Lincoln College Lane) and Turl Street formed a tiny cross at the center of Oxford, and a great deal of colleges were clustered around them. At the end of Ship was the Saxon Tower, the oldest structure in Oxford, which dated to 1040.

"Did you see Bill Dabney that day, Mr. Kelly? Red?"

"I didn't, sir. I had seen him the night before."

"What was he doing?"

"Going to the dance at Jesus College."

"Did George Payson go to the same dance?"

"I don't know, sir."

Lenox thought of the dance card he had found in Payson's room. "How about Payson's scout?"

"He didn't go to the dance, no, sir."

Lenox laughed. "Very good. I meant—did you see the scout that day?"

"I see him every day, sir." The head porter seemed to be growing impatient.

"Could I meet him?"

"He's not here, sir."

"That's odd."

"Not really, sir, begging your pardon. It's his day off."

"Do you know whether the police have spoken to him?"

"They haven't to my knowledge, Mr. Lenox."

Lenox puzzled over this. Suddenly the dance card seemed like another clue for his list. The strange thing about the card was that only one side of the correspondence appeared on it—the porter's response. Had Payson sent his request down on a different piece of paper? But why would he have done that?

"Have you heard of the September Society, Mr. Kelly?"

"No, sir."

"I believe you were in the military, however?"

"Yes, we were, all of us porters. The Royal Pioneer Corps."

"Did you see the battlefield?"

"No, sir, thankfully not. Though mind, I would have done my bit when the time came."

"Of course . . . what can you tell me about Bill Dabney?"

The head porter shook his head apologetically. "We have an awful lot of students, sir, and the only ones I know well are our third-years. Master Dabney was only another face in the long procession. Friendly enough, good pals with Masters Payson and Stamp—I fear that's about the extent of my knowledge of him, sir."

"Did he get much post?"

"Post? I couldn't say, sir."

"And Payson?"

"Oh—now that you mention it, he'd been getting more recently."

"Do you have any memory of it?"

"One queer thing comes back, sir, now that you say it. He had been getting letters, properly stamped, Queen's head on 'em, and then throwing 'em away unopened."

"Why did you notice that?"

"I didn't, sir—Mr. Fallows, another of our porters here, he noticed it, Mr. Lenox."

"Can you remember when?"

"Certainly, sir. About a week ago, I reckon—

and finally Mr. Fallows went and took the letter out of the wastepaper basket to open it, and he found it to be empty!"

"Puzzling, that."

"It is, quite."

"Anything on the letter except the stamp and address? Any markings?"

"Nothing, sir. No return of address."

A signal? How long had Payson known that he was in danger?

"You don't have any mail for George Payson left, do you?"

"None, sir, nor for Master Dabney. Checked straight away, I did."

"Which other porters were on duty the day Dabney and Payson vanished?"

"I was, sir, both days, Fallows on evenings, and with me in the daytime was a chap named Phelps."

"You're alone now?"

"No, Phelps is out checking the staircases and the student rooms. A new system since the unfortunate incident."

"Ah. Well, thank you, Mr. Kelly. I appreciate it."

Lenox left Lincoln and walked the short distance across Turl Street to Jesus College, another of the small to medium–sized colleges along this central artery, not quite as grand as some but beautiful in their own right. Jesus was known for having a large Welsh population (a Welshman had founded it, though officially Elizabeth I held the title of Founder) and for its frequent contributions to the 'varsity athletic clubs. The college also famously owned a huge silver punch bowl from which the Tsar of Russia, the Duke of Wellington, the King of Prussia, and the Prince Regent had formally drunk to signify their defeat of Napoleon in 1814. But Lenox's favorite thing about it was the daffodils that appeared in full bloom on (the Welsh) St. David's Day, the first of March, to signify the beginning of spring. He remembered fondly seeing the daffodils and feeling his heart rise as another cold winter vanished behind him.

Seeing a porter, Lenox said, "I had a note from someone called Rosie Little. Any chance she's still in?"

"Tomorrow morning, sir," said the porter, a jowly chap.

"Thanks."

It was dark as Lenox walked toward the Randolph, his notebook in one hand. The net was drawing tighter, he felt—but around whom?

CHAPTER TWENTY-ONE

In the lobby of the Randolph, Lenox stopped at the front desk for his key, but just as he was going to speak to the manager, he saw Lady Annabelle Payson. With a heavy heart he changed direction and walked toward her.

She was sitting in the far corner of the room, half hidden in the shade and all on her own. Lenox saw as he drew closer to her that her eyes were red-rimmed and that her cheeks had grown paler since he had last seen her. The air of utter defeat in her face was easy for Lenox to take as a personal rebuke.

"Lady Annabelle?" he said.

It took her a moment to look up. "Ah," she said, bowing her head with great dignity, "how do you do, Mr. Lenox?"

"Lady Annabelle, is anybody here with you?"

"My brother is speaking to the police at the moment, but yes, he has kept me company."

"I wanted to apologize, Lady Annabelle. For failing, and of course for George's death."

She didn't contradict him. "Tell me, Mr. Lenox, do you still plan to work on this case?"

"I do, yes." He didn't add: until I drop dead myself, if need be.

"Good," she said, though her eyes were still dull and lifeless, lacking even the fieriness of revenge that Lenox had so often seen in the grieving.

"Perhaps it will be some solace when we find out who did it," said Lenox. "I hope so, at any rate."

After a long, almost reproving pause, she went on, "What I cannot forgive myself for is letting him leave when I met him at Lincoln College, Mr. Lenox. I keep repeating the scene in my mind, and it's beyond my comprehension that I could have let my poor George walk away from my embrace when he looked so pale, so . . . so vulnerable, Mr. Lenox. So vulnerable."

"You couldn't have known what would happen, Lady Annabelle."

"I lost my husband, too, you know."

"I do," Lenox answered quietly. "I remember him."

"But that," she said, her voice a whisper, "was a walk in the park to this."

"Perhaps you could help me, Lady Annabelle."

"Help you?"

"To solve this case. For example, have you heard of the September Society?"

"I haven't, no, Mr. Lenox."

"Does the color red mean anything to you?"

"Not in particular." Her tone was distracted, even faintly annoyed, and Lenox didn't blame her for it.

143

"Did George take long walks?"

"Only in the country, he always said." She laughed in a rather choked way. "Said there was no point walking in Oxford or London, when there was always a pub nearby."

"I see."

"He was awfully sweet, my dear George. The funniest person I ever knew."

"Yes," said Lenox. A moment's silence later, he reached for his pocket. "Do these pen lines mean anything to you?"

He handed her the September Society card that was marked with the black and pink X. Taking it from him, her brow furrowed, and she turned it over several times. She studied it closely. She looked slightly puzzled—the only deviation from the wan, downcast mien her face had borne throughout the conversation.

"It rings some vague bell, Mr. Lenox."

Trying to suppress his eager curiosity, Lenox said, "Can you think of what it might be?"

"Why—I think—only faintly, but I think it resembles the Payson crest."

"The crest?"

"You know, the coat of arms, whatever you call it."

"How so?"

"The crest's a shield in black and pinkish red. George had it on his stationery."

"Black and pinkish red?"

"A bit darker pink than this, but an X shape, yes—the pink for the blood the Paysons have spilled in battle." Though Lenox was worried it might, the thought of blood didn't seem to bother her. "Yes, it looks like a quick, crude rendering of the crest."

"How odd," Lenox murmured, his mind quickening.

At that moment John West, Lady Annabelle's brother, came toward them. After introducing himself and again trying to find a few consolatory words for her, Lenox left them. As he went upstairs, his thoughts moved on to the cat on the seal (seals and crests were certainly flying fast and furious now) of the September Society. It must have been related, the dead cat, to the Society. Every bone in Lenox's body told him that George Payson, or Bill Dabney perhaps—perhaps even someone unknown—had left behind a minefield of clues waiting to be discovered. The cat was one of those clues, like the walking boots, the line of ash, all of it.

Now they were gone, dash it. If only he had thought to make a more thorough catalog of what the room had contained. Perhaps he would go back and look at it again despite the cleaning. The question was why whoever had planted the clues had felt the need to make them obscure, and there was only one answer: The person had known that somebody would search the room after it had been abandoned. The cat was a clever touch, in that case. It would draw the instant focus of anybody who saw it. Perhaps, Lenox mused, that meant that the cat was the least important of the clues—pointing toward the September Society but not in itself the critical puzzle piece. Perhaps it was designed, with the cryptic numbers written on the note underneath it, to seem more significant or baffling than it was.

When he reached his room, Graham was sitting on a chair in the hall.

"There you are, Graham," said Lenox. "Is this my kip?"

"Just here, sir. I acquired a suite with a bedroom and sitting room. If it does not meet with your approval, sir—"

"Not at all, no. Thanks awfully for coming and figuring it out."

"Was the Bodleian a fruitful detour, sir?"

"It may have been. I'm not certain." Lenox related the tangle of uncertainties to Graham as he unpacked the detective's clothes. "The damned thing about it, Graham, is that it might have been a local criminal or a far-flung one, we can't know yet."

"Frustrating, sir. I think you'll find the navy socks are preferable, sir."

Lenox discarded the black pair and donned the navy blue. "McConnell's meeting me downstairs, then? How much time do I have?"

"Half an hour, sir."

"I say, Graham, have you started your investigations into Hatch yet?"

"Not yet, sir. I planned to begin in the morning."

"Could you figure out whether he was in the military? In the East, for obvious reasons? I forgot to look up *Who's Who* in the Bod."

"Yes, sir, I certainly shall. Is he of the correct age, sir?"

"Hard to say. One of these chaps who could be twenty-five or forty-five."

"Indeed, sir."

Lenox, dressed now, shot his cuffs in front of the mirror. His black tie was a bit off center, and Graham tended to it.

"I saw Lady Payson downstairs."

"Yes, sir?"

"It was painful, though that's nothing. She's as broken as I've ever seen anyone." Lenox paused. "This may be the first time somebody has come to me *before* a death." Another pause. "It's a pretty bad lookout, Graham."

"Yes, sir."

"To put it another way—every effort, don't you think?"

"Of course, sir."

"Not that it's ever otherwise." Glancing again in the mirror, Lenox said, "I think I'll have a drink at the bar before I meet McConnell. Steady myself a bit."

"Very good, sir."

"Do you have anything planned? Have the night off, of course. I can draw my own bath and that sort of thing."

"Thank you, sir. I may see one or two of the other footmen from my Balliol days, sir."

"Our Balliol days, Graham. Which ones are still kicking around?"

"Oh, Mr. Bond, of course, Mr. Middleton, and Mr. Dekker."

"Will you buy them a round on me? Here's a couple of shillings." Lenox reached into his pocket and handed the money over. "Tell them I said hello, won't you? And tell Dekker I haven't forgotten him dropping that boiled egg in old Bessborough's lap, won't you?"

With a smile, Graham said, "Yes, sir."

"All right. I'll wander off, then. Hopefully McConnell's solved the whole thing and we can go back to London."

CHAPTER TWENTY-TWO

The next morning, slightly hungover after a merry dinner with McConnell, Lenox woke up to find the soft sun peering through the curtains. The Turf was well and good, but it was nice to sleep on soft sheets and to find his coffee waiting for him on a tray with a vase of nasturtiums. Graham must be awake, he thought. So the careworn detective lay in bed and read for twenty minutes or so, losing himself in the copy of *The Praise of Folly* that he had bought from Mr. Chaffanbrass. The sharp, warm coffee slowly brought him back to the world. By the time Graham had come into the room, Lenox was alert enough to have his mind on the case again. He would devote this morning to speaking to Rosie Little at Jesus College and looking over Payson's rooms again. Then he would take the 11:35 train to Paddington and search out Theophilus Butler and the September Society. It was high time he found out more about both of them.

Graham was laying out a blue suit. "Will this do, sir?"

"Yes, thanks," said Lenox. "Don't know how I managed without you. Are you going to begin on Hatch today, then?"

"I had planned to, sir."

"If you want to jaunt off, I can dress myself."

"As you say, sir. May I inquire after your plans?"

"I daresay I'll scratch a bite of breakfast together downstairs, then set out for Lincoln to look over the room again. Oh, and Graham, I'll be returning to London for the night to follow up on a clue."

"Do you require my company, sir?"

"Don't even think about shirking—I need you to stay here, of course. Who's in charge of the house at the moment?"

"Mary, sir."

"How did Ellie take that?" Lenox's cook was excellent but tempestuous.

"Equaniminously enough, sir."

After eating alone (or rather, with his book and the *Standard*—McConnell had popped back to London that morning), Lenox took a final glance into the mirror by the door and left the Randolph. It was cold but bright, a taste of the autumn ahead, and he regretted leaving his overcoat behind. Fortunately it was only a few minutes until he got to Jesus. It was too early to see Rosie Little, so he turned left toward Lincoln. When he found the porter's lodge, a strange man was there in place of Red.

"How do you do? I'm Charles Lenox."

The man tipped his hat. "Mr. Lenox, sir. You can call me Phelps."

"Hullo, Phelps. Are you the porter who was on duty with Mr. Kelly on the day Bill Dabney and George Payson disappeared?"

"I am, sir, yes. Why?"

"I'm by way of helping Inspector Goodson with his investigation. Here's his note." Lenox handed over that useful passport again and watched Phelps read it. "I was hoping to see

Payson's room once more—and in fact to have a word with you as well, Mr. Phelps."

"Aye, sir?"

"Do you remember seeing Bill Dabney or George Payson that day?"

"No 'or' about it, sir. I saw the two of 'em together, only but once."

"Did you? What time would that have been?"

"Early, like, and that's how I remember it. Neither of 'em was an early riser."

"Where were they?"

"In the Grove Quad, underneath all that ivy along the high wall there. It was around seven o'clock in the morning, I'd reckon, sir."

"Were they talking openly?"

" 'Ad their 'eads together, they did. Whispering."

"Well, that certainly confirms our thinking. Had you reported this?"

"To Re—to Mr. Kelly, sir."

Why wouldn't Kelly have mentioned it?

"Did you catch anything of what they were saying?"

"I didn't, sir, no."

"Have you heard of the September Society, Mr. Phelps?"

"No, sir."

"Anything else you can remember? What did you think of the lads?"

"Liked 'em, sir. Specially Payson, bit of a firecracker, him. We're all passing sad about it, sir. Mrs. Phelps included, mind you."

They spoke a few minutes longer, though Phelps didn't yield any other interesting information. Then Lenox took the key from him and went up to George Payson's room. It looked startlingly different, not so much tampered with as sanitized, depersonalized. The walking stick at its jaunty angle was gone from the chair; the tomato, string, and pen were gone; the books had been neatly gathered from their improbable homes and put in a row; the bed had been stripped. In the silence of the white, chill morning light it all seemed immeasurably sad.

Lenox looked behind all the furniture and in the ashes of the grate, and for good measure he glanced through the books, shuffled through the shapeless clothes on their sagging hangers, and read carefully through Payson's notebooks. They only contained tutorial notes.

Lenox left Lincoln again with a few words to Phelps, who tipped his cap good-bye, and then made his way across the street to Jesus. When Lenox asked for Miss Little, the porter said that she had been expecting him and directed him toward the long hall at the end of the Front Quad. Finding it, Lenox went inside and saw a single woman pinning decorations to the wall.

"Miss Little?" he said, walking toward her.

"Ah—Mr. Lenox, is it? You've received my note, then."

"Yes, that's right. You wanted to speak to me?"

"I did. Call me Rosie, please."

"May I ask how you heard about me, Rosie?"

"To be honest, Mr. Lenox—I—I followed you."

She was an exquisitely pretty young girl, fair, with high plump red cheeks and lovely auburn hair. The dress she wore, blue and long, made her look both young and practical. She was distinctly of the middle class, the daughter of a banker or a local brewer, nineteen and with all the world before her.

"Did you?" he said mildly.

"I'm so sorry, Mr. Lenox, but I did. It's—it's George, you see."

"George Payson."

Two large tears trembled in her eyes. "Yes."

He put his hand softly on her arm and said, "Oh, my dear, I'm so terribly sorry."

At these kind words her composure collapsed and she buried her head in Lenox's chest, sobbing and sobbing.

Presently he asked, "Would you like to tell me what happened?"

She sniffled. "Yes," she said. "I want to help."

"Were the two of you—"

Hastily, she said, "No, no, Mr. Lenox, there was never a breath of impropriety. He was the finest gentleman I ever saw! So friendly, and so gentle

153

with me, and such lovely manners. Once—once —he kissed me on the cheek. But oh, how I loved him, Mr. Lenox! I knew he was only polite, but Lord! How I loved George Payson!"

"Do you mind going backward a little? How do you come to manage these dances?"

Regaining some of her composure, Rosie answered, "It's charitable work, Mr. Lenox. Half of the subscription prices go to the local orphanage. A few of us girls who grew up here do the work to prepare the dances."

"How often do they happen?"

"There's one every Friday evening in term. They rotate around the colleges by twos—that is, each college has two dances and then passes it on. This will be Jesus's second dance; then it will go on to Magdalen."

"The dances rotate through the colleges alphabetically?"

"Yes, Mr. Lenox. George and Bill took out subscriptions from their first week last year, and came to dance."

"Did you dance, too?"

"Heavens, no. I serve punch and tick off names on the subscription list."

"And over time you had a friendship with George," he said.

"Yes," she said, tears welling up in her eyes again. "But I didn't write to tell you about this, I wrote to tell you about Friday."

"What happened?" he said.

"The first odd thing was that his dance card was blank, Mr. Lenox. That never happened."

"What did he do?"

"He stood off to the side, occasionally speaking with his friends, and occasionally having a word with me."

"Did you notice anything else?"

"One other thing, actually—toward the end of the evening—"

"What time would that be?"

"Oh, quarter till eleven, perhaps."

"Go on."

"Toward the end of the evening, I saw him out in the quadrangle here at Jesus arguing with a man older than himself."

"Can you describe him?"

"I can't *really*, no, I'm afraid, because it was dark out. I saw that he wasn't a student straight away from his dress, you see, and from the way he carried himself."

"And you didn't overhear them?"

"No, I'm afraid I didn't. I'm sorry I can't help more. But with what came afterward, it began to seem so strange!" She burst into tears again.

"On the contrary, you've been a great help. And you can trust that we'll do whatever we can."

"I've been so lonesome, Mr. Lenox!" she said, looking up at him with wet eyes.

Lenox didn't speak for a moment, and then said, "How about this, Rosie: You and I shall be friends. Whatever I know, you'll know. I'll write you notes every other day or so and tell you what's happened. A proper friendship."

"Thank you," she said, unable to say anything else.

A few minutes later they parted. Lenox thought of her, all alone over the past days with the terrible secret of her love and its defeat, aching to help, unequipped by her upbringing or her experience in the world to cope with her emotions. And felt at once a great pity for and admiration of her.

He had to catch his train in twenty minutes, but first he went back to the hotel and left Graham a note that read, *Will you please find out whether Hatch attended the Jesus College dance last Saturday? An older man reported there. Thanks, CL.*

CHAPTER TWENTY-THREE

With unwelcome force, the question of Lady Jane returned to Lenox while he was on the train. To distract himself he took his bag down from the rack to find a book—he was alone in his compartment, the train being relatively empty—and found atop his clothes Theophilus Butler's entry in *Who's Who*, copied out in Graham's precise handwriting. He must have done it that morning, remembering that Lenox had forgotten to look into the book. It read:

BUTLER, Maj. (ret.) Sir Theophilus Fitzgerald, KT. *cr.* **1844. D.S.O.;** *born* **1814,** *2nd Son of* **George Theophilus Butler and of Elena Miles** *daughter of* **John Fitzgerald, Dublin.**
Address: **114 Green Park Terrace, W.1.**
Educated: **Radley School and Sandhurst Military Academy; served with H.M. forces 1840/52 (Major, 12th (East Suffolk) Regiment of Foot, 2nd Battalion).**
Recreations: **Military History; Eastern Studies; Musicology.**
Clubs: **Army and Navy; September; Whites.**
Arms: **Ermine, 3 griffins courant, argent; motto: Comme je trouve.**

Lenox noticed that he was from an Irish family, perhaps one that had emigrated to England some time back, at least on his father's side. It was odd for Butler, given his background, to have served in the East Suffolk. Of course, from the profile it was difficult to tell how he would be—

either a bluff, courteous old soldier, completely ignorant of anything to do with George Payson, or the mastermind of the whole thing. He had the Distinguished Service Order, so he was brave, and he had been knighted, so the chances were that he had connections either in court or in the upper stratum of the military hierarchy.

Turning the page over, Lenox saw that Graham had also copied out the entry for John Lysander, the Society's admissions director, and written below it that Peter Wilson, the cofounder of the Society with Theophilus Butler, wasn't listed. Lysander's looked like this:

LYSANDER, Capt. (ret.) John; *born* **1821,** *son of* **Capt. John Lysander and of Louise Wright,** *daughter of* **Homer Allen of Windon Manor, Hants.**
Address: **116 Green Park Terrace, W.1.**
Educated: **Thomas College, served with H.M. forces 1841/49 (Captain, 12th (East Suffolk) Regiment of Foot, 2nd Battalion).**
Recreations: **Military History, Chess.**
Clubs: **Alpine; Army and Navy; September.**
Arms: **Sable, 3 hares courant; motto: Lysanders Lead the Charge.**

Interesting that he lived just two houses down

from Butler—from the look of it they had probably served together quite closely, a friendship
bred in the officers' mess and only allowed to
flourish when both were decommissioned and
allowed to meet again on a slightly more equal
footing. Thinking it over, it seemed odd that a
club should be devoted to such a small group of
men, but Lenox decided to reserve judgment
until he found himself on Pall Mall.

His first destination when he left the train,
though, was Hampden Lane and home. He wanted
to check the post, have a cup of tea, and change
his clothes before he went out again, and he
wanted as well, though he wouldn't admit it to
himself, to check in on Lady Jane. When he
arrived at their slender, homey lane, however,
she wasn't there, and according to Mary, who was
in charge of the house in Graham's absence and
seemed to be filled with a mortal terror of her
new and lofty position, Lady Jane had been away
the entire day. It was vexing: For so many years
she had simply been at hand, and now, in these
days when he most wanted to see her, she was
nowhere to be found. Who was the lean man in
the gray coat that he had seen emerging from her
house? Why had her carriage been in the Seven
Dials?

It was the middle of the afternoon by the time
Lenox left for Pall Mall. He decided to take
the trip on foot, stale as he felt from the train.

London looked its best, too, austere on its high horizon, the cold, white, ancient stone of its buildings agleam in the fading sunlight. On the ground the city traded austerity for intimacy, a kind of companionship in the mass of people along the streets, the shuffling red leaves under the carriage wheels, the brightly lighted rooms just above street level. The briskness in the air was refreshing to Lenox, snapping some red into his cheeks and clearing the fuzziness travel always gave him from his brain. By the time he had turned into Carlton Gardens, the site of the September Society, he felt ready again to clear the corresponding fuzziness of George Payson's death and Bill Dabney's disappearance.

Two small, rectangular brass plates were affixed to the door. One said THE BIBLIUS CLUB plainly enough, while the other only said, rather cryptically, THE SOCIETY. The building was a Regency town house. Its first floor extended behind to about twice the length of the upper floors, so the areas of the two clubs must have been roughly similar. The door was of barred glass and bore one unfamiliar crest (which must have belonged to the Biblius) and one with the familiar cat on it. Lenox only had a moment to gather all of these impressions, because as soon as he paused in front of the building a doorman in a morning suit had stepped out through the door. Behind him Lenox could see a small but tidy entrance, about five feet by five feet, which had two doors plainly leading to the two clubs. The doorman had been having his tea, Lenox saw. He was a middle-aged fellow with graying hair and an intelligent, humorous face.

"Sorry to interrupt you," Lenox said, "but I wondered whether I might pop up to the September Society."

"Are you a member?"

"I'm not, no, I'm afraid. I'm investigating a young lad's death, though, and thought I might be able to see either Theophilus Butler, Peter Wilson, or John Lysander."

"Well, sir, you won't find Mr. Wilson."

"Why not?"

"He's dead, I'm afraid, sir."

"Is he? How did that happen?"

The doorman cleared his throat. "Well, sir, it was suicide by gunshot."

Lenox was surprised. "I see," he said. "Any chance of Major Butler or Captain Lysander?"

"No, sir, the club does not permit nonmembers within its rooms." More confidentially—he was quite clearly a chatty chap who had grown bored with his five-by-five cell—the doorman said, "Neither of them is in, anyway, sir. Both of 'em come most mornings."

Knowing that his interlocutor wanted more to while away a few minutes than to handle the

161

building's business, Lenox only said, "Regular practices, eh? I'm much the same."

"Oh, yes, sir, set your clock by them. Come at ten, they both do, and leave again after lunch. Major Butler goes to the British Library, and Captain Lysander often sees a show."

"Do they? And neither of them ever comes in to get out of the rain, perhaps, and sit by a warm fire?"

"No, sir, as Major Butler goes to White's and Captain Lysander to the Army and Navy."

"Ah, I see. I know the type—like a certain routine—never vary from it."

"Yes, sir. Though mind," said the doorman, reaching back in through the door to fetch his cup of tea, "there are the meetings."

"Meetings?" said Lenox, perhaps a touch too innocently.

"Yes, sir. They come in quite late, sir, even after the Biblius closes at eleven, and meet up in their rooms. And neither Chapman, who serves at the Society, nor me, nor the cooks, nor the charwoman is allowed to be in the building."

"How peculiar!"

The valet tapped his nose. "It is, sir, though mind, they're military folk, and have their own ways about them."

"Any other peculiar mannerisms?"

"Not to put your finger on, sir, though they're a sight more ornery than the Biblius."

Lenox sighed. "Well, I suppose I'd better try to see them in their homes."

The doorman was anxious to prolong the conversation another moment or two and remembered Lenox's errand. "If I may ask, why did you need to see one of the two gentlemen? Did you say?"

"I'm a detective."

"So is it a murder, sir, that you're investigating?" he said eagerly.

"Perhaps—though I'd ask you not to mention it to anybody. Quite confidential."

The doorman tapped his nose again furiously and in general did so much winking and nodding in such a confused manner that Lenox knew his secret was safe. "Scotland Yard, then, sir?"

The "sir" was a bit more hesitant—Lenox looked like a gentleman, but of course an inspector wouldn't deserve quite the same intensity of nose-tapping and sirring. "Oh, no," said Lenox, "merely a friend of the family."

They were on the right ground again. The doorman gave his nose a final, emphatic tap of secrecy. Lenox left his card behind, found out the man's name was Thomas Hallowell, and promised to return soon. As he walked back to Pall Mall, once looking back and up to see whether he could decipher anything from the curtained windows in the top two floors, he thought over what he should do. He could try the two houses at Green Park Terrace, though from the sound of it Lysander and Butler both kept odd hours. Then there was Peter Wilson, the suicide. That had an air of suspicion about it.

The detective took a hansom cab to Scotland Yard and was closeted briefly with Inspector Jenkins, a young chap on the rise in the force with whom Lenox had once briefly worked in the matter of a murdered parlor maid, though Inspector Exeter had quickly taken over the job. Jenkins asked about George Payson and offered whatever help he could give Lenox. He also said that he would send over the coroner's report and the Yard's file on the case as soon as he could lay his hands on them.

Though he had been uncertain of whether he knew Jenkins well enough to ask him for the favor, Lenox was glad that he had. Like many favors, it had bound the two people involved a little tighter, and Jenkins had made it plain that he was happy to lend a hand now and then where he could, while Lenox had made it equally plain that he was always good for a consultation. There were one or two people who trusted Lenox at the Yard, but he felt it was good to have a real friend in situ there, at a place where his work had mostly generated suspicion and surliness over the years.

CHAPTER TWENTY-FOUR

The dim, final strands of sunlight were failing when Lenox returned home from Scotland Yard, but he noticed that Lady Jane's house was bright. He thought he might go over straight away but then reconsidered and went inside his own house instead. Sitting at his desk by the window overlooking the street, he wrote Major Butler and Captain Lysander identical notes, asking in a line or two whether he might call on them either at the Society or in Green Park Terrace the next day in order to discuss a troubling criminal matter in which the September Society played a peripheral role. Sending them off with Mary—still flustered by the majesty of her position in the house and curtsying at nearly every word Lenox spoke—he wondered how the two men would react.

He called Mary in again after he had taken a more leisurely look at several of the letters he had received and only glanced over that afternoon.

"I think I'll dine out," he said to her.

"Very good, sir."

"Could you please keep an eye out for the nine thirty post, and for any return messages from Green Park Terrace?"

"Certainly, sir."

"And is everything here running smoothly in Graham's absence?" He had no illusions about his own instrumentality to the organization of the household.

"Quite smoothly, sir, though of course not as smoothly as when Mr. Graham is here, sir." Evidently thinking this a pretty bright answer, she curtsied with a little stumble.

"All right," said Lenox. "Thanks very much."

Only after these little means of stalling his visit did Lenox rise with the intention of going to Lady Jane's. Damning himself as he did it, he looked his features over in the mirror and tidied his clothes. A sort of heartsickness deep within him rose into his throat, but, as he reasoned to himself, there probably had been a Lenox at Agincourt, and he might as well walk toward certain death just as boldly as his ancestor had.

Kirk, Lady Jane's butler, answered the door deliberatively, as befitted such an oversized man, and greeted the visitor with a grave "How do you do, Mr. Lenox?" Still with some trepidation, Lenox approached the drawing room—only to hear two voices and the rolling, silvery peals of laughter that so clearly belonged to Toto McConnell.

"Charles!" she said effervescently, rising to her feet to kiss his cheek. "How well you look!"

"Thank you," he said. "You look lovely. Is everything well?"

"Oh, I've been having a delightful time listening to my husband talk dead cats over supper." She sighed dramatically and then chuckled. "Still, better than dead fish, which he always rattles on about after he goes north."

Lenox laughed. As it always did, her charm made him feel warmer and somehow more gallant. In turn he greeted Lady Jane, who was more subdued but also had laughter in her eyes.

"It's awfully good to see you, Charles. How is your case?"

"Not bad, thanks. I expect we'll have the solution out soon enough. Sad for Lady Annabelle, of course. She seems a wreck."

"She's going off to spend the winter in France," said Toto. "Apparently for her health. Duch"—this was her nickname for the Duchess of Marchmain—"tried to invite her into London so that she could be among friends, but Annabelle said no."

"Dreadful, that."

Throughout this Toto's face still bore its initial enchantment, which Lenox thought rather odd. Then, however, looking at Lady Jane, he saw that she had it, too. He was too polite, of course, to ask after it, but his old friend spotted it instantly.

"Toto," she said, "you had better tell him the news."

"Oh, Charles, I'm going to have a child!" said Toto. Her whole body was alive with happiness as he congratulated her and was rewarded with a flurry of kisses. "Oh, and I don't know if I'm to mention it, but would you stand godfather to the baby? Thomas wanted to ask you specially. Jane will be godmother, with Duch, of course. I always believed in two godmothers because one always forgets to send presents. Jane, you'll be the one to send presents and little silver cups and things, won't you?"

Smiling, Lady Jane nodded her assent.

"I know it's frightfully popish to have god-parents, of course," said Toto, fairly brimming with joy, "but it's a great tradition in our family."

"I know," said Lenox. "My father stood as your father's."

"That's right! At any rate you'll just have to do it, and the two of you will make a delightful pair on the altar—of course you'll come to the baptism—and, Charles, I *do* hope it's a girl, don't you? They're so much nicer I think."

"Thomas must be awfully happy," Lenox said.

"Oh, he is! He was sorry to leave Oxford when I called him down, but he is!"

In Lady Jane's face, which he could read so well, Lenox saw that she hoped the baby would be the panacea that Toto and McConnell needed to cure their marriage's intermittent discontent —and he partook of both the overt happiness in the room at the news and this quieter, naturally unspoken happiness underlying it.

The conversation moved on to baby names (Toto liked the thought of Henry for a boy, and the list of girls' names she liked was close in length to a biblical genealogy—including Margaret, Anne, Anna, Elizabeth, Louise, and dozens of others, all of them to be immediately replaced by a dozen nicknames when they were actually implemented) and then to what schools the child would go to as a boy (Eton, though Lenox made a strong case for Harrow) and what sort of person the child would marry if it was a girl (one just like her father). The room was full of goodwill and happiness, and though Lenox was delighted for Toto and McConnell, a small, ignominious part of him was sad that he didn't have the same kind of joy in his bones.

At one point in their conversation, Toto asked Lenox what he meant to do for dinner.

"I thought I'd go to the Devonshire and hunt up a companion or two," he said.

"Nonsense! Have dinner with Thomas—I'm going to eat with Duch and Jane later to celebrate, and probably a few other people. I can't bear to think that he'll be all alone, fussing over his poor dear dead animals. Won't you take him out and have a bottle of champagne or something?"

"Terrific idea," Lenox said. "In fact, perhaps I'll

invite a few others, too—Hilary, Dunstan, perhaps my brother, that sort of a crowd."

"Brilliant!" said Toto and then resumed her exegesis on the perfect shade of yellow paint she would put into the nursery if the child was a girl.

Lenox excused himself and stepped out of the room to write a few notes, to McConnell and about five others, naming a restaurant in Piccadilly called Thompson's, which he knew to be cheerful. He was looking forward to it himself. Between the death of George Payson and his reticence with Lady Jane he hadn't realized how low his spirits had gotten, despite his determination to direct all of his energy into the case. One too many glasses of wine and a night of good company would be just the thing, he thought, to leave him ready for a fresh try the next morning.

"I've written the notes," he said, coming back.

"Oh, good," said Toto.

"Will you be in London long, Charles?" Lady Jane asked.

"I won't, I'm afraid. Too much of the case is in Oxford—I'll have to return tomorrow. But it will be over soon, I hope."

"I hope so, too," said Lady Jane, with something indeed hopeful in her voice.

But here again the line separating friendship and love was unclear, and he couldn't decipher her feelings, usually so plain to him. He wondered for the thousandth time about the man in the long gray coat whom he had seen visiting her, and for the thousandth time reproached himself for his vulgar curiosity. The special misery of undeclared love again rose within him, but he pushed it back down and listened intently to what Toto had to say about February birthdays and their astrological luck.

Toto and her news were what both prevented and saved Lenox from speaking to Lady Jane alone, of course. But there was a moment toward the end of their conversation when Toto went off to look in the mirror in the hallway and all of the unsaid words underneath the two old friends' conversation began to fill the room as slowly and surely as rising water. Just when Lenox had built up some particle of courage Toto came back—and the two of them left Jane a little while later, both promising to return soon.

CHAPTER TWENTY-FIVE

The next day, his higher spirits worth a terrible morning head, Lenox woke up to a note and a visitor. The note was from Captain Lysander. It was written on heavy paper with the September Society's seal embossed in the upper right-hand corner and Lysander's name at the bottom, and said:

Mr. Lenox,

By all means come see me, though I don't know how much help I can be to you. I shall be in Green Park Terrace at 2:30 this afternoon. Incidentally, Major Butler, in case you desired to speak to him as well, is out of town.

Yours &c,
Captain John Lysander,
12th Suffolk 2nd

Funny, thought Lenox, that he would mention Butler. Had Hallowell, the Society's doorman, mentioned Lenox's visit there? Perhaps.

The visitor was just as mysterious. For propriety's sake, it was a footman, Samuel, who had given Lenox the note and announced the visitor, not Mary. The card he bore on his tray only had the name John Best written on it, without any further explanation. So this was the man who had been dogging Lenox's steps, leaving his card at the house every few days.

"Did he say anything else? The name doesn't ring a bell," Lenox said as he dressed, pausing now and then to sip the lifesaving cup of coffee on his table.

"No, sir," said Samuel, "though he assured me that you knew him."

"Did he? Cheek, that—I haven't the foggiest idea who he is. Are you sure he isn't asking for money or selling tastefully designed Christmas wreaths?"

"He assured Mary, sir, that he was on no such mission."

"Dress?"

"Quite high, sir."

Lenox shrugged. "I must see him, I suppose. If you haven't already, offer him something to drink and tell him I'll be down in a moment."

He ate a ruminative apple slice—no sense in hurrying to see a man who had come at this early hour—and checked a list of what he would do that day. He would look at the coroner's report, if Jenkins had sent it; he would meet with John Lysander in the afternoon; he would call on Lady Jane; and then he would take the train back to Oxford, where Graham would hopefully have completed his research about Hatch. It was the third of these tasks that reigned in his mind. Sighing, he took a final sip of coffee and put on his tie.

When Lenox went downstairs, he found a man of perhaps twenty-two or twenty-three, dressed quite well, who said, "Where's Graham, then? I've been curtsied roughly a thousand times by a creature called Mary."

"John Dallington?" said Lenox, much surprised.

"No other. I thought John Best was a lovely touch, though. Had a hundred of the cards printed up."

"What for? Why have you visited? Not that I'm not always happy to see you, of course. It must be a year or so."

Lord John Dallington was the youngest of the Duke and Duchess of Marchmain's three sons, and a notorious anxiety to his parents. In person he was short, trim, handsome, dark-haired, and deep-eyed, with an amused look always lurking in his face and an air of boredom in how he stood. In his buttonhole, as ever, was a perfect carnation, his trademark. He looked a bit like Napoleon, in fact, if Napoleon had decided to drink at the Beargarden Club every evening rather than conquer Russia.

His reputation across London was set; he was known to be the most determined drinker, party-goer, and cad in the West End. Instead of entering the military or the church, as most third sons might have done, he had elected to idle until he discovered what he wanted to do in life. Such a discovery would have shocked everyone, however, and though Dallington gave the impression that it was daily expected, even his partisans admitted that a long life of dissolution seemed most probable.

Lenox sometimes met Dallington in Marchmain House in Surrey during hunting season, and less often in London. Lady Jane, on behalf of her friend the duchess, had once asked Lenox if he might talk to the lad, but Lenox had put his foot down smartly and averred to his friend that under no circumstances would he be dragged into a conversation doomed to end in failure and, worse still, awkward silence. However, the mountain will now and then come to Mohammed, and here Dallington was, and at this early hour. For Lenox, it had the same surreal quality as running into the Emperor of Japan in the Turf would have.

"I was hoping to speak to you about something, Mr. Lenox. You know my father is fond of you, and I've always liked you, too—I haven't forgotten, of course, the timely half crown you delivered to me before I left for school, and which bought me many an illicit cigarette in those early days—and I have something serious on my mind."

"Do you?" The pronouncement would have made happy news for the duke and duchess. For Lenox it was simply perplexing.

"Though I left my card before, at the moment I'm especially keen, because I know you're working to find out who murdered George Payson."

Surprised, Lenox said, "I am, yes."

Dallington paused, looking as if he were weighing in his mind the best means of expressing something larger than his powers of articulation. At last he said, "As you may have heard, I've been casting around for a career that I fancy, and while I'd love to make the governor happy and became some dratted vicar or general, the idea that keeps returning to me is that I become a detective."

There was a long pause. "I'm astonished," Lenox said, and he had never spoken truer words.

"I've had my wild times now and then—more than my share perhaps—and I don't think I'll give them up, because I like them too well. But I have also always had a very fine sense of justice. It's really the highest praise I can give myself. Criticism is easier, of course. I'm a spendthrift—I play with girls' hearts—I drink too much—don't give a whit for the family escutcheon—don't always listen to the mother and father. Still, though, weighed against all that, for as long as I can remember this sense of justice, of fair play, was what I liked best in myself."

"I see," said Lenox.

"Part of it is the playing fields of Eton sort of thing, that old sense of never ratting and always sharing out and that, but I also remember earlier examples. As a child I always confessed to my crimes when there was any chance of another person getting blamed. Which was out of character, as I never minded the crimes themselves, you see."

"But to be a detective takes more than that—it takes as well doggedness and humanity, John. And humility."

"You mean to remind me that I'm a dilettante, of course. I don't deny it. Still, I feel deeply that this is the profession I'd like to follow. I wouldn't take your time lightly."

"Your parents will be upset."

"No doubt—but then again, they might be pleased to see me settling to something, and of course there's no worry over money."

"That's the other thing that would worry me about your following this path, if I may be frank."

"Of course."

"The victims of murder are a variable lot, as variable as any set of mankind you'll find. Finding justice for George Payson is well and good, but what about the cabman who beat his wife and died of a blow to the back of the head? Will you follow the clues in a case like that? What about the louse-and-dirt-covered body in a ditch by the side of the road?"

Very openly, Dallington said, "I can only promise that I'll try as hard as I know how to treat every case equally. At any rate, I mentioned Payson for a reason—he was a fresher in Lincoln when I was spending that fourth year at Trinity, and I saw some of him and always rather liked him. It was seeing a mutual friend of ours the other day that finally galvanized me to come make this proposal."

"Proposal?"

"I'd like to apprentice myself to you."

There was another long pause. "I assumed you meant to ask for advice about joining Scotland Yard."

"Oh, no, of course not. For the same reason you didn't. Men of our rank could never serve there, could they?"

"Yes, I see that," Lenox said. Again he paused, turning it over in his mind. At last he said, his words measured and contemplative, "I find it difficult to reject what you've asked of me. And it's a large request—I can't hand you a magnifying glass and see you off. The reason I find it difficult is that mine is a neglected profession. I would scarcely say so if you hadn't asked me this question, but it is, in my mind at least, both one of the least respected professions among our kind of people and one of the most important and noble in its purpose. If you are a detective and a gentleman, expect to be unheralded—misunderstood except by your friends, and even by them sometimes—looked on as somewhat odd, if harmless. It will help that you have a position and money, as it has helped me, but it won't save you from a certain, rather hard to bear kind of disrepute."

Dallington nodded. "I won't mind."

"Won't you? I hope not."

"I haven't yet. You couldn't fathom the things that are said of me, you know. The most incredible falsehoods!"

"Yes," Lenox said. He sighed. "You had it in mind to begin straight away?"

"Yes, I did. As I say, because of Payson, poor chap."

"Would you mind giving me the morning to consider what you've said and what course of action to take?"

"Oh, certainly," said Dallington, suddenly jolly again. "I'm absolutely famished, and I thought I'd pop round to the Jumpers and have a spot of breakfast if any of the lads are there."

"You're welcome to stay for breakfast here—"

"Oh, no, I wouldn't like to impose—and really, I think I had better let you alone. My absence, I reckon, will improve my campaign."

He laughed a high, youthful laugh and bade Lenox good-bye, promising to return at noon. Before the door was shut, however, Lenox knew that he would assent to Dallington's request. For several reasons: because he believed what he had said about the nobility and neglect of the profession, because the solitary life of the detective at times weighed on him, because he really did like the lad, and most of all because he was generous, and found it difficult to decline any earnest and thoughtful appeal, whatever it might be.

CHAPTER TWENTY-SIX

The morning post arrived—Lysander's note had been delivered by hand—and brought with it the coroner's report on Major Peter Wilson's suicide. The accompanying note from Inspector Jenkins offered whatever aid the Yard could muster, and Lenox found himself with two new and amenable colleagues in less than twenty-four hours.

It was a dull document. The jury had been unanimous in its verdict and the coroner had strongly endorsed their decision, and to Lenox's untrained eye there looked like very little that could possibly be askance about it. So he put the report in an envelope and sent it with a short note to McConnell, to see if the doctor, better used to such language, could make anything out of it. Then he wrote to Jenkins and thanked him for the report. After a last gulp of coffee, he went into his study and answered the correspondence that he had received while in Oxford. There was a letter written in painstaking English from a French scholar inquiring about life in Hadrian's court, a subject on which Lenox was something of an expert, and another from his old Harrow friend James Landon-Bowes, who in

Yorkshire was happily raising his children and farming.

Before he knew it noon had come, and there was a ring at the door that resulted in Mary's presenting Dallington.

"Hullo again," the youth said cheerily, sitting down in the chair Lenox offered. "Have you thought much about what I asked?"

"Yes, of course."

"Right-ho," said Dallington, and while he seemed airy, there was a look of intentness about him that gave Lenox hope.

"I'll agree to it."

"That's more like it!" said Dallington.

"I'll agree to it, but only if I have your word that this isn't some passing fancy. Your solemn word, Dallington, with all due respect."

"I give my solemn word, Lenox, and delighted to do so."

"Very well. You asked me whether or not you might help solve the mystery of George Payson's death. Well, it's likely that you'd only prove a liability to me, but you'll have your chance."

"Lovely!"

Lenox jotted down a name and address. "This man's friend claims that he's gone out of town, though I find it highly doubtful. I'd like you to try to find out whether it's true. For heaven's sake, though, don't follow him to Pall Mall or his club—any of his clubs."

"Right-ho," said Dallington, looking at the paper. "Theophilus Butler."

"Yes—and please avoid *asking* anybody if he's there who might tell him that someone was looking for him."

Dallington nodded and laughed. "Clear enough," he said. "Footwork—looking out—just the sort of thing I need to practice."

Lenox sighed. "It isn't practice, though."

"Oh, no—of course not."

"And don't push the matter. If you can't discover where he is, leave it."

"Just as you say. Goodness, though, thanks." Dallington grinned. "I'm dead excited."

"Do you read the police report in the papers?"

"Sometimes."

"Read them every day, all the papers. Crimes always repeat themselves."

Dallington noted it in a small leather journal he had brought out.

"The agony column, too—those brief messages at the end of the newspaper, you know. More happens in those messages than in all the streets of East London put together."

"Agony column . . . police report . . . all papers. Got it," he said, binding the journal again. He stood up and thanked Lenox profusely. They had a short conversation about what equipment he might need—the older man recommended a variety of the clothes that existed along the subtle scale of class, a pocket ruler, a pocket magnifying glass, good boots, and the friendship of a good doctor. He saw Dallington off with a hearty good-bye that masked his trepidation at their fledgling project. It was no time to disrupt the system he had, he thought—but the milk was spilled.

At half past two that afternoon, Lenox presented himself at Lysander's door. A man tending toward old age and with a military air answered the door, probably Lysander's one time batman, Lenox thought. They went together into a snug but comfortable living room with a fireplace and chairs on one end. Nearby was a bookcase full of military histories. Glancing over the rest of the room, Lenox took one of the chairs and waited. Presently, Captain John Lysander came out and greeted the detective.

He was a distinctly military man, with a trim mustache and tidy whiskers, a scar on his neck that looked like it had once been painful, quite black hair, and utterly average features. He wasn't tall, but he stood quite upright, jutting his chest out, and it gave him an authoritative air. His clothes were informal but clean and creased, puttees of the standard postmilitary variety. No doubt he would exchange them for a more proper suit when he went out but felt at ease in them at home. His bearing was neither kind nor unkind, but efficient. Lenox had seen his type a hundred times, both good and bad.

"How do you do, Mr. Lenox? May I offer you some coffee or tea?"

"No, thanks."

Lysander nodded to his man, who retreated. "Well, how can I help you?"

"You may have heard something of the death of George Payson, Captain Lysander."

"Indeed I have. Terribly sad. I never went to the 'varsity, of course, and in the military men die at that age many a time, but never so senselessly."

"I don't suppose you knew him, did you?"

"No, I didn't. And I can't quite see what connection you suppose I might have to the young man."

"Or Bill Dabney?"

Lysander's face was blank. "No, nor him."

"You're a member of the September Society, aren't you, Captain Lysander?"

"Indeed I am, and it's saved many of us returned from the East from losing touch and helped us in making that—well, call it that uneasy transition back to civilian life."

"Quite a military atmosphere there?"

"Yes, indeed. As we like it."

"It's probably nothing," said Lenox cautiously, "but I have a duty to follow every possible clue."

"Quite right."

"And I found in Payson's belongings several mentions of the September Society."

"Did you!" If Lysander's shock was feigned it was done rather well.

"I wondered whether you could think of any connection between the lad and your group."

"I wish I could help you, but I can't think of any possible link. We're only an assembly of twenty-five or thirty, Mr. Lenox—I suppose the exact number, if you want it, is twenty-six—and keep much to ourselves. We have our friendships outside of the Society and inside the Society, and the two rarely meet. Of course, this young man couldn't possibly have served with us, and it's most unlikely that an uncle or cousin would even mention such a small organization to a lad who had no prospect of joining. We firmly intend for the Society to die out with us."

"I see," Lenox said. He took a different tack. "Major Butler is out of town?"

"Yes, I'm afraid he is."

"Did you know I had written to him as well?"

Lysander laughed. "I did, but no cause for suspicion. I know that you detectives often interpret every small unknown as guilt, but I only heard of the note you wrote Major Butler because we live in such close proximity and our houses trade a good deal of talk."

"If it's not impertinent, Captain Lysander, why do you live so closely together?"

"Ah—well, Major Butler served rather longer than I did. I was injured outside Lahore, you see.

185

When I returned my parents had been dead a year, and I had inherited a comfortable sum from them, and decided to settle down in London, as so many ex-servicemen do. I had a few friends here from my school in Hampshire and a few others from the military, and I belonged to the Army and Navy, and thought I'd get along all right. So I moved into this flat, with its modest few rooms, counting—correctly—upon spending a good deal of time at my clubs and that sort of thing."

"I see."

"When Major Butler returned in '52 he came to see me. He had been my commander in the East, but we were always pretty pally, and when he said he hadn't anywhere to stay—well, you see. I offered him my spare room here. He declined in favor of a hotel, but through my landlord I put him onto the free rooms a few doors down."

"Ah—that makes a good deal of sense."

"It suits us both, as we're close to our clubs and to Piccadilly. And then, our valets served together as well, both of them, and it's nice for them to have each other's company."

"Awfully considerate, that."

"Well, as I mentioned, the transition to civilian life can be difficult."

"Certainly. Could you tell me about Peter Wilson?"

Lysander's back went up at this. "I don't see

how that question could possibly be relevant to whatever it is you're investigating, Mr. Lenox."

In a conciliatory tone, the detective said, "I had hoped to speak to him, you see."

"Well—he's dead. He killed himself. It was the damnedest thing that ever happened. I loved old Wilson like a brother."

"I'm sorry to have brought it up. I only thought you might be able to tell me why he killed himself."

"I don't know. And I wish I did."

"Again, I'm sorry."

"No, no . . . in fact, I'm sorry I can't be of more help with your case," said Lysander.

"Not at all—it was a dark horse, as I say. Thanks awfully for your time."

"Don't mention it," Lysander said and walked Lenox to the door.

As he said good-bye and walked down the stoop, Lenox wondered about the man. He was personally quite agreeable, not at all volatile, and he seemed honest. He might have been either a banker or a bank robber, from his demeanor. The only thing that seemed clear was that if Lysander was a criminal, he was an exceptionally level-headed one, exceptionally cool. There was little emotion in him. If he was a criminal, Lenox knew, and shuddered to think it, he would be capable of nearly anything.

CHAPTER TWENTY-SEVEN

Green Park, a shamrock-colored rectangle that lay behind the Houses of Parliament, was warm and beautiful that afternoon. The willow trees bent toward the lake, their lowest branches just brushing the water, and the park's lone wanderers and couples alike walked more slowly than they had along the fast city blocks, stopping to watch for a while. Lenox always liked to watch the swans gliding serenely, birds with just the mix of beauty and danger that humans like in wildlife—for a swan, of course, could break a man's arm.

Another curious fact about them was that every swan in England belonged to Queen Victoria. Not many people knew it, but poaching swans was an offense the crown could punish. The official swan keeper to Her Majesty wrangled the birds in the third week of July every year, when they were served at the Queen's table and a few others across the isles, in Cambridge, Oxford, York, Edinburgh. The swans were mute, but at their deaths they found voice and sang, and the long line of wranglers always claimed to be haunted by the sound. It was the origin of the term swan song.

Lenox pondered the bizarre customs of his beloved country as he walked toward Toto and McConnell's house. He had omitted his congratulations from the note he sent to McConnell with the coroner's report in case the doctor wanted to announce the news himself.

When Lenox arrived at the vast house, McConnell and Toto were in the small anteroom by the door with Lady Jane. They only used the room with their closest friends, preferring its intimacy to the rest of the house's grandeur. When they invited him in, McConnell stood up.

"Hullo again, Lenox.

"I can't stop beaming, can I? By the way, Toto and I are delighted that you'll be the godfather. Here, sit down, sit down."

Lenox laughed and took his place on a highly fashionable blue and white sofa that was Toto's pride and joy—or had been at any rate, before young Henry or Anna or Elizabeth or whatever the baby would be called. The room smelled buttery, like tea and toast.

"How are you, Charles?" Lady Jane asked.

"Quite well, thanks, and you?"

"I say, Lenox," McConnell cut in, "I haven't had time to look at the coroner's report you sent over. We've had visitors all morning, distant aunts and things, or I would have."

"It's not pressing by any means," Lenox answered.

189

"I'll look at it this evening, though, while Jane and my wife go to the doctor's." He turned to Toto. "Do you really mean to go every day of your pregnancy, darling? You do realize that I'm a doctor, after all."

Toto laughed. "Of course I do, you dear man, but Dr. Windsor takes care of all the babies and he's ever so cheerful about it and I like him to reassure me. Anyway, you'd rather neglect me for dead cats and coroner's reports."

"Yes," said Lady Jane, "what is the coroner's report? You've been secretive, Charles."

"Have I? Not intentionally, I promise. It's only that there's not much to tell, unfortunately. There's a tiny club called the September Society that may be bound up in George Payson's murder, and one of the Society's founders killed himself, I'm sorry to say. I sent McConnell the verdict on his death to see if it looked suspicious. That's all."

"It's too sad," said Lady Jane. "Poor Annabelle —to have both her husband and her son die in such odd and violent ways."

As she said this Lenox looked carefully at his friend and saw again the same sorrow that had lived just beneath her exterior for the past few weeks, and again wondered what it was that could reduce her eternal cheer to its threadbare outward appearance; and wondered why an air of secrecy hung around her; and wondered who the man in the long gray coat was.

With a charming pout Toto said, "I scarcely think murders are as celebratory as toast. Have some, won't you? And Shreve"—their butler, standing somnolently in the hallway—"be a lamb and bring a bottle of champagne. What's a nice one, darling?"

McConnell turned to Shreve and ordered a '51 Piper. "I don't mind a glass. Charles?"

"Of course," said Lenox.

The champagne came, and all but Toto had a glass—she was content to put her nose to McConnell's glass and give a small sneeze of protest. They looked so happy that Lenox almost turned to Lady Jane and asked her to marry him there and then. Soon, though, the company broke down into two pairs as Thomas and Toto argued good-naturedly about the baby's name and whether it would go to school in Scotland or England, if it was a boy, that was, while Lenox and Lady Jane resumed the conversation that had been ongoing between them for their entire lives.

"I feel I haven't seen you in years!" she said. "Is it dreadful to be up there on your own?"

"Graham came up, kind soul that he is, but of course I miss home." He just barely resisted the urge to say "and you."

"Is the case very hard?"

"The hardest I've ever had, I should say."

She took his hand and said, "It will turn out well in the end. You'll see to that."

He believed her. "I'm sorry to have been pre-occupied."

"Oh, not at all. I've missed our visits from house to house, but Mrs. Randall has supplied her company in your absence."

Both of them laughed at this old joke. Elizabeth Randall was a widow of about ninety, well known for staring out of her drawing room window (which looked out onto Lenox's and Lady Jane's houses) and quietly passing judgment on their visitors. It was never a surprise to Lenox when he met Mrs. Randall on the street and she inquired nonchalantly about the particularly scruffy young man in the stovepipe hat she had seen, or the dark-looking woman in the crimson dress—even when the visits were weeks old. Her complete shamelessness was almost endearing.

"One thing that's nice, though, is to see Oxford again."

"Is it? That was the dullest time of my life, of course, not yet living in London and without the diversion of all you young gentlemen who had gotten to go out into the wide world."

"They have dances now, apparently."

"Do they! My mother would be appalled."

"Yes, and it seems as if they're a pretty raucous business."

"I've been meaning to visit Timothy there."

"Do you have letters from him?"

"Oh, short, polite ones, doubtless full of affection, but never with much news in them. I crave news."

Lenox was the only person in the world who knew about Jane's allegiance to Timothy Stills, a poverty-stricken lad, abandoned by his mother, denied by his father, who belonged to some forgotten cadet branch of Jane's noble family. She had heard a whisper of him and gone to Manchester a dozen years ago to find him near starvation, living on what he could beg with an aunt who tolerated his presence only for what money he brought in. Jane had taken him back to London instantly, and then arranged for his schooling and had him to visit every Christmas and during the summer holidays. She never concealed his identity, but neither did she bruit it about, as some might have.

"Shall I look in on him when I return?" Lenox asked.

"Would you? You're such a dear, Charles. He's at Oriel. I'll write him that you're coming."

"Have you been worried about him for some reason?" Lenox asked.

"Not at all," she said, and her unhappiness remained unspoken another moment longer. "But tell me more about Oxford, won't you?"

Lenox told her about visiting the Turf again, about his old friend Caule's ghost story, about seeing Balliol and eating at the Bear with McConnell, and suddenly, as he told it to his friend, laughing along the way, it became real to him, and he felt better about it. Of course he would solve the case—and of course he would ask her to marry him.

They both left a little while later, Lenox promising Toto that he would think over the dozens of names she had asked his opinion of, Lady Jane promising to be at Dr. Windsor's at five for Toto's appointment. McConnell told Lenox again that he would send the results of the coroner's report up to Oxford, and after a number of other little reminders and last words, they all parted.

"Well! I certainly am glad for them," said Lady Jane, stepping into the cab that Shreve had hailed. "They seem to be awfully happy."

"Yes, and after things had gotten worse," Lenox added. "Will the change be permanent?"

"It's just what Toto needs, I should say, something to dote on and love and make dozens of small but significant decisions about. And it will give Thomas an heir and less time with his thoughts. Yes, I think it will be permanent."

"I certainly hope you're right."

They rode along, the two friends, until they had come to Hampden Lane.

"Are you definitely going back to Oxford, Charles?"

"Can't be helped, I'm afraid."

"Do stop in on Timothy, then. And hurry back

afterward. I won't be able to see you again before you go if I'm to meet Toto at her doctor's office."

They stood in front of their adjoining houses, the light dimming. "I meant to say, Jane—is everything quite well?"

Hurriedly, she answered, "Oh, yes, of course. It always is. Now, good-bye, Charles!"

Lenox walked back down her stoop and up his own. It was dark, and he knew that he had ahead of him a long train ride across the bleak landscape of an autumn night in England. Still, it wouldn't do to put it off until the morning.

Sitting by the fire in his study, waiting as Samuel packed his bags and the driver rubbed down his horses for the trip to Paddington, Lenox read distractedly over an essay he had written for the upcoming Roman Historians' Conference, which was meant to take place in Vienna in a month's time. His tickets were booked, and he was pleased with his essay, which had to do with childhood in Augustan Rome. A friend and correspondent from Cambridge, Bertie Flint-Flagg, had sent it back in the post with his congratulations and a few minor corrections. He also mentioned a term-time teaching fellowship available at Magdalene, a small college with an excellent reputation in classics, which he thought Lenox might be suited for. As perhaps the premier amateur historian of Rome in the Isles, James Hawthendon aside, Flint-Flagg wrote (and this threw Lenox into a slight dudgeon), he really ought to try his hand at academic life. Suddenly Lenox had a vision of himself with a pipe, a small back garden, a spacious study in Magdalene or Clare or Caius, a wall full of books, the companionable presence of other scholars—and perhaps it was seeing Dallington that morning, but even as he envisioned that happy life, even as his heart leapt at the prospect, he knew that he could never abandon the hard and taxing work that won him so little worldly respect, and that he knew to be as high and noble as any calling.

CHAPTER TWENTY-EIGHT

McConnell's report on the inquest of Peter Wilson arrived at Oxford the next evening. It had been a discouraging day for Lenox. Inspector Goodson's sergeants had searched to the south of the town past Christ Church Meadow, not quite as far as Faringdon and Didcot, asking in pubs, post offices, and inns, but nobody had seen Dabney or Payson. Lenox's suggestion had been well reasoned, Goodson said when the two men met, not adding that it had failed nonetheless.

"Did you search the fields?"

"Aye, and asked the locals too. Nothing there."

"Perhaps it's best to restrict the search—bring it back in within a quarter mile of the meadow and search that quarter mile very thoroughly."

Goodson shook his head. "We don't have the manpower. We'll have to follow other leads."

"What has there been?"

"We're focusing now on the man who met Payson at the Jesus College dance that Saturday evening."

"Just so. Anything on him?"

"That's a bit better—but only a bit. We've tracked him to an inn at Abingdon, we believe, and he left his name there as Geoffrey Canterbury."

"A man of at least small literary knowledge, then."

"Aye, *The Canterbury Tales*, we thought so, too."

"Any further description of him?"

"Only that he looked about fifty, dressed well, had very dark hair, a mark on his throat, and carried a heavy pocket watch that looked to the landlady—Mrs. Meade—expensive, perhaps ornamental. He seemed to check it and handle it constantly."

"Still, better than nothing. What did he leave as a forwarding address?"

"Only a steam liner bound for India—which, it

turned out, departed a month ago for Delhi."

"Was he tan?"

"Pale."

"And not military by the look of him."

"No, not according to Mrs. Meade."

This conversation had taken place at the police station a little after one o'clock. Waiting for Dallington, Graham, and McConnell all to report back, Lenox had no choice but to resume his dull research at the Bodleian. Nothing else had come to light, and he had given it up as a bad job a bit after four. Now it was five, and a bellboy had brought in McConnell's note with the evening post. Graham was still out on Hatch's trail, but had assured Lenox he only needed one more day to see what he could find out about the elusive professor.

The parcel contained three things: a short note on yellow writing paper, a more formal letter on long paper, which evidently appraised the coroner's report, and then the report itself, which Lenox would have to return to Jenkins at Scotland Yard. The short first note turned out to be from Toto. It read:

Hallo Charles! I'm with Jane (it's about 9:00 in the morning here, when shall this get to you?) and she thought we ought to tell you that I'm healthy and that I mean to call the baby Malory if it's a girl. Isn't that a sensible and lovely name? Malory McConnell—I think it sounds awfully well. P.S. Do return soon, and stop Thomas poring over reports all day! Affectionately, TM.

Lenox laughed and folded the note back in half. He paused for a moment, then put it in his leather correspondence case. At any rate Lady Jane had been there at its writing, so it deserved preservation. Smiling again at the folly of the mind in love, he turned to McConnell's more serious note.

Hello, Charles. Thanks for letting me have a look at this. I may as well say straight off the bat that I don't think it's the kind of thing that will instantly solve your case—in fact the coroner, Bellows, did quite well with a tricky matter. As near as I can tell, Peter Wilson probably did commit suicide. But there's some room for doubt, which may perhaps be of interest to you.

Wilson died in Suffolk, at the country house of a friend, Daniel Maran. It was September of last year, and the two men as well as half a dozen others were evidently escaping from London for the weekend—you can no doubt decipher all of that in the report your-self. Wilson went off on his horse one morning alone, taking his air rifle with him. He would have known how to handle guns himself, of course, having hunted since youth and served in the Suffolk 12th. The gun was a light one, suitable for small game. And in fact he was ultimately found in a thicket of mature woodland that Maran used as a pheasant cover. The horse returned home; Maran formed a search party, and they found Wilson dead.

The angle of the gun is the one thing that forced Bellows to the conclusion of suicide, rather than merely accident. The gun was angled up slightly so that the bullet hit his right cheek—from a distance of two feet or so. This seems to mark a clear intent on Wilson's part. However, a small part of me is uncertain that this was how he would have killed himself—it was a position which would have forced him into an awkward half-kneeling stance, as the gun would have had to rest on the ground. Looking over my files, I find that it's almost unique as an angle of entry in most suicides by air rifle. On the other hand, murder in the same way would have been *relatively easy for somebody in the undergrowth.*

Weighed against this, though, is the overwhelming fact of the position of Wilson next to the gun when Maran found him—Wilson was lying across the gun with his hand still tightly gripping the weapon that killed him. It would be very difficult to manage a body to make it fall in that way—a shot from the ground would have probably sent Wilson staggering backward.

One other thing supporting the theory of suicide: Pheasant hunting doesn't begin until October, and Maran's game-keeper insists he would have found it poor sport. Wilson went out there for a reason other than hunting, it would seem.

Sorry this isn't more helpful—Thomas

Scrawled beneath the doctor's signature, in less precise handwriting, was the following:

Incidentally, you'll find a note from Toto here—no doubt you'd do well to ignore its entreaties, but I'll leave that to your discretion. TM.

Lenox was grateful to McConnell for his diligence, but the results were disappointing; the detective felt as if he were reaching for something substantial, only to find himself grasping the air every time. Still, it might be that Dallington could find something useful about Maran.

Maran. Didn't he know that name? Tossing the letter on his desk, Lenox stood up. Hurriedly he put on his coat and left the room, leaving his candles burning.

He left the Randolph and found himself on Broad Street, ignoring the students let off of their tutorials coming from Balliol and Trinity, striding past them toward the Bodleian. He went straight in and up to the Reading Room, where he pulled out *Who's Who* from its spot on the bookshelf where he had left it. He found Maran easily in the book and read over the entry twice, copying it out carefully in his spiral-bound notebook the second time. Well. Daniel Maran was without a doubt a member of the September Society. The most important so far, perhaps. He had served in the 2nd Battalion, 12th Regiment of Foot, Suffolk, just as Wilson and Lysander had—a captain. Unlike them, though, he was no mere retired military man, in and out of his clubs.

Back at the Randolph, Graham had returned. He was in Lenox's rooms, laying out an evening suit; Lenox was to dine with McConnell's friend Radley, the one who had telegraphed down to London about Payson's death.

"Any luck?" Lenox asked.

"Perhaps, sir," said Graham. "I thought I might organize my thoughts while you were at supper."

Having waited so eagerly for information about Hatch, Lenox was suddenly unconcerned. "Of course," he said, waving a hand. What *was* this Society devoted to a long-forgotten battle? Why was anybody but an old codger or two at the Army and Navy Club worried about it? Above all, how was it related to Payson and Dabney? Dabney—there was the lead to follow, now that none of the others seemed to have panned out. He would speak to Goodson about it in the morning. Were Dabney's parents even in Oxford at the moment?

"Have you heard of Daniel Maran, Graham?"

"No, sir, I don't think I have."

"I just read up on him. A thoroughly undistinguished military career, followed by an unexpected and unexpectedly well funded stand for Parliament." Putting a cufflink in, Lenox went on, "He's a government official now. Works at the War Office Building on Whitehall Place, just by Scotland Yard. Do you know it? Opposite the Horse Guards building, if you've been down there. I imagine that he reports directly to the minister there."

"How did you hear of him, sir?"

"He's a member of the September Society. And the master-general of the Ordnance."

"If I may ask, sir—"

"The master-general of the Ordnance is a Member of Parliament, usually in the cabinet, in fact—and the only member of the British military who doesn't have to report to the commander in chief. It's a tremendously powerful and influential position. He arranges for the procurement of artillery and supplies, manages our fortifications . . . millions of pounds pass through his hands every year. It used to be Baron Raglan, you recall."

This was a famous general who had done well in the Crimean War, and whose name was a byword for military integrity throughout the Isles. It disturbed Lenox that the quality of the man occupying the position had fallen off so precipitously. Maran had done little of note besides finding himself in Parliament before attaining the position.

"My goodness, sir," said Graham—for him as violent as language could become.

"Yes, I'd reckon he knows every secret about the British government that's worth the having. My brother described him to me once as the most dangerous man to cross in all of Whitehall."

CHAPTER TWENTY-NINE

Supper with Radley was interesting, and better still it was distracting. A professor of biological sciences at Worcester, he had great enthusiasm for McConnell's work as an amateur biologist. His own passion was birds. For much of the meal he had laid out the objections to the theories of evolution that Charles Darwin and Alfred Russel Wallace had proposed a few years ago and that were still widely debated in the scientific community. Probably impossible, though very clever, was his conclusion. "The best we'll say of Wallace and Darwin is that they gave us new ways of thinking about animal growth, which could spur on other, more plausible theories." He appeared to be in a diminishing majority, however, and Lenox reminded himself to ask McConnell his thoughts on the matter. In all, though, Radley was a genial, undeniably good sort, and their conversation was pleasant, if heavy on birds.

After supper Lenox had gone for a long, thoughtful stroll around Addison's Walk, the path that wound narrowly around a small island within the grounds of Magdalen College. It was a beautiful ring that led away from and then back to the college, the ground level and only inches away from the quiet, rolling Cherwell River. He remembered its pristine beauty under fresh snow from his undergraduate days; once, despondent over some long-forgotten exam, he had gone to the Walk at dawn and come out feeling better, slightly better. This evening he had smoked his pipe and thought about the case, the cool air clearing the wine from his head, a don passing now and then, the view of Magdalen Tower up in the middle distance . . .

Just back in his rooms now and removing his coat, he said to his butler, "Well, Graham, if you have any questions about the blue chaffinch or the gray-rumped swallow, I imagine I can answer them for you pretty exhaustively by now."

"Thank you, sir. Perhaps some other time."

"Sensible. Swallows and chaffinches are good in their way, of course, but too much of them is inadvisable."

Graham had given him a glass of brandy, and Lenox was sitting in his shirttails in a blue high-backed chair near the fire. He invited the butler to sit down opposite him and take a glass; Graham assented to the first offer but declined the second.

"Hatch, then," Lenox said.

"Yes, sir."

"I hope you've found something interesting out?"

"I think I have, yes, sir."

"Go on."

Graham looked at the notes in his lap. "The gentleman is called John Braithwaite Hatch, sir, Bingham Professor of Chemistry. Aged thirty-eight. Born and grew up in North London, a rural area near Ashburton Grove. Educated at Westminster College, having earned a scholarship. On to Lincoln, Oxford, after that. Stayed as a fellow after finishing his undergraduate coursework, and soon became a don."

"Much distinguished as a scholar?" Lenox asked, cradling his brandy in his hand.

"He was, sir, yes, though he hasn't published anything in two years."

"I see."

"His servants universally ascribe his current stagnation to his love of drink, sir."

"I'm not wholly surprised."

"What I have to report otherwise is concise but I hope useful, sir. You told me that you thought Mr. Hatch had lied to you twice, about George Payson's cat and about the last time he had seen the missing gentlemen. I can add to your statement two extremely suspicious facts. The first is that he saw George Payson on the morning of his disappearance."

"Good Lord!"

"Yes, sir, I was as surprised as you are."

"Where did they meet?"

"At a coffee shop about halfway between Worcester College and the Ashmolean Museum, sir, a place called Shotter's."

"Shotter's? What sort of name is that?"

"After the proprietor, sir, one Peter Shotter."

"Ah. How did you find this out?"

"Mr. Hatch spends most mornings in the Lincoln College senior common room, according to a gentleman I met who works there, sir."

Every college's professors had a senior common room, the graduate students a middle common room, and the undergraduates a junior common room. They were all similar, filled with couches, fireplaces, and always something to eat. Usually the senior room, though, held the college's treasures—its single Michelangelo cartoon or notable Greek vase.

"But that morning he didn't?"

"No, sir, he did not. I asked a maid in Mr. Hatch's house where he had gone, and all she knew was that he had gone down Beaumont Street. I inquired at the shops on that road and struck lucky, sir."

"You're a marvel, Graham. How long did they talk? How do you know it was Payson?"

"According to Mr. Shotter, the two spoke for about fifteen minutes. He knew Mr. Payson, sir, and identified Mr. Hatch from my description, though he couldn't say that he had ever seen him before that morning."

"It sounds almost as if Payson instigated the meeting. A spot he was accustomed to, where his face was known, I mean."

"Yes, sir."

"Did you find out anything about a connection between Hatch and the September Society, by any chance?"

Graham shook his head. "No, sir, I'm afraid I didn't."

"No fault of yours. What clubs does he belong to?"

"Only the Oxford and Cambridge, sir."

"Never served in the military, I take it?"

"No, sir."

"Did you find out anything about his relatives?"

"Yes, sir, though nothing which might help the case, I fear. His mother is living, father dead. He is an only child and has two living aunts in Yorkshire, both childless."

"Father's profession?"

"A barrister, sir."

"Successful?"

"Not successful, sir, but not a failure."

"I see. Well, Graham, thank you."

"I have one more piece of information, sir."

"Yes?" Lenox had been poking at the fire, feeling suddenly sleepy, his brandy mostly gone, but now he looked up. "What else did you find out?"

"Professor Hatch has an unassailable alibi for the time frame of the murder of George Payson."

"Given by?"

"Numerous people, sir—to begin with, his servants."

"Go on."

"However, sir, the afternoon before the murder he went for a walk in Christ Church Meadow. It appears, sir, that he went beyond the meadow to the south, where you and Inspector Goodson had speculated the two young gentlemen might be hiding out."

"That's right," said Lenox. His whole attention was on Graham, and he had moved to the edge of the seat, his hands interlocking, his hair untidy, his face intent.

"He reappeared in the meadow after about fifteen minutes, sir, according to a park guard there. When he had left through the lower meadow he had a parcel."

"And when he returned?"

"He no longer had it."

Lenox sat back low in his seat, suddenly pensive. He stared at the fire for a minute, perhaps two, Graham silent as well. Then he stood up with sudden energy.

"The question is whether he was taking something to Payson and Dabney, or just to one of them, or to . . . Geoffrey Canterbury. Or to some other person. The murderer."

"Precisely my thoughts, sir."

Lenox, pacing, his face red now from the heat of the fire, said, "Did anything else occur to you? About Hatch, about the case? Is there any other information about him? I feel as if I'm missing some small piece here . . . some key into the whole thing."

Graham coughed softly. "I have a little more information, sir, but that's all, and none of it terribly helpful. Here," he said, passing a sheet of paper to Lenox, "is a list of the people who usually attended Mr. Hatch's parties. On its reverse you'll find the dates of the last several."

Lenox nodded. "Thanks, Graham. I'll track them down. That will be useful." After another moment of silence, still pacing, he suddenly sighed and said, "Well, I suppose I'll go to bed. Was there any late post, by the way?"

"Only this, from London, sir."

He passed Lenox a heavy envelope. It was from Dallington.

"Excellent. All right, thanks, Graham—first-rate work. Sorry to seem so distracted, you know. This case is bothering me, really bothering me. But you've opened up a whole new vista. I mean to tell Goodson straight away tomorrow morning, if you'll come with me."

"Of course, sir."

Lenox paused. "And when we're done—all our thoughts toward Morocco!"

"Indeed, sir," said Graham, with the slightest of smiles.

"Good night, then."

After Graham had withdrawn, Lenox sat at the desk by the window. He left the note for a moment and stared out into the sky. A clear night, a crescent moon. Another sigh, and he turned his attention to Dallington. The note was characteristic of Lenox's new pupil.

Good news, then, Lenox—or bad, as you choose—Butler was certainly in town on the evening you asked me about. The chap couldn't have been more conspicuous if he tried, in fact. Attached find a list of his activities (dry stuff, but to each his own). Thanks for the chance of doing it, really. If there's anything else I can help with, send word by return—or at your leisure. Cheerio, Dallington. P.S.: No charge for the services, though my mother's desperate to see me paid. Droll, isn't it? She sends on her regard.

Lenox laughed at the postscript and scanned the attached list, which seemed to be in order. Admirable quickness on the lad's part, as well. Perhaps an apprentice would be useful after all.

CHAPTER THIRTY

The next morning, Lenox saw Inspector Goodson. They spent about an hour aligning their knowledge of the case, Goodson working primarily in Oxfordshire, his energy at the moment devoted to finding the man who called himself Geoffrey Canterbury, while Lenox's interest was now mainly in the September Society.

Lenox wrote a note to Rosie Little, updating her and encouraging her to be brave, then went to see Timothy Stills, Jane's cousin at Oriel, for a pleasant half hour. As he walked away, his mind turned to his own troubles: Lady Annabelle had reappeared on the scene and was speaking vocally to anybody who would listen about both Goodson's and Lenox's incompetence.

Most important, Bill Dabney's parents had arrived from Birmingham, or rather nearby Kidderminster, a town on the River Stour famous (it was a dubious fame) for its carpet factories. Mr. Dabney, a squat, solid man with a Midlands accent that made every word sound heavy in his mouth, was a farmer. He grazed cattle as well, and did both jobs prosperously from the fashionable look of his fluttery and tiny wife, who spoke in a high-pitched voice. Lenox met with them at their hotel in St. Giles Street at a little after ten thirty.

"Of the Sussex Lenoxes?" were the first words of Mrs. Dabney.

"Yes," said Lenox.

"A pleasure to meet you," she said, the appraising look gone from her eye. "I was saying to Mr. Dabney only the other day that a visit to Sussex would be just the thing for us. The air there is clean, very clean indeed, and I've heard the parkland is handsome, very handsome indeed. And all the small villages!"

There was a great deal more like this before Lenox was able to turn the conversation to their son, and then it was Mr. Dabney who answered.

"What is he like?" said Lenox.

"Alive, we pray."

"I should think he is, Mr. and Mrs. Dabney."

"Do you?" Now it was the farmer's turn to bestow an appraising glance upon Lenox. "I hope you're right."

"It would help to know what he was like—what he looked like, what his personality was like, whether he would go anyplace special besides home in a crisis."

"For the last question, no, I don't think so—he loved Oxford and Kidderminster most, always said he'd finish in one of the two places. He was a happy child, Mr. Lenox, loved to play on the farm, he did. Knew every animal by name, plowed every row of seed by my side. Which isn't to say he neglected his studies, however."

"Always very bright," added Mrs. Dabney. "Studied very hard, and earned his place at Oxford quite easily."

"Did you ever meet Tom Stamp or George Payson?"

"Yes indeed, he brought them to Kidderminster," said Mrs. Dabney. "We have a house to accommodate a number of guests."

"How long did they stay there?"

"A week, Mr. Lenox, last year. Then went down to Stratford for two nights. Over winter break."

"What did you make of George Payson?"

"Lovely manners," said Mr. Dabney. "A fine young lad. Took an interest in the farm as well."

A picture was forming in Lenox's mind of Dabney's character. Solid, proud, middle class, and above all intelligent—that was the part of his personality that everybody from Hatch to Stamp had mentioned. He decided to move on to a more speculative sort of question.

"Would he be the sort of lad to follow George Payson simply out of loyalty? If this case centered on George, for example, rather than the other way around"—Lenox was thinking of the Jesus ball—"would it be like Bill to drop everything to help a friend?"

"Oh, yes," said Mrs. Dabney—but was halted

215

by her husband's obvious introspection. All three of them fell into a momentary silence.

"Yes, I think so, Mr. Lenox," he said finally. "You see, in the Midlands we're slower to change. My family has been on the same farm for three generations. We don't tend to flash between London and Oxford and the country-side, really. We like to get used to things. We like to stay put. We're not changeable."

"I see," said Lenox.

"So I think the answer is yes. Bill would have been very loyal to his friends. Almost stubbornly so, I'd reckon." He paused. "But with that said, Mr. Lenox, if in fact this matter *was* primarily about George Payson, bless his soul, why would Bill still be gone? Wouldn't he have come back?"

Instantly Lenox saw where the younger Dabney's sharpness came from.

"A point well taken, Mr. Dabney. I think the answer must be fear. Perhaps neither lad realized how serious the matter was until George Payson was murdered. If I understand what Bill is like, he may have been savvy enough to recognize the danger and go on concealing himself."

They spoke for about twenty minutes longer, and over the course of that time Lenox saw the tremendous sorrow and worry that underlay Mr. Dabney's deliberate manner and Mrs. Dabney's flightiness—the anxiety about their only son. He disliked seeing people at their weakest, their most vulnerable, as his job continually forced him to do. Did it give him a skeptical attitude about human beings? It wasn't impossible.

He thanked them when they parted and promised to keep in close touch. Leaving them at their hotel, he went to the Bodleian, where he did another hour of fruitless research. Just before getting up to go find some lunch, he wrote Goodson a short note, saying that he no longer thought it possible that Bill Dabney had been behind George Payson's death, as they had once speculated. It seemed improbable after that meeting.

He fell ravenously to a chop of beef with potatoes, peas, and gravy at the Bear and had a glass of shandy with it. After polishing it off he sat at his old table, initials carved into its surface, and drank a coffee while he looked out the window. The days had been getting colder, and the warmth of the coffee was renewing. In the warm, low-ceilinged Bear, he felt almost content—though all the while knowing that the case, getting colder by the minute, awaited him outside.

Before going back to the Randolph to consult with Graham—who he thought should perhaps shadow Goodson on the trail of Geoffrey Canterbury—Lenox took a quick walk through the old stone courtyards of Corpus Christi, close by the Bear.

Corpus was perhaps the most learned college,

famous for its classicists and humanists despite being the traditional terrain of the Bishops of Winchester. Erasmus, with whom Lenox was at the moment wrestling as he read *The Praise of Folly*, had once famously praised its library for containing books in Hebrew as well as Latin and Greek. Balliol had always been more outgoing, more athletic, than places like Corpus Christi, the reason it produced more politicians and explorers than writers and clergymen. Still, Corpus was a small gem, like one of its giant neighbors, Merton and Christ Church, in perfect miniature. Peering in through the windows of the library he saw rows of students with their heads bent over Homer, Herodotus, Cicero, Josephus. It gave him pleasure to think of them so gravely setting out for lives devoted to knowledge, to the great tradition of thought—it gave him pleasure that this went on even after George Payson's death.

Back at the Randolph there was another note from Dallington. It was somewhat surprising:

Dear Lenox—in lieu of further instructions from you I spent a bit of time thinking about the note under that blighted cat, and think I may have come up with something. At school we used to have the Eton cross-tip, a code we wrote notes in so that they'd be indecipherable to the Beaks. Just substituting numbers for letters, really, like this:

$$x/1/2/3/4/5$$
$$1/a/b/c/d/e$$
$$2/f/g/h/ij/k$$
$$3/l/m/n/o/p$$
$$4/q/r/s/t/u$$
$$5/v/w/x/y/z$$

You catch the drift, I'm sure—the letter k would be represented as 25, or the letter v would be 51. We had to combine i and j to make it work. Oh, and an x in front of a number meant it was simply a number (so you could write "Meet at 330" in code without some ass wondering what 330 meant). Well, have another look:

$$x12/43\ 21\ 31\ 25/x2$$

Plain as day, that translates to:

$$12/SFLK/2$$

At first I thought it was rot but then I asked the pater what he thought, and he said why of course it must be the

12th Suffolk, 2nd Battalion—which needless to say rang a bell. Have you looked it up yet? The regiment and battalion of your lads, Wilson and Lysander. According to my encyclopedia, the 12th Regiment of Foot was raised in 1685 as the Norfolk Regiment of Foot. Got madly decorated for the Fourth Mysore War (sounds like a laugh) in 1799. Currently commanded by Robert Meade. Hope this helps. Here at the ready. Dallington.

Lenox had been meaning to look up the 12th Suffolk 2nd to see if any other names were familiar. He hadn't, but upon reading this he left the room quickly. Why would Payson leave two clues, both the September Society card and this note, pointing to that regiment, that battalion? Would he have counted on somebody—perhaps Hatch, perhaps Stamp—recognizing the Eton cross-tip? Dallington had been at Eton, but was it common to other schools as well, the code? It had been remiss of him not to research it.

It took very little time in the Reading Room of the Bodleian to find a military history of the last hundred years devoted to the 12th Suffolk, which contained at least four battalions. Rapidly flipping through the pages, Lenox read that the 2nd usually had about eight hundred men at a time, which would mean about fifty-five officers, which would mean that in the last century there had been some three hundred officers in the battalion. A page was cited where their pictures and names were given. He flipped to it and almost at once found Lysander, then searched for his picture—younger, but without a doubt him.

Then, more methodically, he scrolled through the fifty-five names. Twenty-six of these would form the September Society. (Why was it called that? His mind racing, Lenox asked himself all the questions he had been saving.) Henry Nelson, Mark Noakes, Matthew Ottshott, Tim Patterson . . .

Lenox froze.

The next name in the list—he read it, reread it, triple-checked it.

James Payson.

Could it be? It must be right—yes, it was right.

James Payson had served in the 12th (Suffolk) Regiment of Foot, 2nd Battalion.

CHAPTER THIRTY-ONE

Now, a while later, sitting on a bench in Balliol, Lenox watched the students mill around him. Gossip had long since run wild about Dabney and Payson, and he overheard many students talking about the two now and then, though the majority of conversation was still devoted to boat races and undergraduate plays, rugby and tutorials. His mind was going over and over the few dim personal memories he had of James Payson, smoothing them out like water over rocks; there had been a period of six months or so when their London sets had mingled, and Lenox and Payson had seen each other once or twice a month, a desultory acquaintance springing up between them.

His people were from Worcestershire, near Evesham, where they maintained a dilapidated castle that had been given to the family by George II after some ancient service done to the crown during the War of Jenkins's Ear. He remembered this because Payson had always made a joke about the absurdity of the war that had founded his family, so to speak. (During a fraught time in the relations between Britain and Spain, a sea captain named Robert Jenkins had been captured by Spaniards and had his ear cut off; when he came back and triumphantly showed it to the Houses of Parliament, the Prime Minister —Walpole?—had declared war. Lenox knew at least that much of the story from his schooldays.) Payson had been the second son and black sheep of his family—fiery tempered, commonly found in low company. It was inevitable that he would find his way to London, given those traits, and having been sent down from Oxford, for public drunkenness, he had somehow acquired a place in—well, in the 12th Suffolk 2nd, as it would seem.

He had been handsome, tall, upright in his bearing, with a mustache and a forthright manner, but his eyes had always looked dangerous. When he had convinced Lady Annabelle West to marry him, people had predicted ill of it—and after six months of hard use she had fled from him, seeking refuge in a small town in Belgium, where her brother moved to protect her. She was three months pregnant, and other than a somewhat startled state of mind had been in decent health. By the time the baby was born in Brussels, six months later, James Payson had gone to India with his battalion. The book had said of that time that the battalion was by and large bored, despite occasional skirmishes with the locals. On their return two years after leaving England, they had left behind twenty men and two officers dead, James Payson one of them. The book didn't give the reason for his death.

Indeed, if Lenox remembered correctly, the reason had always been somewhat obscure. As he had originally heard the story when at Oxford, Payson had been shot dead for cheating at a card table with his fellow officers, but the regiment's commander had hushed matters up. Another story had it that Payson had been killed in battle, some skirmish with local rebels on the border between India and that bloody area of Bengal that the British East India Company had just claimed in the Sepoy Mutiny a few years—perhaps a decade—ago. Whoever shot him, and for whatever reason, he had arrived in England with a bullet lodged just above his heart. Lenox and Edmund, who had known Payson slightly, had been to the memorial service in London, though not to the funeral in Evesham. In death Payson had acquired twice as many friends as in life, and the papers had reported about his death extensively. Perhaps, Lenox thought, he'd ask Dallington to go back and track down their reports.

Trying to align the facts in his mind, he thought: Well, Payson would have been eligible for the September Society—which might mean either that some benefit or some evil would accrue to his son—which might mean that the younger George Payson had been killed out of revenge, perhaps, though surely a long-dead feud wouldn't have been reason enough—and was this why they hadn't killed Bill Dabney?

Suddenly he realized that of course George Payson *had* been leaving him clues all along, because there was the September Society card with black and pink lines on it, the crude image of the *Payson* arms. It had obviously linked his father, with whom he would have been most likely to associate the crest, to the 12th Suffolk 2nd. Same with the note underneath the cat.

How daft I've been, Lenox thought. I have to return to the clues he left, see what they mean.

Then he thought about the man all the undergraduates at Lincoln called Red—James Kelly. For that had been the second shock of the afternoon. After finding James Payson's name in the officer's rolls, Lenox had gone back and scanned the name of every man who had served with him. There, listed as a transfer from the Royal Pioneer Corps, was James Kelly.

Red. He had been in India—with Lysander, with Butler, with Payson. What could be more likely than that they would delegate a murder, give the order, and watch it done as they had so many times?

And how had Red ended up at Lincoln at the same time as James Payson?

He thought about these coincidences for a

while, until finally, stopping a passing under-graduate with a wave of his hand, Lenox said, "Do you mind if I have a quick word?"

"Not at all," said the lad, who had big ears and red cheeks as well as a fiercely cut head of blond hair. "Are you looking for your son?"

"No," said Lenox, half regretting the word, "no, I used to be here at Balliol, and I'm visiting for a day or two."

"Having a jolly time, I hope?" said the young man patiently.

"Yes, thanks. Good to see it all again. At the moment I was wondering—if I wanted to take a long walk hereabouts, where would you recom-mend I go?"

"Well, sir," he said, "there are two options. You could walk up north, just walk past Wadham and keep on, and then you'll reach the parks. Beautiful cricket pitch there, though they reckon they'll build a new one, and a fair amount of meadow to walk about on. I often walk the leas there myself."

"Sounds charming. What's the other?"

"Just past Christ Church Meadow is a fair bit of open field and stream, plus of course the Thames —or rather, the Isis, as you'll remember we call it here."

"Do students go there often?"

He nodded. "Many students walk there, cer-tainly."

"Perhaps I'll try that," Lenox said. "Thanks very much for your help."

"Not at all."

"I'm Charles Lenox, by the way."

"Hopkins," the lad said. They shook hands. "Gerard Manley Hopkins. A pleasure to meet you. Have a good walk—I'm off to see my professor." With a wave he tramped off toward the Balliol lodge.

Lenox was thinking of the muddy boots and walking stick Payson had left in such an oddly prominent spot of his sitting room. What did they indicate? Along with his harried, anxious attitude when he met his mother just before disappearing, perhaps that he already knew the trouble he was facing—that he had already walked past Christ Church Meadow, looking for a place to hide? Even that he had met Geoffrey Canterbury before the ball at Jesus?

Lenox left Balliol and started walking down Broad Street. It was midafternoon by now, and it occurred to him that perhaps he should return to London. Goodson was in charge on this end, and to Lenox's eyes everything seemed to indicate the participation of the September Society in London. Hatch aside . . . but then, perhaps he would leave Graham here to keep an eye on Hatch—and, more important, Red. Could he ask Graham to look after the porter, too?

He stopped in to see Goodson and told him

about finding George Payson's father's name in the rolls. They had a long conversation about its significance.

"Any luck with Canterbury?" Lenox said at last.

"A constable in Didcot may have traced him to that neck of the woods, but I'm not hopeful. He'll have disappeared already. I'm thinking of taking your advice, doing a closer search behind the Meadow."

"I don't think it can hurt," Lenox said and told him about the walking stick and boots in Payson's room.

"I confess," said Goodson, "that I'm a little low in my spirits. Nobody has come forward to say that they saw something; nobody can find this Canterbury fellow."

"I felt the same."

"Yes?"

"That's why I thought I might track back down to London to follow the September Society lead—this Payson lead."

"As you wish."

"There's nothing I can do here?"

"No, I don't think so."

"You'll keep an eye on Hatch and Red?"

"Aye."

The two men shook hands and said good-bye. "For now, anyway," Lenox said.

"Keep in close contact."

"I will."

Outside, Lenox turned his footsteps toward the Randolph. Canterbury, he thought—what could have compelled Payson to meet Canterbury?

Then he stopped.

What had the description of Canterbury been? Dark hair, a big pocket watch, a mark on his throat? Why did that ring a bell? Then he realized: He had just met a dark-haired man with a scar on his neck.

He ran back inside to see Goodson. "Look," he said, "I think I may know who Geoffrey Canterbury is."

"Who?"

"John Lysander."

"The chap you met with?"

"Exactly. I think he convinced Payson to meet him somehow—invoked his father's name, something like that."

"Why would he have lingered hereabouts, then, rather than going straight back to London?"

"Because it's what Geoffrey Canterbury would have done, perhaps? And the opposite of what John Lysander would have."

"Can you furnish a more exact description of this Lysander?" Lenox did as he was asked. "All right, then," said Goodson. "I'll take it to Mrs. Meade."

"Excellent," said Lenox.

He returned to his room at the Randolph in a pensive mood and instructed Graham to pack.

CHAPTER THIRTY-TWO

On the train once more that evening (the trips were becoming tedious) he thought about what he would do in London. First, perhaps, he would find out whatever he could about John Lysander and James Payson. Or better still, he would have Dallington handle Lysander, because he and Lenox had already met.

Oxford an hour behind him, he almost missed it—the quiet implacable towers that stood on against time, the low murmur of people on the sidewalks, the perennially festive pubs that were always greeting a new wave of students just past some looming obstacle, an exam, an essay . . . and above all the companionable feeling of a university town, of a place that centuries of students have come to frightened and left feeling that they would always belong. The fields on either side of the train, golden in the late light, felt like the border between that simple life of his undergraduate days and these more complicated ones; for, as always, his thoughts had revolved again to Jane.

Pure sentimentality, thought Lenox—but smiled as he did.

He forced himself back to the case and for the

rest of the train ride sat low in his seat, eyes hooded, trying to untangle the skein of connections between Red Kelly, John Lysander, Professor Hatch, Bill Dabney, and the dead father and son.

From Victoria he took a two-wheeled hansom cab, thinking first that he would go straight to Hampden Lane, but after a moment he decided to drop in on Toto and Thomas.

He found them again sitting quietly in the small anteroom by the door. It was a happy scene upon which he stumbled. The remnants of an informal supper were just being taken away, and Toto was writing letters at a small correspondence desk, while just by her McConnell was sitting on the sofa reading. Lenox saw this from the outside, the firelight dancing in the dim windows, and almost turned away, but rang at the door instead. Shreve showed him in.

"Charles, how good to see you back. Any progress?" This from McConnell.

"Some. A great deal, in fact, if only it will lead us to the murderer—and to Dabney, of course." Toto had stood up to kiss him on the cheek. "You're still in good health, I hope?"

"Oh, yes, the doctor's quite proud of me—apparently I've unconsciously done everything right. I think that's an absolute sign that I'm meant to be a mother, don't you? Although it's a bore to skip my favorite foods. I don't like that bit. Still, think, in seven months you'll be a god-father!"

"What present ought a godfather to give his godson, do you think?"

All three of them were sitting now, Toto with her feet up on the couch by McConnell, Lenox in a chair opposite. Very definitely, she said, "Oh, you must give her a silver porringer! We're expecting a christening bowl from Vix, you see."

Lenox took this to refer to the Queen of the United Kingdom of Great Britain and Ireland, Empress of the Isles, Victoria.

"That's jolly, then," he said.

"If she'll do it. I expect she shall, Father will speak to somebody. But I would find it auspicious." McConnell rolled his eyes in a way calculated to irritate his wife, and she smacked his hand softly. "Thomas, if you want to raise little Malory a heathen—"

"Malory, is it? Have I agreed to Malory McConnell? Well, she'll grow up to be a washer-woman, but I'll love her anyway," said the doctor, though happiness was etched into his face.

"Take it back!"

Laughing, Lenox said, "Perhaps the Queen's washerwoman, at any rate. That will be a conso-lation."

"But listen to us," said Toto. "Charles, where do you think you're going to travel next?"

232

"Morocco!" he said and expounded on the merits of that country for a little while longer.

"Morocco! Oh, no, Malory's godfather can't go to Morocco."

"But it's awfully beautiful, Toto, I promise."

"Promise all you like!"

They rattled on in this way for a few minutes more. Presently, McConnell said, "By the way, Charles, did you get that report on Peter Wilson that I sent you?"

"Yes, thanks. It was helpful."

"I wish I could have been more conclusive."

"Well, in any event it showed that there are some grounds for suspicion."

"Quite slim ones, perhaps."

"By the way—does either of you remember George Payson's father?"

Both of them shook their heads. Toto said, "I wasn't born, I don't think—or only one or two."

"And I'd have been in Scotland still, or at school."

Lenox sighed. "No matter; I only mentioned it because I'm going to track down the report of his death, and if it wouldn't be too much trouble you might have a look at that, too."

"Yes, of course," said McConnell. "Foul play?"

"There's always been some doubt about it, actually. I always heard he was shot over cards, but that may be a myth."

"Oh, Charles," said Toto, suddenly perking up,

"won't you have a bit of supper? We've just had ours, but we haven't had coffee yet—or rather, Thomas hasn't, I'm not meant to at all any longer."

"Thanks, no," he said. "I must get home. I only wanted to say hello—and to check that you were in good health."

"Oh, I don't think I could be healthier or happier in a million years!"

The truth of this in the face of both his friends gave Lenox a moment's happiness, even as his brain prowled around the edges of the case.

CHAPTER THIRTY-THREE

A few minutes later he was in another cab, bumping homeward. A glass of wine wouldn't go amiss, he thought, and if he saw lights on next door he might drop in on Lady Jane. The next morning he would go straight to work again—well, perhaps he'd drop by the bookshop, then straight to work. What should he read next? Something contemporary, perhaps, something fresh . . .

As the cab pulled into Hampden Lane these idle thoughts vanished. The street was ablaze with light, crowded by carriages, and on one stoop—Lady Jane's stoop, he realized, his heart plummeting—were two bobbies, speaking to a servant.

"Stop here!" said Lenox, and roughly handed the driver some indeterminate amount of change. He picked up his small bag and flung it over his shoulder, then ran the twenty feet to the small stretch of sidewalk where his house joined Jane's. There was a confusion of people on the street and no real order to things. Spying Mr. Chaffanbrass, he said, "What's happened?"

"I don't know," Chaffanbrass responded. He was bright red and looked out of sorts. "Somebody's been shot, but everybody seems to be all right!"

Horror and relief flooded Lenox's mind at once; of course, he would have to ascertain the truth for himself. In his heart was a prayer for Jane's safety: a deep, almost unconscious prayer. He moved roughly through the crowd of onlookers toward the door. Looking up he saw to his consternation that one of the policemen on the stoop was Inspector Jenkins, who had given him the coroner's report on Peter Wilson's suicide. As Lenox climbed the stairs he rapidly tried to think whether Jenkins would be there without anyone dead, or at least injured.

"Jenkins," he said, coming to the top step. The door to the house was open and every room was brightly lit, giving the place a look of midnight panic. "What's happened?"

"Lenox, hello—everybody's all right. Only one injury, and that superficial."

"To whom? To whom, Jenkins?"

The inspector looked at his pad. "Annie, a kitchen maid."

"What happened?"

Again Jenkins consulted his pad. "Apparently a man knocked on the door, face covered by a kerchief, brandishing a revolver, and pointed it menacingly at this housemaid. He dropped a note at her feet, and then as he turned to leave the gun went off. It struck the stone eave of the door and ricocheted back off, grazing Annie on the shoulder."

"Did she get a good look at him?"

"No, unfortunately."

"Fainted?"

"On the contrary, she chased him halfway down the block, the plucky old girl."

"May I go in? Is Jane—Lady Jane Grey—inside?"

"She is, but . . ." He looked dubious.

"We're old friends—please ask her."

Jenkins nodded to his constable, who went inside and checked. On returning, he said, "Looks all right, then," and with a grateful nod Lenox pushed his way inside. He saw Lady Jane sitting on her rose-colored sofa, all alone. Instinctively he dropped his valise and ran to be beside her, embracing her shoulders as he sat.

"Thank God you're safe" was all he could manage to say.

She didn't seem at all surprised by his unusual actions and hugged him in return. "I'm quite all right," she insisted. "Only a little shaken."

A little shaken!

"How is Annie?"

"They've taken her away to Dr. Brooke's."

That was the doctor on Harley Street whom both Jane and Lenox routinely visited. "Where was she hit?"

"The bullet grazed her arm, just by the shoulder. I came back to find Kirk and the police here, and she seemed the sanest of all of them. Said she only needed a bit of iodine."

Here she gave out and buried her face in Lenox's shoulder, crying.

"What is it?" he said. "What?"

"I wish I had half her courage, Charles. Look at this."

She reached into her pocket and produced a note. Lenox read it twice, trying to be clear-headed. It read: *Tell your friend to leave Payson in the ground, or we'll be back.*

237

CHAPTER THIRTY-FOUR

W hat do you think the Yard can do, Jenkins?" said Lenox. It was half an hour later, and the two men were standing on the street. The crowds had begun to dissolve, the stream of startled neighbors at the door had slowed, and in Lady Jane's house the servants were all having a glass of brandy under Kirk's supervision. Jane herself was still in the drawing room, with the recently arrived Toto and the Duchess of Marchmain at her side.

Briefly Jenkins consulted his notepad. "Not much, I fear. We only have one description of the man, and that's a vague one—we just managed to figure out his height and weight, but they're average."

"Nothing, then."

"Well, whoever murdered George Payson has made the mistake of involving the London police force. We'll give you and Inspector"—again Jenkins's eyes scanned his notes—"Inspector Goodson all the help you need on this end. You've described the September Society to me, and we'll put a constable near Lysander's house, watch his comings and goings for a few days. And we'll shake out our usual East End gangs, see if they know anything. Which is always possible."

Lenox shook his head. "It's a pity there's no more to be done."

Jenkins nodded. "Yes. Still, everything turned out as well as it could have."

"That's true."

"We'll leave a rotation of constables in front of these two houses as well, for a few days anyway."

"Well, thanks—you've made this a lot smoother than it might have been."

"Cheers, Lenox. And I say, please do keep me up to date on the case. I shall want to find out who did this very much."

They parted with a handshake, Jenkins to speak to his men and Lenox to return inside. The inspector was doing as well as he could under the circumstances, but it was infuriating that someone had threatened Lady Jane's house with a gun—in fact shot her servant!—with relative impunity.

Inside there was some normalcy to the voices of Lenox's friends. As he paused in the hallway he overheard Toto talking about her baby again, Thomas chiming in with an occasional low word of wit, and Jane laughing at all the two of them said. Good of them to try to cheer her up; and even better of her to try to reassure them that she was already cheered. Was he blinded by love, or was it only to himself that she had shown her true fear, her true emotions? He hoped—feeling ridiculous even as he did, for he wasn't generally given to over-the-top Arthurian chivalry—that he was worthy of her confidence. He hoped his love was enough.

"Everything all right in here?" he said, speaking to Jane alone as Toto, the duchess, and Thomas were once again buried in the controversy over the name Malory.

"Yes," she said, laughing and slightly rolling her eyes toward the couple. "Things have gone back to normal rather quickly, as you can see."

"I've spoken to Jenkins."

"Have you?" she said lightly. "What has he said?"

She was wearing a pale green dress, simple and straight, and her pretty face betrayed no anxiety; and when he looked at her lovely curling hair and long, proud neck, his heart nearly burst.

"Only that they would try to track the man down, and that they'll have a rotation of police constables set in front of our houses. But I think you'd probably better visit your brother, don't you?"

The Earl of Houghton, whose house was only a mile or two from Edmund Lenox's, was a well-intentioned, studious, and thoughtful man, but without Jane's lightness; a man who took his responsibilities and position too seriously to be like her.

"I don't think I shall, no. It happens that I can't leave London at this particular moment, and then, why give them the pleasure? Surely if there are constables here the person won't dare return."

"Probably not. It was probably only a message to me—and for that I apologize again."

"It's not your fault that there are madmen in the world. It's not your fault that somebody killed that poor boy in Oxford."

"But it is my fault for holding you so dear."

In the moment of silence that followed this comment, Lenox's and Lady Jane's eyes never left each other. The other three broke off their conversation and looked at the pair of them. At last Toto said, "Is everything all right with the policeman, Charles?"

"Oh, yes," he said, tearing his eyes away from Lady Jane's to look at her. "They'll put somebody by the house for a few days. And I've said to Jane she should visit her brother for a little while."

"Oh, *don't* leave London, Jane, you can't!"

"She'll have to if it makes her feel safer, darling," said McConnell to his wife. Then he turned to the rest of them. "In fact, if you prefer you can stay with us for a few nights. Just until things are as calm as usual."

"Now *that,* as my father would say, is a ripping idea." Toto beamed. "Please do, won't you, Jane? We'll make you ever so comfortable. And nobody will be there but you and me, because

Thomas looks at squids in his microscope all day! And we'll have lovely things to eat and read novels and see our friends if we feel like it."

McConnell half laughed, half grimaced at the depiction of his daily life, but otherwise seemed enthusiastic, and Toto looked utterly delighted.

"Shall I, Charles?" said Lady Jane, delaying her friend's happiness momentarily.

"It's an excellent idea, I should say. It would make me easier in my mind."

She turned to Thomas. "Then I will, thanks. Only for a night or two."

"Or a week," said Toto doggedly. "Consider staying for a week, at least."

"Perhaps three nights. I can't stay more than that or people will think I'm afraid of going home."

"Well—three nights to be going on with," said Toto and hugged Jane.

"McConnell," said Lenox, "shall we leave them for a few minutes?"

The two men stepped outside. All but Jenkins and the two constables who were on the first watch had left, and Jenkins was getting ready to go.

"Keep in close touch, would you Lenox?" he said.

"I shall—I'll write to you once a day with whatever progress we have if I can't come see you."

"Excellent."

Turning to his friend, Lenox said, "You will keep an eye on Jane, won't you?"

"Yes, of course."

"Exactly. I actually wanted a word on another subject as well. Are you still friends with Harry Arlington, at the War Office?"

"Yes—you know that."

"I was going to ask you a favor. I need to see the file of a soldier who died twenty years ago. In the 12th Suffolk 2nd."

"Is this about the case?"

"Precisely."

"Tangentially, I assume?"

"From the age? No, in fact it's at the heart of the matter."

"I'll write to Harry straight away when I get home. What's the soldier's name?"

"James Payson."

McConnell looked appropriately taken aback. "The lad's father? How does he figure into it?"

"He would have been one of the tiny number of men eligible for the September Society, had he lived."

"I'll write him tonight," said McConnell. "If you go by tomorrow morning, he'll certainly have gotten my note."

"Thanks, Thomas."

"Not at all."

CHAPTER THIRTY-FIVE

After several sunny, seasonable days, the next morning was gray. Just as Lenox stirred into a first, dreamy kind of wakefulness, rain began to drop softly against his windows. It reminded him somewhere deep in his mind of his first days at boarding school, when as a thirteen-year-old he had sat at the desk in his tiny room feeling lost in the world. Soon enough he had made friends, but the desolate feeling of that rainy autumn had always remained with him.

The late night seemed like a dream—it had been almost one o'clock when he had put Jane, Toto, and McConnell in a carriage. Afterward he had restlessly inhabited his study for another hour or so, but at last he had gotten to sleep.

At just past nine he went downstairs. He wrote a few notes, including one to Rosie Little, and then went to the table in his dining room. His eggs and toast were waiting there, and he dug into them hungrily, relishing their buttery taste and following it with swallows of hot tea. The rain had gotten louder, and by the time he finished eating it was lashing across the empty streets on a high wind. He decided to run across to the bookshop and risked doing it without an umbrella.

"Well," said Mr. Chaffanbrass, sitting by his hot stove reading when Lenox entered, "look what the cat dragged in. Has Noah started to load up his ark yet?"

"No talk of cats, please, if you have a heart. Too frighteningly apt."

"Quite a noisy affair last night, wasn't it? It was lucky that Annie was only scratched."

"Do you know her, then?"

"Oh, yes. She often stops by for a word or to pick up a book for Lady Grey."

There were several customers patrolling the bookshelves that ran from floor to ceiling, and one of them came up to the front desk now. He had the look of a genuine bibliophile, something intangible in the way he held the book just so, lightly but at the same time as if he never wanted to lose his grip.

"How much for this, sir?" he asked, his eyes keen.

Peering over the man's shoulder, Lenox saw that it was a battered but ancient edition of Lavater's *Physiognomy.* "Three crowns, and a bargain at that price," said Chaffanbrass.

The transaction took place, and the man left.

"Do you know who that was?" Chaffanbrass asked.

"Who?"

"Charles Huntly."

"I don't think that rings a bell."

"Do you remember Princess Amelia?"

"George III's daughter? Something of her—she died during my father's lifetime."

Chaffanbrass nodded. "When I was a boy. They wouldn't let her marry her true love, Charles Fitzroy, but they had a child anyway. Illegitimately. That son was Charles Huntly's father."

"So then—"

"Yes, exactly. Great-grandson in the direct line to George III. Mad King George. They've kept him as a commissioner in some part of South Africa, but now he's made his fortune and returned. It all would have been a great palaver in your grandfather's time."

"Is he a book lover, then?"

"He certainly is. When he was poor his uncle's manservant came in to pay his tabs now and then. Old Prince Adolphus, the Duke of Cambridge."

"Does he have any children?"

"Oh, a dozen, I expect."

Chaffanbrass rambled on about the royal family a little bit longer—a favored subject of his—and then Lenox was able to ask about a book. Something recent, he said, and not quite as taxing as Erasmus. Chaffanbrass said he knew just the thing, then presented Lenox with about ten books. After a few minutes the detective left with a new volume under his arm, *Felix Holt, the Radical.* It had only just come out.

When he left he saw that the rain had subsided, and he was able to dash across the street without getting too wet. Just as he reached his own door, however, he saw something disheartening: The same tall, thin man in the long gray coat he had seen coming out of Lady Jane's house before was there again. This was the second time. Who was he? Could he be the cause of that sorrow Lenox had detected in his friend?

It was in a duller mood that he ordered his carriage and departed to see Harry Arlington, McConnell's friend at the War Office.

Arlington received Lenox in his usual jovial way. They had met once or twice before, though they had never spoken at length. He was a large man, tall and broad-shouldered, who had been forced into the military by his father straight out of school and spent his lifetime flourishing there. He had become a general three years ago, and two years after that become the military secretary, the senior military assistant to the secretary of state for Defense. He spent his days appointing colonels, considering court-martials, judging applications to Sandhurst, and overseeing Her Majesty's Bodyguard of the Honorable Corps of Gentlemen at Arms, who protected the Queen, performed ceremonial duties, and also still, 350 years after their creation by Henry VIII, served on regular duty. He called the work dull but in fact was perfectly suited to the somewhat nebulous position he occupied between Parliament and the armed services. He was about fifty, in the pink of health, with five daughters and a string of horses in the country. In all he had done very well for himself. His best friend had once been Arthur McConnell, Thomas McConnell's uncle, with whom he had entered the Coldstream Guards as a lad of seventeen. Arthur McConnell had died in the Crimean War, and since then Arlington had kept a close watch over his (as he called McConnell) honorary godson.

His office was massive and daunting, with a large window behind the desk overlooking Whitehall. The flag of the Lilywhites was on display next to the Union Jack on one wall, and on the other was a row of full-length portraits of former military secretaries. Arlington put Lenox at ease straight away, offering him a cigar and a handshake.

"Toto's pregnant, then, Mr. Lenox? And I hear you're to be the godfather? Well, well, congratulations."

"Thank you, General. They seem awfully happy."

"Call me Arlington, call me Arlington. Are you related to Edmund Lenox, by any chance? I come across him in my work in Parliament here and there."

"He's my brother," said Lenox, once again

marveling at Edmund's hidden life in government.

"Wonderful fellow. Now, I have the file here which Thomas wrote to me about." His manner became suddenly grave, as he took a folder out of the top drawer of his desk and tapped it thoughtfully against his palm. "And I can't help noticing that the name is a familiar one."

"The lad at Oxford?"

"Exactly, Lenox, exactly."

"You won't be surprised to hear that the errand I'm on is related to his death. I'm investigating it, helping the police there."

"I see. And how do you think that the death of the boy's father however many years . . ." He peered into the folder. "Nineteen years ago—how do you think that may be involved?"

"Have you heard of the September Society, Arlington? For retired officers of the 12th Suffolk 2nd?"

"I haven't, no."

"A small club of men. But they keep turning up in unlikely places. Daniel Maran—you know that name, I'm sure?"

Arlington's brow darkened. "Yes, yes I do. We run on parallel lines, and the less I deal with him the better, as I find it."

"He's a member of the Society. It would be too complicated to explain it now, in full anyway, but I think George Payson's death may have some link to his father's death, and I wanted to look into the file."

Arlington turned so that he was in profile to Lenox and looked out through his window. "In this room I make decisions," he said, "which affect my country—my Queen—every day."

"Yes," said Lenox.

"To give you this would be to break a hard and fast rule, you know. You have no claim to that file."

"I understand."

Arlington turned back to him. "But your brother could legally request it." Lenox was silent. "My rule of thumb here has been total honesty. I've been guided entirely by the rules that bind me. I can't change that now. But I'll send the file to my friend Edmund Lenox this afternoon." He put the file back in his top drawer, and with a firm nod the subject was closed. "Now, have I heard correctly that Toto wants to name the child *Malory?*"

CHAPTER THIRTY-SIX

When Lenox returned to Hampden Lane he found Dallington, carnation firmly established in his buttonhole, his feet up near the fire in Lenox's favorite armchair, evidently feeling quite at home. He was smoking a cigarette and reading Punch with a small grin on his face.

"Entertaining?" said Lenox.

Dallington turned to him. "Oh—your maid put me in here. Hope that's all right. Yes, it is, rather," he added, gesturing toward the magazine. "What's that parcel you've got?"

There was a rectangular package under Lenox's arm, wrapped in brown paper and tied with string. "Oh," he said vaguely, "just something."

"Your powers of description would put Wordsworth to shame." The small grin had grown wider by now. "At any rate, I didn't come here to josh you."

"Didn't you?" Lenox sat down opposite his pupil. "What a lovely surprise."

"I wanted to ask about the servant who got shot."

"Oh—yes, it worked out as fortunately as it could have."

"I'm glad of that."

"The wound wasn't serious at all."

"I saw the bobbies outside. They looked at me as if I might be returning to the scene of the crime when I sidled up here. By the way, you got my note about Theophilus Butler?"

"I did—and about the 12th Suffolk 2nd, thanks. Both a big help. In fact, I'm glad you're here. I wanted to talk about another assignment."

Dallington's eyebrows arched inquisitively. "At your service, of course. Everything's gone well enough so far, give or take."

"This task might be a bit more delicate—closer to the heart of the case."

"May I ask what it is?"

"Do you remember I told you about Lysander?"

"Yes, of course."

"I think perhaps he murdered George Payson."

"What!"

"Yes. At any rate, I think he met with Payson before Payson disappeared. Who knows what they talked about."

"Why? What would his motive have been?"

Lenox laid out the trail of clues connecting the younger George Payson, his father, and the September Society. "So you see, you've asked the precise question Goodson and I have been asking ourselves . . . motive."

"What can I do?"

"You can put together as accurate a record as possible—you really can't be too meticulous—of this last week of Lysander's life. We know, or at least I think I know, that he was in Oxford this weekend, and we know that he and I met two days ago. The rest will need to be sketched in."

"Any advice?"

"Only that it would be much better that you fail miserably than that you succeed and at the same time tip Lysander off."

Dallington nodded, his face grave, transformed since only a moment ago. Lenox recognized a flicker of that fire of curiosity and—well, anger that he felt in himself when he worked on cases like this.

"I understand."

"I hope you do. Please don't speak to his servants, or anything like that. Hard evidence, his name in the club register—you don't belong to the Army and Navy, of course? No, well, you'll know somebody who does. Ask the conductors on the Oxford train, speak to the man who sits on the bench in Green Park all day and watches that row of houses Wilson and Lysander live in—you know they live two doors away from each other?"

"Yes, of course. What man, though? In Green Park?"

"I was speaking figuratively. I mean—be imaginative."

Dallington nodded again, though less certainly. "Yes, I see what you mean. I'll do my level best at any rate."

"Lovely. Oh—and look Lysander up in *Who's Who* for a bit of background information. Do you have it? Because it's somewhere on these shelves . . ." Lenox peered around the bookcases.

"Father has it, I'll ask him."

"All right. And remember—caution. The case's

demands have to be more important than any-body's ego, yours or mine. It's no use trapping him dead in a lie if he's already on a train to Moscow by the time you have."

"Thanks, Charles. Your trust means the world to me."

Dallington took up his copy of *Punch* as he said this, and suddenly Lenox saw the young lord for what he was: a boy. Not five years out of school, and already the misery of his parents, a notorious failure. His bantering manners and air of worldliness—not to say weariness—somehow masked a truer part of him. A part that had already come to the surface in flashes during his brief working relationship with Lenox. Whether it would stay there was another matter entirely.

Dallington left, and Lenox was alone. He sorted through his post, discarded most of it, and then picked up his parcel and went toward the door. He was going over to Jane's house.

Kirk greeted him with his usual measure of corpulent politeness, then said, "I am sorry to say that her Ladyship is not at home just now."

"Oh, I know. I was hoping to see Annie, actu-ally."

Kirk raised his eyebrows almost imperceptibly. "Yes, sir," he said.

"If it's not an inconvenient time for her, that is."

"No, sir, I'm sure it's not."

"She has recovered some, then?"

"Very well, sir, yes."

"If she's retired—"

"No, sir, she is situated in the second upper drawing room."

Kirk led Lenox up a long flight of stairs to a wide, rather drab room, prettily furnished, on the second floor. Lady Jane lived primarily in two places: her morning room, a small, beautifully light square where she wrote letters and took her breakfast, and the drawing room Lenox knew so well. This room was new to him. Annie was perched on a long chaise by the window, facing away from the door, her arm in a sling. She didn't appear to be doing anything particular and tried to crane her neck to see who had entered. Kirk bowed and left the two of them alone—commenting quietly to himself, no doubt, on the impropriety of the situation.

She was a plump woman, rosy-cheeked, maternal in bearing, with the strong arms and sloped back that a lifetime of labor bestowed on so many women of her class. She wore a cheery bonnet and a long, plain gray dress.

"How do you do, Annie? I'm Charles Lenox." She made the best curtsy she could from her compromised position, and Lenox sat in a chair that had been left close by. "I recognize you, of course, but I'm not certain we've met properly."

Awkwardly, he took her outstretched hand.

Then he handed her the parcel Dallington had asked about, saying, "Oh, this is for you, incidentally—just to pass the time."

She opened it deliberately and cooed over its contents: a few penny dreadfuls, several women's magazines Lenox had sent Mary to fetch, an ivory-handled comb, and a wax-paper-wrapped bundle of chocolates he had bought himself.

"Why, thank you, Mr. Lenox. How kind of you!"

"Oh, no—we've all been ill," he said, smiling. "The hours do drag on. I remember receiving just such a parcel from my mother when I was at school. It made all the difference."

"As this shall, too, sir, I'm quite sure."

"Really I wanted to come apologize, however, Annie."

"Oh, Mr. Lenox," she said skeptically, "please don't think about it."

"Really; none of this would have happened if it weren't for me. I'm sorry. If I can ever do you a good turn, simply say the word, won't you? I do wish it had happened to me rather than you."

"Don't mention that, sir. As my lady pointed out, you had no more control over this madman than I did. And to be honest"—her voice fell to a whisper—"it hasn't been all that bad, having a vacation. Mind, I'm not saying I'd do it again, but it hasn't been all *that* bad."

Lenox laughed. "Still—for all that, I am sorry."

As he walked down the stairs a few minutes later, he was glad it was over. It had been an awkward transaction. He wished that he might have expressed himself more eloquently— impressed upon her more urgently how sorry he was that he had endangered her. Even how fearful he was that he had endangered Lady Jane.

Of course, though, that was impossible. Their stations were too far apart. He went home and answered one of the letters he had received. Mary came in to ask him whether he would have his lunch in or out, and he decided that he would try to drop in on his brother, Edmund, and perhaps get the file Arlington had sent over. No, he told her, he would eat out. He gave her the letter to post and, asking for his carriage, said he would be reading until it was ready to take him to the Houses of Parliament.

CHAPTER THIRTY-SEVEN

The Parliament of the United Kingdom was by no means a perfect body, but it was getting better—had gotten better, in fact, in Lenox's lifetime. He could remember the infamous borough of Old Sarum, which in 1831 had elected two Members, and in doing so overcome the notable handicap of having only eleven residents.

But the Reform Act of 1832 had finally abolished Old Sarum and places like it. (The town of Dunwich, in Suffolk, for example, had also elected two MPs in 1831 despite literally not existing, an impressive feat; while it technically had about two dozen voters, the town itself had long been claimed by the waters of the local river.) Now, only thirty years after the reforms, which had been unimaginable to his grandparents' generation, more and more people had suffrage, landowners could only vote once, and the Earl of Lonsdale no longer had the right to name nine Members completely on his own. In all it allowed the House of Commons to become more forceful in its dealings with the House of Lords—allowed the people, in other words, to be more assertive with the noblemen. Taken together, the years of that era had added up to a gradual reclamation of rights that was on par with the Magna Carta.

As he looked up at the famous long facade of the Palace of Westminster (its formal name) just above the rolling Thames, he thought for the hundredth time that the highest service an Englishman could do was to work in this building, to serve here with honesty and compassion and patriotism. At Balliol his friends had called him "the Debater" because of his tendency to make long and ardent speeches about civil reform and imperial restraint. His friends and family had all assumed he would find himself within these doors before too long. Yet here he was, nearly forty, and no closer than he had been twenty years past. It was a deep, mostly healed-over wound. He was reconciled to his profession, loved his profession. Still, just as his heart rose every time he caught a glimpse of Big Ben, it fell when he had to sign in as a guest at the door.

Lenox found his older brother in the anteroom just by the actual chamber of the House of Commons sitting with two or three other Members, heads huddled together, quite obviously speaking about something of importance to the party. He held back in the doorway and waited for their conversation to end. The House was down, of course, until the evening, and there was quiet in most of the building. He felt slightly out of place. After only a few seconds Edmund looked up and saw him, flashed him a smile, and made his excuses to his compatriots.

"Charles," he said, "I'm very glad to see you."

Lenox's brother looked very much like him, tall, with a good head of brown hair and sparkling, curious eyes, but while the younger brother was slender, the elder was ruddy and heavyset from years of country life.

"How are you, Edmund?"

They shook hands. "Not bad, not bad."

"You look a bit knocked about."

"Do I? Late nights in here, I expect. I miss the country. But how's this business in Oxford going?"

"Are you having lunch with anybody?"

"I am, yes—but come along, won't you? Only a few chaps from the Board of Trade, the War Office, all our party. Russell. You'll know one or two of them."

"Wouldn't it disrupt your work?"

"No, not at all. Purely social."

They had paused in the hallways that connected the street, just by the Thames, to the beehive of rooms around the House. "I shall, then, thanks," said Lenox, and they moved inward once again toward the famous Parliamentary restaurant called Bellamy's.

Edmund's group was at a large table to the rear of the room, far from the prying eyes of the entrance. By the table there were two large windows overlooking the swift, gray river, but nobody looked out that way. Edmund introduced Lenox to the people he didn't know—his friend James Hilary was there and greeted him warmly—but had read of in the papers. There was the promising young MP Jonathan Brick, a great orator and defender of the poor from Warwickshire, with a melodious South Midlands accent, and also Lord Russell, whom Lenox knew slightly and who had only just served a year as Prime Minister. Russell had stepped down after trying to introduce a reform bill which his own party had opposed—scandalously, in Lenox's view. An angry mob in Hyde Park that July had agreed.

At the luncheon there were also several back-benchers, men Lenox knew and recognized, men useful to the party in small, unglamorous, and utterly practical ways. Peter Anthony, a soap manufacturer from Birmingham, was one, and so was Donald Longstaffe, a man with no aspirations other than to belong to good clubs, Parliament being one of them. His talent was for gossip, a currency always redeemable in politics.

The Liberal Party missed its founder, Viscount Palmerston, who had died just the year before. Besides being politically gifted and uncannily savvy, Lord Palmerston had been a figure around whom Liberals could unite: Having begun as a Tory, he had decided upon the necessity of a new path and forged it himself. As an orator nobody in either party had surpassed him. Lenox would never forget Palmerston's bold stance in favor of the revolutions that swept the Continent in 1848, support that lent legitimacy to the rebellious armies in Italy, France, and Hungary. It was a noble belief in the idea of constitutional liberties that had driven him. Yes, they missed Palmerston. The party missed its talisman.

In the meanwhile the Conservative Party had its own still-living leader. The current Prime Minister, the Earl of Derby, was serving his third (nonconsecutive) term, and all agreed that the Liberals had to find somebody quickly who might match him both in rhetoric and vision. Brick was one candidate; Hilary another, at any rate in time; and William Ewart Gladstone, though rather puritanical for some tastes, was a third, though he wasn't present at the luncheon.

"What are we all speaking about?" Edmund asked.

Out of deference they all waited for Russell's answer. None forthcoming, Brick said, "Oh, all the usual catastrophes. Derby's evil plans. Gladstone's speech yesterday evening."

Hilary said, "Derby may mean to steal our reform bill—yours, I should say, Lord Russell. He wants to greatly increase the franchise, anyway, reading between the lines of his speech of last week."

Edmund nodded. "Yes, that seems to be so."

The attention the table granted Edmund was not deferential, as with Lord Russell; but it was somehow individualized, specific, respectful. The entire table took up Hilary's point, debating it back and forth. Once, Russell said, "Well, if he does it, good for him," and everyone nodded vigorously and then disagreed. Lenox chimed in once or twice energetically, and when he did

Brick looked at him rather appraisingly. Between them they finished three bottles of claret, which went a long way toward the establishment of good feeling at the table, and by the time they stood up they all seemed to agree about something not quite spelled out but nonetheless significant. All in all it left Lenox confused, but at the same time with the feeling that the language was one of subtexts, which it would be easy to pick up.

"What did you make of that?" Edmund asked, clapping his brother on the shoulder as they walked down the long corridor toward Edmund's office.

"Was anything accomplished, exactly?"

"Oh, Lord, no! We simply wanted to begin talking about this reform bill we're expecting next year. Needed to find out what Russell thought."

"He seemed unruffled."

"That was the right form on his part."

A man, dark, short, and striding quickly, approached them. Edmund said hello to him.

"Oh—yes, hello, Lenox. I can't speak at the moment—something—something quite important. Forgive me."

"Not at all," said Edmund, and the man walked on.

"Who was that?" Lenox asked.

"Daniel Maran."

"What! That's a strange coincidence, to lay eyes on him."

"Not that strange, of course—he haunts this little building. I must see him at least once a day. Why are you so surprised?"

"He may figure into this case of mine."

"How so?"

Lenox quickly told Edmund what the September Society was, about Wilson, Butler, Lysander, and the shooting accident at Maran's property that killed Wilson. He also mentioned that he had come by in part to see the file Arlington had sent over, and reminded his brother about James Payson.

Edmund's brow furrowed. "That's quite strange, you know, about Maran."

"Oh? Why?"

"I could swear—yes, I feel certain that only the other day he was closeted with that man Lysander when I wanted to see him."

"What do you mean?" said Lenox keenly.

"I popped into his office to ask him a question or two—I was with James Hilary, actually—and he said he couldn't meet, and then introduced us to Lysander in a rather hurried way."

"When was this, Edmund?"

"Oh, last . . . was it last Thursday? Yes, I think so."

"Why have you been dealing with Maran?"

"Oh, just a small task they've asked me to do

—nothing important, mind you. A few matters of ordnance. Some strange spending there, it would appear—though nothing that can't be sorted out. But listen, Charles, what about Lysander?"

Lenox's mind was racing, and he answered his brother's questions distractedly. When at length they reached Edmund's small, cluttered office, he sat down and jotted a few notes. Then he took the file on James Payson, which Edmund had found on his desk. It was thin and looked inconsequential. Lenox scrambled backward in his memory for some further recollection of James Payson in his early days of marriage but couldn't remember any. He opened the folder expecting disappointment but still half hoping for a breakthrough. After a bit of boilerplate, the report of the 2nd Battalion's medical staff read:

Already there are rumors in the camp about Captain Payson's final hours, some of them quite outlandish . . . it is the consensus of this panel that these rumors should be encouraged while a deeper investigation of the circumstances of Captain Payson's death is undertaken, for it seems to us certain that, first, the subject was not injured by the enemy, and, second, that he may well have been the victim of foul play, intended to simulate suicide . . . whether or not this turns out

*to be the case, the death is not one which
redounds to the credit of the 12th Regiment
or the 2nd Battalion, and we believe that
precautions should be taken against the
revelation of the true facts of the incident
in order to maintain morale . . . please see
our initial findings below . . .*

Following this introduction the report went on
for some time, describing in great detail Payson's
wound and how it might have been sustained.
Lenox scanned this quickly and flipped to the
second page of the report, an addendum from
the same pen, which read:

*After further investigation we must con-
clude that our original report's conjecture
about Captain Payson's death was incor-
rect, and that in fact he was a suicide . . .
it may be seen that the angle of the shot,
while unusual, was not impossible . . . in
re the question posed about the scars on
his face and chest, an animal had obviously been at the remains between
Payson's death and the discovery of the
corpse, not surprising given the emaciated
state of the domestic animals in this
region . . . the scent of aniseed around the
body points to canines . . . added to the
peculiarity of Payson having wandered off*

alone, quite out of his usual routine, we are forced to believe that he killed himself with aforethought . . .

Lenox read over the report a second time; his brother was sitting at his narrow window, tapping the ash of his pipe outside as cold air blew into the room. Nevertheless Lenox flushed as he read on, slowly realizing how this twenty-year-old description of James Payson's suicide corresponded with McConnell's report on the suicide of Peter Wilson. Was it possible that these two men, drawn from the same small circle of a battalion's officers, had died in the same fashion, under the same cloud of uncertainty, coincidentally? No, of course it wasn't. Of course it wasn't.

Above all it was eerie that James and George Payson's deaths were so similar: both bodies found in public fields, their bodies mauled, their lives over at the age of twenty.

"This damned Society," Lenox muttered. "Look here, Edmund, I don't suppose I can take this folder with me?"

They had both seen that Arlington had marked it NOT TO BE REMOVED FROM GOVERNMENT PROPERTY.

"You know, I'm not sure you should, Charles. I hate to say so. Is it quite important?"

Lenox waved his hand. "Oh, I understand, of

course—look here, would you mind if McConnell came in and had a look at it?"

"Not at all—as long as he does so before the end of the day."

"Then I'll fetch him right now. I won't come back myself, Edmund—thanks awfully for lunch, and I'll see you as soon as this business is resolved, all right?"

"Yes, all right. You can't explain?"

"I wish I could," said Lenox, taking his coat and heading for the door.

CHAPTER THIRTY-EIGHT

As he stepped out of his carriage by McConnell's house, Lenox heard a piano and a clear, melodious voice accompanying it.

It was Toto, playing and singing. Her spirit was captured in music, often: evanescent, chatty, generous, warm. He almost hesitated as he knocked at the door, loath as he was to cut her off. Then again, Arlington's file would only be with Edmund for the rest of the day.

"Charles!" she said. "You see how frivolously we pass the time."

"Good for the baby, to hear such sweet sounds. Where is Jane?"

Toto looked cross. "Where is she ever! As

secretive as the sphinx, and always in and out. I should chain her to this piano. But how's your case?"

Lenox looked to McConnell. "In fact, I came here about it. Do you think you could go to my brother's office and look over a file he has there?"

Toto looked unhappy at the request, but McConnell nodded. "Of course. What's it all about?"

Briefly Lenox explained what he thought was the similarity between Wilson's death and Payson's. "I'm not sure, however, and I could use your opinion."

"I'll go straight away."

"Thanks very much. I have to be off as well— let me give you a ride."

"Perfect."

In the carriage, Lenox said, "Thanks for your letter to Arlington, by the way. He thought it best to send the file through official channels, rather than handing it over. Sensible enough I suppose."

"Don't mention it. How did you find him?"

"I liked him. He seems to be straightforward about things. He says exactly what he means."

As he dropped McConnell by Westminster Abbey a moment later, Lenox said, "Do you want to come around to see me afterward?"

"Yes—it shouldn't be above half an hour, if the file's as short as you say."

"I'll be waiting for you, then."

At home Lenox sorted through his post and found that there was a report from Graham about Hatch's movements in the last day or two. It read:

Mr. Lenox—

Per your request, I have closely followed the movements of Professor John Hatch since your departure. Unfortunately he has done nothing untoward; his routine seems to be very set, a limited range of motion including his rooms at Lincoln, his laboratory, and the lecture hall. I shall continue to observe him but have little hope of a breakthrough. Unless I receive instructions to the contrary I will return to London tomorrow.

It would be best for Graham to return, certainly. Lenox sighed. If Lysander and the September Society were responsible for killing George Payson, *why?* What did Hatch know that he wasn't revealing? And where on earth was Bill Dabney?

There was also a note from Inspector Goodson. It was very brief but made Lenox more hopeful than anything had in days.

Have found a small campsite just by

the meadow, due 100 yards south in a thick grove of trees. Sign of habitation some days old. Remnants: some food, a bright red lock of hair, and a thick, straight line of ash. Thought the latter two might interest you. Please report any findings, as we have lost Canterbury and no sign of Dabney. Goodson.

Before he had time to think about this, there was a knock on the door, and he knew it must be McConnell.

The doctor was drenched. He came in smiling ruefully. "Don't suppose I could have a cup of that?" he said, gesturing toward the tea tray. "Something hot would go down well." He took the towel that Mary had just arrived with and managed to make himself slightly drier.

"Come over by the fire," Lenox said. "Only milk, right?"

"Right."

They sat opposite each other in the brown armchairs by the fire, Lenox quickly removing a small stack of books he had left on the one he never sat in.

"Was I right, then? About the report?"

"Yes," said McConnell, removing his flask and taking a slug with a wince, "you were absolutely right. There's no question about it. Unless

James Payson and Peter Wilson's regimental training encompassed a uniform lesson on the proper way to commit suicide, they were both murdered."

Though he had known it was coming, Lenox's composure lurched a bit. "Murdered?"

"That's as clear as I can see it. I wanted to come over here first, but then I'm going to go see the coroner who worked on Wilson's case and ask his opinion."

"I wish you wouldn't, just yet."

"Why?"

"In a day or two it won't matter—next week, say—but at the moment I don't want him calling in Daniel Maran and the rest of this damned Society for testimony about that weekend, asking them about George Payson."

McConnell nodded. "Yes, all right. By God, it's pretty grim all around."

"Yes. Pretty grim."

"Have you heard anything from Oxford?"

"They found the place where Payson and Dabney were hiding out behind Christ Church Meadow." Lenox handed his friend Goodson's note. "Everything seems conclusive enough, and at the same time completely baffling. Why would this Society care after twenty years that old James Payson's son was sitting around studying modern history in some innocuous college? And it has to be Payson, doesn't it? He was the one killed; he's the one with the link to this group; Lysander was in Oxford. And yet, and yet . . ."

"It'll come clean soon, I've no doubt," McConnell said consolingly, giving the note back.

"I suppose you're right. Jane's doing well, incidentally?" said Lenox.

"It would put anyone's back up to have their maid shot, but she's doing remarkably well, yes."

They spoke for another few moments, but as soon as he had drunk his last drop of tea, McConnell stood up and said he had to go. Lenox could see his eagerness to return to his pregnant wife, and envied him it.

"Sorry to have taken you away from home, but the file couldn't leave Edmund's . . ."

"Oh, not at all, I was glad to get a look at it. One of the queerest means of murder I've ever heard of. By the way, what do you make of that missing sheet? In the file on Payson?"

"Missing sheet?"

McConnell had been halfway out the door, but he turned back fully to Lenox now. "You must have seen that there was a third sheet in Payson's file. In the War Office's file."

"I confess I didn't."

"Yes—in all that useless information on the bottom of the first page it said $1/3$, the second said $2/3$ . . . I suppose I got used to looking there when I practiced medicine."

"Unforgivable on my part." Lenox shook his head. "What do you think it was?"

"Could have been anything—a meaningless addendum, the solution to the whole problem. I don't know. But if it were meaningless, why would it be gone?"

CHAPTER THIRTY-NINE

That evening at eight forty-five, Lenox put on a swallowtail coat and white evening tie, his SPQR cufflinks, a black waistcoat, and last of all his black patent leather shoes, buffed by the shoe-and-lace boy who came by once a week. Boats were steaming toward the New World, merchants were taking stock in Yorkshire, and railroads were being built one spike at a time so that Lenox could stand at his mirror in the city at the center of the world, preparing himself for the evening. But for better or worse, none of that was on his mind.

He straightened his tie with one last nudge of his knuckle, turned, and went downstairs. His carriage was waiting on the curb, but he didn't hurry to it as he usually did; he looked over a neat stack of papers on his desk once more, put them into a brown leather case, donned his heavy overcoat, and only then went outside, with Mary wishing him well. It was a special evening.

The SPQRs met once every two months, sometimes less and never more often, in a large room, windowed on two sides, at Boodle's. Of all his clubs—and by now Lenox belonged to some seven or eight—Boodle's was the most prestigious, and the one he visited least. Lenox's ancestor the late eighteenth-century Prime Minister the Marquess of Landsdowne had founded it. People there tended to be somewhat staid, a departure from the club's earlier days when Beau Brummell had made his last bet there before fleeing to France and the Duke of Wellington had taken his evening meals there with a choice friend or two, guaranteed for once of no adoration. It was placed well, at 28 St. James's Street, and even clubmen passed it with a reverentially silent step, contemplating their slim chance of entrance; the days were long gone when the club was whimsical and un-self-important enough to be named, as it had been, for a beloved waiter.

"Mr. Lenox," said Timothy Quails, an institution himself, in the doorway of the club. He held the door open.

"Thanks, Quilts." Somehow that name had stuck to the doorman. "Am I first?"

"Last, sir, save one."

He emphasized the word "one" strangely,

and Lenox knew whom he meant. He mounted the back staircase two steps at a time and entered the SPQRs' usual room with a smile at the five men seated at the round table in the corner.

"No sign of our seventh yet, according to Quilts?"

The other five men stood up and crowded around him, smiling and offering their hands in turn. Some of them he only saw at these meetings and some he saw every day, or nearly every day. All of them were his close, close friends; after nine years, he could have gone to any of them with any problem and been assured of their confidence and sympathy. The club was seven for precisely that reason. They were Lenox; young James Hilary, the MP, whom Lenox had proposed, and whose third meeting it was; Sir John Beacham, an engineer and student of Brunel's who was only slightly older than Hilary, and considered in his profession to be immensely promising; Thomas Weft, who was kind, poor, shy, and brilliant, but had only a sinecure at the Naval Office, procured for him by an SPQR, to show for it; Lord Hallam, the terrifying, imperious inventor and scientist who had introduced McConnell to the Royal Society; and, sixth, Francis Charles Hastings Russell, Liberal Member of Parliament for Bedfordshire, founder of the SPQRs, and agricultural theorist, who would become the 9th Duke of Bedford when his father died.

Then there was the seventh member of the club, who came in about ten minutes later while the other six men sat at the table talking. He was Edward, the Prince of Wales and heir apparent to his mother's crown. Though he had come late to scholarship—for the SPQRs' common interest was Roman history—at Christ Church he had been keen, and he and Francis Russell had been friends. That he knew the least of the seven was no obstacle; doors opened at the sight of him that would have been closed shut to the battering of money and even position, usual position. He was candid, friendly, and yet slightly remote. Theirs was his only intellectual pursuit. The rest of the time, married though he was to Princess Alexandra, he was with women and friends, living the life of a playboy.

"Marius," said the future duke, and was first to shake the prince's hands.

There were a few hard and fast rules of the SPQR, and one was that names didn't matter. Weft and the prince could shake hands, for those few hours, as equals, Aurelius and Marius. Lenox was called Julius, and when the prince came to him the royal lips moved slightly: "Well, Julius, how goes it in Oxford?"

"Well enough," said Lenox, momentarily dumbstruck.

"I wish you all luck there. This is still England . . ."

The meeting opened with a ceremonial glass of Roman honeyed wine, which the chef at Boodle's prepared a week in advance. Russell said the traditional opening words.

"Gentlemen, welcome again to this tiny club of ours. Tonight we honor the long dead, for the happiness and instruction they bring to our short lives. Drink with me once, and be my friend forever."

For supper there was soup, fish, steak, and finally Boodle's orange fool, made of sponge cake, orange, lemon, heavy cream, and sugar; it tasted delicious with a glass of champagne. Talk over supper was general and avoided their common interest, which was reserved for the postprandial hour. They talked about politics, horses, friends, hunting, cricket, books, their lives. Over dessert everybody was responsible for a paragraph of praise and celebration of the person to his left. Lenox spoke of Beacham, the engineer, with fond and witty brevity, and in turn had to listen to Weft's encomium.

The great hour, though, was the brandy hour. When it arrived they all felt slightly more solemn, unbuttoned their cuffs, gave great sighs of contented fullness, and sipped their drinks to the accompaniment of a lecture. At this meeting it was Weft's turn, and the young scholar gave a lively account of gossip's role in the second Catiline conspiracy (he was a great lover of Cicero, Weft). The speech met with thundering applause and a lively round of questions. Even the prince asked a question—rare for him—on a minor point of Senate history and was congratulated on its aptness. Lenox challenged Weft's translation of a line of Sallust and gained the small concession from the room at large, though Weft stuck with his original reading. Hallam brought forth an exceedingly rare Roman coin he had acquired at auction and, as a first order of business, made a present of it to the SPQRs, which was greeted with many toasts and great excitement.

("A silver didrachm of Claudius," said Hallam authoritatively. He was reckoned to know of such things. "You can all see the uneven cut, as well as Claudius standing in his four-horse chariot. From A.D. 46, would be my guess. One of the rarest early coins."

"But where shall it be housed?" Hilary asked.

"If the palace will do, I can arrange for its presentation and safekeeping," said the prince with a noble turn of his head. "It shall come to every meeting."

Nobody would say otherwise, though Hallam looked slightly crestfallen, and indeed there was much excited talk about a possible SPQR collection—and then a long argument about whether Cambridge or Oxford was a better ultimate location for the hypothetical archive.)

Then there was a motion from Russell to cap the total number of members at any one time at eight, except in the case when a legacy of the seven original members present, or more specifically a son or grandson, had a sufficient interest and knowledge of Roman history to gain admittance to the group.

Now, this was a controversy. A faction comprised of Lenox, Hilary, and Beacham suggested that the number be higher—twelve, say—though with no obligation to reach the cap, because there might well be two deserving candidates to come forth in the future. Russell pointed out that compatibility was as serious an issue as knowledge, and that the group would begin to grow too generic if it got much larger, without the bonds of friendship that they all enjoyed. The prince, Hallam, and Weft all said that they could see both sides of the argument, with Weft leaning toward Russell's side, Hallam the other way, and the prince refusing to commit. This was all very vexing to Russell, who had expected to sail through the vote unanimously. Eventually, though, he agreed to compromise on the number nine. Everyone conceded that finding *three* eligible candidates in their lifetimes was unlikely, and so nine became the number. Weft added that they didn't even have an eligible candidate on the horizon and expressed his doubt that the issue would become problematic anytime soon. Still, it had been a pleasing argument and given them all time for another glass of brandy, and so none of them regretted it.

Lenox gave the closing remarks. These were different each time, and responsibility for them rotated among the men. In general they were meant to pledge the renewal of every man's friendship with every other. He removed a sheet of paper from the thin brown folder he had brought, and read.

"Gentlemen," he said, "we come here every two months to celebrate the ancient culture which all of us love. And if I may say so, they are six of the happiest nights of the year for me. I read something of the old texts every day—Virgil, Polybius, Tacitus, Ovid—and I may say that they are common in my life. But it is uncommon to meet with a small group of other people so sympathetic and friendly, so lively and intelligent. It is uncommon that we all feel at ease with each other, in our short interactions together. It is uncommon that we have this felicity in our lives. As Marcus Aurelius pointed out, we are only passing creatures—but happy and fortunate ones. Please raise your glasses with me that these passing hours of our lifetime are so blessed with good spirit and friendship."

The applause bespoke recognition, somber, affirmative, and genuine. They raised their glasses, their room visible as a small square of light in the late darkness of the city.

CHAPTER FORTY

Who *was* Major Peter Wilson, late of the 12th Suffolk 2nd, cofounder of the September Society, and recently deceased?

The next morning was rainy, too, and after rising late (and slightly foggy-headed), Lenox in his slippers and robe had taken himself to his old thinking post by the fire. Sipping his cup of tea, he pondered Wilson's strange and superficially senseless death. Wilson must have had a good pension, had certainly had a distinguished career, and enjoyed—theoretically—a group of close friends. The more Lenox thought over the idea of suicide, the more improbable it seemed.

When he finished his breakfast, Lenox donned a blue morning coat and set out to walk the short distance to Park Lane. He had decided to pay another visit to the September Society's (and Biblius Club's) talkative doorman.

The rain was thin and driving, bitter, and the buildings along St. James's Park looked gray and dull, lifeless even where they were dimly lit.

A rolling fog had appeared, too. It became denser as Lenox came nearer the Thames, until the streets were almost impenetrable beyond a few feet. When he reached Carlton Gardens and the stout building that housed the two clubs, he found a different, older doorman present.

"Hello there. I was hoping to find Thomas Hallowell here?"

"He's not on for another half hour, sir."

"Isn't he? That's too bad. Any idea where he might be at the moment?"

"Probably down the pub, sir, having a bite of breakfast."

"Which one would that be?"

"The Royal Oak, sir, just through that alley."

"Thanks very much."

Like so many pubs in England, the Royal Oak was named for the oak tree in Shropshire in which Charles II had hidden from the Commonwealth troops after a key battle in the Civil War. It was an undistinguished pub, with a brass bar, charred wood tables, and low lamps that were always guttering and shifting, casting a sallow light over the dark room. Lenox found Hallowell eating ham and eggs with a mug of coffee at the bar, a vast napkin spread over his chest to avoid disturbing his neatly turned-out suit of clothes. He looked up at the detective when the barman, who had a massive mustache that was wet with beer, asked what Lenox was drinking.

"A half of mild, then," said Lenox and put his change on the stile.

"Mr. Lenox?" asked Hallowell, looking disconcerted.

"That's right. Hope you don't mind my coming to see you."

"No, not at all—only I don't know anything else about the murder, or I would have come to see you."

"Actually I know a bit more, and I was hoping to ask you a question or two."

The man looked doubtful.

"Nothing to incriminate anybody at either club—only background, you see. We're all pushing in the same direction, the members of the club and me and you. But you know them. Like their privacy, don't they?"

He nodded knowingly. "Aye, that's right."

"So they might not recognize quickly enough that we're all on the same side."

Thomas nodded again, and Lenox knew that he had license to ask his questions. "What I really want to know about is Peter Wilson, Tom."

"Major Wilson? He was a nice enough old chap—quite military, you know, very orderly and all."

"Did he get on well with all the others?"

"In the Society?"

"Right."

"Yes, he seemed to. He was close with a chap

284

named Allen—Lieutenant Allen, we call him."

"A regular?"

"No—not a regular, exactly, but came in pretty often with the major."

"Who are the most regular Society members?"

"Oh, there are seven or eight."

"Major Butler? Captain Lysander?"

"Yes, certainly."

"Major Wilson?"

"Not as often—about half as often. Though they all come in for the meetings."

"Meetings?"

"There's a Society meeting every month, and they usually get a quorum then—three-quarters of the members. We have to stay late for those. But for the September meeting, we get the night off."

"Has that just happened? The September meeting?"

Hallowell shook his head. "Not till Monday. I've been looking forward to the free night."

"Do you know anything about the meeting?"

"No—oh, except by courtesy the Biblius don't come, either. Same way when the Biblius have their meeting, in June. Though we doormen are meant to be there *then*."

"How about the cook and the footmen? Do they go to the September meeting?"

"No, sir, only their personal butler, who was in the military with them—a private, I guess, we call him Private Dove."

"And he's there for the September meeting?"

"Oh, he's always there. Lives in the attic."

Changing tacks, Lenox said, "And Major Wilson, he was sound? More polite than Lysander, for example, or Butler?"

"Yes, sir, I'd say so."

"Did he ever seem low in his spirits?"

"Oh, no, sir, the opposite—he was the only one who always had a good word for you. About the weather, about the society pages . . . nice to have a few minutes pass by in conversation, it was. I was sorry to see him go."

The man obviously had a brightness and quickness that were going to waste in his job. The perfect spy, in other words.

"Would you mind meeting again, Thomas? I can't say how helpful you've been."

He nodded circumspectly. "Yes, I suppose."

"Can I generally catch you here around this time?"

"Generally."

"All right. Good. Excellent. And you must let me buy your breakfast—the least I can do."

Lenox laid a few more coins in the bartender's palm, nodded to Hallowell, and walked past the drinking men, slumped low at their tables, and out again into the gray, wet air. It was almost a relief after the dismal and smoke-stained pub.

When he returned home wet, Mary fussed over him, taking his coat and shoes and thrusting him by the fire with a glass of hot wine, which he took a sip of and then ignored. The fire was bright and lovely, though, and again his thoughts fell to the case, circling and circling around its perimeter, looking for the hidden point of access to its heart. Could it be as simple as a scar on a neck—was Lysander Geoffrey Canterbury, and was Geoffrey Canterbury the murderer? What were they after, these people? How did they all live so comfortably on their army pensions—beyond their army pensions? (For, of course, Green Park Terrace was an exclusive and expensive place.)

Nearing noon, just as he had taken up *Felix Holt* to read, there was a knock at the front door. He first heard Mary go to the door and then a low, unclear, but obviously urgent conversation that pulled him out of his chair. He stood indecisively, trying to hear the murmurs. After a moment Mary pulled open the double doors of the library, and Lenox saw that the person at the door had been George Payson's friend and Bill Dabney's roommate, Tom Stamp.

"Tom, how can I help you? Have a seat, have a seat."

The young man looked pale. "Mr. Lenox, I couldn't turn to anybody else."

"Why, what's happened?"

Stamp paused and gulped for air; obviously he had made haste in coming. "I think I'm going to be killed—I think they're after me, whoever they are."

"Why do you think so?"

"Look at this."

Stamp produced a September Society card.

"Turn it over," he said.

On its reverse was written, *Who can you trust?*

CHAPTER FORTY-ONE

D o you recognize the handwriting?" Lenox asked. "I suppose not—perhaps a better way of asking the question is: Do you think the writer was trying to disguise his handwriting?"

It was some minutes later, and Mary had produced a glass of brandy and the dusty bottle for Stamp, who was slumped low in the other armchair by the fireplace. Ashen and dismayed, one of his two best friends recently dead, he seemed worlds away from the jovial and high-spirited young man Lenox had met in Lincoln's Grove Quad less than a week ago. There was no fight in him—at the moment, anyway.

"Oh, I don't know," said Stamp. "Who can say?"

"It's important—could it be Dabney's handwriting? Hatch's?"

"No, no, I don't think either of them. If it is

disguised, it's so the police can't match it down the road, I bet."

Well, of course, Lenox thought, for the first time in their unproductive conversation verging on impatience. But would somebody from the September Society be so incredibly brazen? Dallington's report on Lysander's whereabouts for the last week would be useful about now.

After another desultory half hour of interrogation, most of it devoted to Lenox reassuring Stamp, the detective left his young friend with a chop and a glass of decent Madeira for a late lunch. They had decided that Stamp would go to an uncle in the north for a few days, if not until the case had been solved. Lenox bade him farewell and left, intending to find his brother.

First, though, he stopped at McConnell's. He found the doctor, his wife, and Lady Jane in the small anteroom again. Jane was knitting something—a shawl for Toto, as it turned out—and when he heard the familiar, intimate sound of her needles clicking he almost dropped to one knee and asked her to marry him then and there. He didn't know how many more small moments of her goodness, of her strength and intelligence and well-ordered generosity, he could take.

"Well," said Toto, the instant all the formalities had been disposed of, "we've decided on a name."

"Have you?" Lenox asked, arching his eyebrows at McConnell.

"Oh—well, I suppose, perhaps," said the doctor.

"Perhaps!" Toto said this to her husband accusingly. "Don't backslide now! The name is Margaret. I think it's ever so lovely."

"No doubt of it," said Lenox. "Jane, does it have your approval?"

"She suggested it, so there." This was Toto. "And none of you can say a word against it or I'll never speak to you again."

"What an unkind fate that would be," murmured McConnell into a glass of—Lenox's heart fell—was it Scotch?

Toto didn't seem to mind, though, only chiding him to be kinder and then moving to Jane's side to see how the shawl's infant stages were matching her pregnancy's.

"I say, Lenox, do you mind a quick word?" said McConnell.

"Not at all."

The two men retreated a few paces away, settling by a small glass and mahogany bookcase with a brass key in its lock. "I had a word with old Harry."

"Did you?" This was a reference to Arlington, who had arranged for Lenox to see James Payson's military file. "All in order, I hope?"

"Oh, yes—nothing amiss at all. But about that third sheet."

Lenox's interest was suddenly intense. "Yes?"

"Well, this hardly seems to be more than confirmation—but the last person to request the file was Maran."

"Good gracious."

"Yes."

"How did you convince Arlington to tell you that?"

"I guessed at a few names, and one of them was correct. Apparently it hadn't been taken out in a decade, up until a month ago. After that Maran took it out, then held it over for an extra day."

"The third sheet, then, must have been his doing."

McConnell grimaced. "I wish it were that easy. According to Harry's secretary—an assiduous young chap from Peterhouse, name of Backer— he checks all outgoing and incoming files for errors, missing sections, and so forth. The Payson file went out to Maran and returned in its original condition."

"How can that be?"

"Your guess is as good as mine."

Lenox was silent for a moment.

"Back to the women?" McConnell suggested.

Before he left, Lenox managed to sneak in a word with his old friend and new beloved. Absurd, of course, that his face felt flushed and his heart was racing, when he had spoken with her a thousand times, a hundred thousand times —absurd, that was, but true.

"I see nothing of you any longer, Charles," she

said, her voice sensible and steady but not, he thought, without beauty. She wore a plain brown dress and a pink ribbon in her hair, which complimented the pink in her cheeks. "I hope you haven't dropped me."

Lenox laughed. "Better that I did than you found your way to danger again."

"Not much better," she said and squeezed his hand.

Saved—and ruined—by Toto. "Is Marian better, after all?" she asked. "I did love Maid Marian when I was a girl. Marian McConnell."

"Malory, Margaret, Marian—are you determined to make this girl's name into a nursery rhyme? Girl! What am I saying! What if it's a boy!" said McConnell.

"Oh, if it's a boy we'll call it Thomas, but I do hope it's a girl!"

"If I were the Earl of Cadogan you wouldn't say that."

"That's why I thank the Lord every evening in my prayers that you're not the Earl of Cadogan. Well, that and his awful drooping chin."

This forced a smile to McConnell's face. "Well," he said, relenting a bit, "how about Elizabeth."

"Elizabeth! That *is* dear! Jane, do you like it?"

Before the conversation got carried away on another tide of speculation, Lenox took his leave, thanking McConnell as he did so for having forged another link (as Stamp's strange and flustered appearance had) in the increasingly strong chain between the September Society and both Payson father and Payson son. But why? Why? Motive was the great mystery here. Motive, and the whereabouts of Bill Dabney.

When he arrived home Stamp had gone, replaced in the armchair by Dallington, who was again reading a copy of *Punch*. Strange how quickly his presence had come to seem natural.

"Oh, hullo, Lenox," he said. "Been out for a swim?"

"It's raining, actually."

"You didn't fall in anything?"

Despite himself Lenox laughed. "Have you found out about Lysander's week?"

"Yes," said Dallington. "He's not our man, unfortunately. At least, he didn't wield the garrote that killed George."

"Can you be sure of that?"

Dallington consulted a small notebook, bound in calf's leather and full of surprisingly careful writing. "On the precise day in question he was in the city of Bath, visiting an elderly aunt who lives in the Royal Crescent and intends to leave him her small fortune."

"Did he spot you?"

"No, he didn't."

"Ah, excellent. How did you come by your information?"

"The usual mix—train conductors, shop sales-men."

"I must say, I'm impressed by your precocity."

"I've read a lot of mystery stories, you see." He pointed at *Punch*. "These magazines are my weakness."

"Your one weakness, then?"

Dallington grinned devilishly. "That's right."

"What else did you find out about Lysander?"

"Nothing all that interesting, unfortunately. He keeps up a pretty steady daily routine between one or two clubs, a restaurant called Marilyn's, which is just by St. Martin-in-the-Fields, and Major Butler's house."

"Butler's back on the premises?"

"Never left."

"Of course, of course. Does Lysander have a girl? Someone he strolls around Hyde Park with?"

"Not as far as I can tell. His life seems pretty monkish. He's forever reading some long, dull history of the wars nobody cares about."

"Which are those?"

"Oh, in the East, or the little wars when Spain got snippy, those. Give me the Crusades."

"Or *Punch*."

"Or *Punch*. Exactly."

"Thanks, Dallington. That's a great help. Now, would you mind another task?"

The young lord shook his head.

"There's a chap called Maran . . ."

CHAPTER FORTY-TWO

W hy September?

Over supper at home, Lenox kept lowering *Felix Holt* to ask himself that one question. The club was called the September Society, it had its formal annual meeting in September—but there was no explicit link between the club's purpose and its name. After pushing his plate aside, he walked to the farthest bookcase in his study and pulled down volume *S* of the encyclopedia.

A small assortment of facts about the month of September: It is the month of the autumnal equinox; its birthstone is the sapphire; its flower the morning glory; in 1752, September 2 was followed by September 14 because of an alteration in the calendar; Queen Elizabeth was born on the seventh of the month, 1533; Samuel Johnson had been born on the nineteenth, 260 years later; the Great Fire, of course, as he had discussed with Chaffanbrass; William the Conqueror had landed on English soil in late September 1066; dozens of harvest festivals had happened for thousands of years in September; the traditional month to dine on goose; acorns on the ground traditionally indicated a snowy winter; on Holy Rood Day, the fourteenth, children were by long custom permitted to leave school so that they could gather nuts.

Lenox read this with mild interest. For good measure, when he returned volume *S* of his encyclopedia to its usual slot he took down volume *R* to look up the color red, as he had been meaning to do. The information was interesting: Red was the first color the cavemen had used in their paintings, for example; in cartography red was the symbol of Britain's empire; the Roman armies, as Lenox had known, wore red so that their blood would be invisible, a valuable illusion both for morale and against an enemy; the Queen's new "mail boxes" were red; in Russia, red had always been the color that denoted great beauty. Interesting, but useless. It seemed clear that those red objects referred to Red Kelly— and it seemed clear that he needed to turn his attention back to the porter.

As he held the book in his hand, there was a knock on the door. A moment later Mary appeared with Inspector Jenkins again in tow.

"Hello, Lenox, how do you do?" said the youthful gentleman. "I hope I'm not disturbing you after your supper?"

"No, not at all, not at all. Won't you come in?" The two men sat by Lenox's desk. "You handled that little Emerson matter?"

"Yes."

"It was Johannsen, of course."

"How did you know?"

"The papers. I would have been to see you if it hadn't come clear."

"How's your own work?"

"I was just thinking about the case when you arrived, actually. Without much success I'm afraid."

"That's what brings me round, actually. I wondered whether you might take a short trip with me."

"Of course. Where to?"

"To Fulham."

This was an area of London southwest of Charing Cross, near Hammersmith Bridge. Its reputation was improving to an extent, but at its pinnacle of debauchery in the last century it had been a place full of gambling houses, brothels, and drinking establishments where the infamous Regency cads had run riot to the consternation of their elders. It was still liveliest far past dark, particularly by the river. Lenox had been on two separate cases there, one involving the assault of a prostitute, the other the robbery of a saloon by a masked man who had eventually turned out to be the oldest son of and heir to the Earl of Downe.

"Fulham? Is that so?"

"On the case," said Jenkins quickly. "A matter involving the case."

"I should hope so," said Lenox, smiling.

"Shall we discuss it on the way? I have a brougham outside."

As they went south toward the Thames, Jenkins told Lenox more about their mission.

"I'm taking you to see a very interesting man named Laurence Matte. German by ancestry, though he and his father were both born in Hertfordshire. He grew up quite poor—father kept a struggling stables for carriage horses—but when he was eighteen he invented a new kind of breech-loading rifle mechanism and sold the patent for a great deal of money."

"Eighteen!"

"His father kept guns and horses for some of the minor gentry without their own land, and the lad's job as a boy was to clean the rifles. He's told me he invented the breech-loader by the time he was thirteen but had to wait to apply for the patent. He may have been boasting, though. He's a terrible boaster."

"With some cause, at any rate."

"Indeed. Well, he took the money he made and with about half of it bought a nice pile of a place near his childhood home, filled it with paintings and furniture and flatware, installed his parents there as resident caretakers, and promptly left. He invested half of the remaining money, and then with the quarter of the patent payment he had left he moved to Fulham, and he's vowed to stay there drinking and gambling until it runs out. Then, he says, he'll move back to the country and marry, perhaps become a local magistrate."

"Good Lord, he sounds fascinating! How on earth did you come across him?"

"This is where your interest may lie, in fact."

"Rest assured, you already have my interest."

"We received a report of repeated gunshots in the basement of his house. A bobby went out to look, and it turned out that he had a firing range underneath his house. He was terrifying his maid by shooting all night. Drunk, oftentimes. It was above the bobby's head, and I went and had a look at him. Well, we fell into a long conversation, and I really found him most interesting."

"I should say so."

"He believes in something called ballistics, you see, Lenox."

"What's that?"

"Do you hunt?"

"Certainly."

"Then you'll know that all rifles have helical grooves running down their barrels, which give the bullet its peculiar spin coming out of the muzzle. Matte believes that it's possible to identify a gun simply by studying a bullet that has been fired from it. I tested him informally with a few bullets we had used in a recent case, and he was dead on."

Lenox was puzzling this over in his mind. "It

just . . . just seems possible," he said slowly. "Perhaps."

"And yet nobody at the Yard would listen to a word I said!"

"That can scarcely surprise you."

"Can't it?" Jenkins sighed. "I love my work, Lenox, but I sometimes fear my colleagues are living in the past. This revolution of industrial technology we're undergoing will change police work forever, mark my words. Yet I can't persuade anybody even to listen to a man like Matte, who may very well have made a major breakthrough in criminology! Maddening—simply maddening. I think of leaving now and then, you know."

In a gentle, commiserating tone, Lenox replied, "That's precisely why you must stay, Jenkins. It's your work to bring your colleagues into the present."

"Well, either way, here we are," said Jenkins. They had pulled up in front of a small and eccentrically designed house. "I've told him we're coming. He'll be downstairs in his basement. I've made him soundproof the walls, anyway, or his neighbors would have gone mad."

Matte was a tall, good-looking chap with blond hair and a straight posture. He was also almost certainly drunk.

"How do you do, how do you do?" he asked jovially. "Has Jenkins told you all about my discoveries? If only the asses he works with would listen, I could save them all hours upon hours of useless work. But will they? No! Of course not! The greatest invention of our time, under their noses, and they won't even put down their newspapers. Asses," he said again, shaking his head as if they were more to be pitied than censured for it.

The basement was a fascinating place; otherwise normal, at its center was a table full of various guns. One wall was entirely covered with hideous oil portraits, all of which were riddled with bullet holes.

"Dreadful, aren't they?" said Matte when he saw Lenox staring at them. "I buy 'em from a lad who thinks he has real talent. I feel sorry for him. He paints pictures of all the prostitutes and tries to sell them down in the West End. Nothing doing, though."

"I've shown Laurence the bullet that lodged in the wall after it hit Annie, Lenox. Laurence, have you taken a look at it?"

"Oh, that, yes." He retrieved it from the table full of guns. "I'm afraid I can't be terribly specific—I can only tell you that it's from an old discontinued line of service revolvers. It's been to the East, and before it shot this maid Jenkins mentioned, it hadn't been used for a decade. That's why it accidentally discharged, old age."

"What!" said Lenox, for once entirely shocked. "How on earth can you say that?"

"Easily enough. Its type is obvious from the grooves it left on the bullet. The firing mechanism was rusty and slightly off center, which can come with long disuse, and the barrel was coated with fine clay, such as you find in the East. A disgusting way to take care of a gun, mind you."

"Are you certain?" asked Lenox. "The East?"

Jenkins was clearly thinking the same thing. "The September Society."

"Oh, certain enough," said Matte distractedly. He had taken up a gun and was cleaning it with a practiced, almost gifted hand. "The worst part of it all is that I didn't even invent internal ballistics! Some chap thought it up about thirty years ago, in 1835. But I've certainly perfected it. Tell everyone you know, won't you? It's important."

Shortly afterward they left Matte in his basement with their thanks. It was late, and the carnival of iniquity was visible in the low lights by the river where the saloons had just opened.

"Interesting fellow, isn't he?" said Jenkins.

"Reliable, though, you think?"

"As I say, I tested him. He seems to be almost perfectly accurate to me. I've come to trust him implicitly despite his oddness."

As they rode back toward Piccadilly and the West End, the two men had a long discussion about the bullet and the September Society, agreeing at the end of it to keep in close contact as they decided on a course of action.

"We have a real interest in this case, as I mentioned," Jenkins said when they had reached Hampden Lane.

Lenox knew that Jenkins was referring to himself, rather than the Yard, and felt touched. An ally, that was what the young inspector was proving to be. "I'll write you tomorrow morning," he promised and said good-bye.

As he climbed the stoop of his house Lenox thought of a long night's rest. But in the front hallway he found Mary in a state of intense anxiety, pacing and waiting for him.

"Sir, sir!" she said when he came in. "There's a man here!"

"Who is he?"

"I daren't say!"

"Where is he?"

"In your study, sir, eating all the food in the house! He insisted, sir!"

"Take a deep breath, Mary. Has Graham not returned?"

"No!"

"Well, let's see who it is."

Lenox strode into his library and found a young man, covered in dirt, hair shorn close to his head, clothes disheveled, and eating, as Mary had said, from a massive plate of food. "I'm Charles Lenox. May I help you?" the detective asked.

The young man rose slowly and swallowed his mouthful.

"Perhaps," he said, in a surprisingly educated voice. "I'm Bill Dabney."

CHAPTER FORTY-THREE

Now," said Lenox. "May I ask you a few more detailed questions?"

"Of course," said Dabney. His voice had been polished by Oxford; it lacked the deep melodious quality of the Midlands his father's voice had, but he was proving just as affable and thoughtful.

Lenox had instantly asked three questions when the two had first faced each other in the library. They were: Do you know who killed George Payson? Does anybody else know where you are? And: What happened? To these Dabney had replied: no, no, and that he wasn't quite sure. Then Lenox, seeing the pathetic state of the lad's clothing and the hunted, fearful look in his eyes, had put off his curiosity and asked Mary to draw Dabney a bath and find him some new clothes.

It was about an hour later now, nearing eleven at night, and he looked like a new man in a pair of gray trousers and one of the thick green Scottish sweaters that McConnell's mother (one of the most charming and eccentric people Lenox had ever met) had sent him for Christmas the year before.

"How did you find me, to begin with?"

"After Payson died I was in Oxfordshire, roaming around the countryside, working toward London. I reckoned that I could disappear more easily here than anywhere else. And I was—I am —terrified by how quickly things went from mysterious to tragic. I have no idea how it happened."

He seemed to be telling the truth. Inwardly, Lenox sighed. Obviously Payson had taken much of the truth with him when he died. "You made it here, evidently."

"Yes, I did. I thought of going to Stamp first, but then it occurred to me that everybody knew we were friends, and at any rate I didn't want to endanger him. So I sent him a card, a September Society card (I had a few, you see, which I nicked off George, just in case—he had been leaving them everywhere), and I wrote on the back of it 'Who can you trust?' He came straight to you, and I watched you for a day and thought about whether I could trust you. But Stamp had. So I decided to take the risk."

That explained that mystery. Stamp could probably return to London in peace.

"What *is* the September Society? How was George involved?"

Dabney threw up his hands. "I don't know."

"Why don't you tell me what happened, then, from the beginning?"

"It all started at the Jesus ball. Stamp, poor chap, had to study for a makeup midyear exam. Collections, they call them at Oxford. So only Payson and I went to Jesus. Stamp and I—we kip together, but you'll know that—we had noticed George was distracted, wasn't quite himself. At the ball I confronted him about it."

"After he met with the middle-aged man out in the quad?"

It was Dabney's turn to look startled. "Exactly. I asked who the man was."

"And what did Payson say?"

A look of sadness came into Dabney's eyes— of deep sadness, of a new, unfamiliar sort that had only just come into his life. He didn't seem close to breaking down; rather he seemed as if he were just beginning to realize what had happened, now that he had been able to stop running. "Oh, Lord, I wish he weren't dead. What's gone wrong?" He buried his face in his hands.

Lenox was silent for a moment, and then said, "Bill?"

"Oh—yes—he only said, 'He knew my father.' Which was odd, as Payson never spoke about his father."

"And what then?"

"He said to me, 'Dabs, something has gone

wrong' "—here again the lad paused, devastated
—" 'and I may have to vanish for a few weeks.' I
asked him what he meant, and he said that some
mystery had arisen about his father and this—
this September Society, whatever that is, and
then he told me not to worry any more about it.
That he had left trail enough in his room if anything went awry."

Lenox cursed under his breath. "Did he ever
mention that trail again? In his room?"

"No."

"Did he ask you to go with him?"

"On the contrary—I said I was going to go
with him and he told me I couldn't. We had
breakfast the morning before he left, and he only
said that I shouldn't worry about him, that I
couldn't go."

"Then how did you?"

"I caught up just after he had seen his mother.
He looked horribly pale and jittery, and I followed him out past Christ Church Meadow."

Lenox nodded. "South."

"Precisely. Finally, after the bridge—you know
the one, just over the Cherwell down past the
lower fields—I simply tapped him on the
shoulder. I told him that I was coming whether
he liked it or not."

"Good of you," said the older man softly.

Dabney shrugged. "It didn't help. Not in the
end."

"And what did you do?"

"We slept relatively close to town, just past the meadow. He had some food, and I went out and got a bit more at a shop by Magdalen Bridge where not many students go. The next day he went and saw the man again."

"At the Jesus ball."

"Lord, you're omniscient."

"You didn't go with him?"

"I did, yes, but George said that I had to hide."

"What was his attitude like—Payson's?"

"Hopeful, actually. Jittery, as I say, but he also seemed hopeful. He seemed relieved." Dabney paused. "Stamp and I always wondered about George's governor, you see. There were all sorts of rumors. I had the sense that George finally felt proud, for some reason."

"Proud?"

Dabney nodded firmly. "Yes, proud—and as if it were an adventure, not as if he were afraid. He didn't seem at all afraid."

"Can you describe the man he met with?"

"Not well, because I didn't catch much of his face. Average build, I should say. Dark hair. Whiskers, and perhaps a mustache, though perhaps not. On his throat was—"

"A scar?"

Dabney looked again surprised. "Yes, exactly. A red scar."

"Lysander," muttered Lenox. Yet according to

Dallington he couldn't have actually killed Payson. Or could Dallington have missed a trick?

"Who is that?"

"A member of this Society, the September Society."

"Ah. So."

"I'm afraid I have to ask you something difficult now, Bill."

A grim look came onto Dabney's face. "About his death. Right."

"Yes," said Lenox.

"I had gone to get food, you see. We were just running out, and we agreed it was much better that I risk being seen than that he did. It was around nightfall. When I came back with the food, he was—he was dead."

Now Dabney did weep, and once and for all Lenox struck him from the list of possible suspects. For his tears were entirely genuine, born out of a grief that surpassed not only words but the years of upbringing that had taught him to keep a stiff upper lip.

"You took his body to Christ Church Meadow."

"Yes," said Dabney, taking the handkerchief Lenox offered him. "Yes, I carried him into the meadow. Our hiding space was just between a grouping of trees, and it was awfully well hidden. But I wanted his body to be found, because I wanted the police—and you, I suppose, though I didn't know you existed—to figure it out straight away."

"You didn't want to come forward yourself?"

"No."

"I can see why you wouldn't, of course."

"It was simply so shocking—so shocking to find him there. Suddenly it all seemed so much different than what we had been playing at. I had had no idea it was serious. And of course I assumed that they would want to kill me, too, whoever had done it, because George might have confided in me."

"Yes, of course."

"So I put his body in the meadow and then I ran for it. It took days of walking—I hadn't very much money, you see, because I thought we would only be gone a short while—and a bit of scavenging—and then I couldn't quite turn to old Stamp, because I didn't want him to become a target . . ."

Exhaustion seemed to overtake the lad. Again he buried his head in his hands.

"We'll push you upstairs to bed in just a moment," said Lenox. "I know how tired you must be. But are you fit to answer another question or two?"

"Oh, yes, yes."

"Did George say anything at all about the man he was meeting with? About the Society?"

"No, he didn't. I wish I had asked."

"I take it you cut your hair and changed into the clothes you had on as a means of disguise?"

"Yes, exactly."

"I thought so. Tell me, what did you speak about? Out beyond the meadow?"

Now the phantom of a smile came into Dabney's eyes. "We talked about old times. About when we were freshers. About what spring would be like, this year, when we had written our exams and we could simply punt all day and go to the Bear and have pints to drink." Another short sob, which he managed to cut short somewhere in his chest. "Lord, I can't believe it's happened!"

After two or three more inconclusive questions, Lenox led Dabney upstairs and put him in the guest bedroom; in only moments there was a deep quiet from within.

As for the detective, he went back downstairs. The candles guttered out, and long after midnight he was left staring into the embers of the fire for light, as a comfortless rain beat against the window.

CHAPTER FORTY-FOUR

It was almost noon when Dabney woke the next day. Lenox had spent the late night and the morning devising a plan of action; it depended on one man, but he thought it might just work.

He also had half a dozen questions he had forgotten to ask Dabney the night before. The foremost of these was about Hatch. When the lad had finished eating his breakfast (prepared by a wrathful Ellie, who thought that once the master started asking for eggs and kippers at noon the apocalypse couldn't be far behind), Lenox began that line of inquiry.

"Did he deliver a parcel to you, out in the Meadow?"

"Who—old Hatch? No, I don't know anything about that. I certainly didn't see him, and I don't think he could have spoken to Payson without my knowing about it."

"Are you certain? It would have been on Sunday afternoon. And the two of them met at a place called Shotter's just before Payson disappeared on Saturday."

"Did they?" Dabney seemed perplexed. "Professor Hatch was decent for a laugh and a drink, but I doubt that he would have been

312

George's choice as a confidant. I very much doubt it."

This exchange immediately led Lenox to reevaluate his thoughts about Hatch. He had to some extent discounted the possibility that Hatch was guilty, even as an accomplice. It had seemed logical to assume that Hatch had been helping his troubled young friend, bringing him a parcel of—what, food? Clothes? It seemed feeble now. Quickly he wrote a telegram to Graham, requesting that he remain in Oxford another twelve hours.

"Another question, then," he said to Dabney. "What do you mean to do? I've met with your parents, and while they've handled it admirably, they're of course frantically worried. I'm inclined to send them a telegram instantly. I fought against the instinct after you had gone to sleep last night, out of respect for your free will."

Dabney winced. "Please, please don't. I have a good reason."

"What's that?"

"Listen, when will all this be over, do you reckon?"

"Not later than Monday evening, I should say."

"How can you know that?"

"I have a plan in mind that should force things to a conclusion, one way or another."

"Tuesday morning, then, as early as possible. I'll write them then."

At half past noon, Lenox set out to execute his new plan. He walked with some trepidation for Pall Mall and the row of clubs along it. As he drew close to Carlton Gardens and the September Society (and Biblius Club), his uncertainty increased, and he decided to wait until after his lunch. At the Athenaeum Club he had turkey on the joint with cranberry sauce and mashed potatoes—heavy but sustaining in the weather, which continued cold and wet—and read the *Cambridge Journal of Roman History.*

The Athenaeum was a place for people accomplished intellectually rather than socially, and many of the people in the dining room were reading similar journals on any number of subjects. While its members were still largely drawn from the landed classes, some had arrived on the merit of their achievements. For example, in the late 1830s, when the club had been in a difficult financial position, its board had decided to admit forty less well born men from a waiting list. Thereafter known jocularly as the Forty Thieves, their number had included Dickens and Darwin. Lenox liked this tradition in the club—one dedicated to Athena, after all, the goddess of wisdom whose cunning had guided Odysseus—much better than he liked the tradition of exclusivity at Boodle's, where the SPQRs met.

At half past one he finally made his way out,

nodding to the familiar faces he saw on the way, and started for Carlton Gardens.

At the September Society, however, he did not find Hallowell as he had hoped, but the second, older doorman who had directed him once before to the Royal Oak.

"After Hallowell again, sir?"

"Yes, actually."

"He won't be at the Royal Oak now, I shouldn't imagine, sir. His shift doesn't begin for another hour and a half."

"I see."

"Would you like me to leave word for him that you called?"

"No, that's quite all right. Thanks."

Lenox decided to check the Royal Oak anyway. He turned up his collar against the rain and once more walked down the slender alleyway which housed the pub.

It was as he had left it, dim, the walls dampening a constant murmur of voices, and in the air the steamy warmth of a wet day brought indoors. In fact, the people at the tables might not have moved at all since he had last been there. The man with the large mustache was still behind the bar.

"Hello," said Lenox. "I'm trying to find Hallowell. You may remember I was here—"

"In the back," said the barman, pointing with his thumb.

It was a stroke of luck. Hallowell was reading a newspaper at a rear table, a full pint of Guinness before him. When he looked up and saw Lenox, his face fell slightly—and who could blame him? What had begun as a conversational acquaintance had become dangerously uncertain.

"Really, sir," he said as Lenox approached, "I've told you all I know about Major Wilson. I haven't thought of anything else."

Lenox sat down. "Of course, and I'm sorry to bother you again."

"It's not a bother, sir, but it may be more than my job is worth."

"Have you read anything about this business at Oxford?" the detective asked, pointing at the newspaper Hallowell was still holding.

"Some, yes, sir."

"I know I've asked you to go against your conscience, but a great deal is at stake, you see. A lad died, a lad of twenty."

"Yes, Mr. Lenox."

"In part it was my own fault. I knew something was afoot before he died, young George Payson, and I couldn't stop it from happening. But I may be able to stop it from happening again."

Hallowell nodded slightly

"I need to ask you a larger favor, Thomas."

"Sir?"

"It's not about Major Wilson. It's about the meeting tomorrow."

"The September Society's meeting?"

"Yes, precisely."

"But I won't even be there, sir. As I told you, we receive the night off."

It was time to level with the man. He was sharp enough, clever enough, to see that things had changed. "I told you that I was working in the same direction as the Society, whether they knew it or not, didn't I?"

"Yes, sir."

"That no longer appears to be the case."

Hallowell blanched. "Sir?"

"I think somebody in the Society is responsible for George Payson's murder—perhaps several other deaths, too."

"Sir, I can scarcely credit—I mean to say, I know these men, it's not possible."

"I'm afraid it is, in fact. And I need you to sneak me into the club before the meeting so that I can spy on them all."

"No, sir, I simply cannot—"

"But you must!"

"I simply cannot, Mr. Lenox—"

Lenox's temper rose. "They shot at my friend's house, Hallowell! Did you read about that in the papers, on Hampden Lane? They threatened a woman with no involvement in the case—they've killed an innocent lad—they probably killed Major Wilson—you must!"

For a moment there was silence at the table.

The paper fell out of Hallowell's hands, while in the front bar the voices grew suddenly louder and a wave of laughter rose and fell among the house's patrons. Outside, Lenox saw through the small window above him, the rain had stopped.

At last, almost imperceptibly, Hallowell nodded. "Yes," he said. "All right."

Relieved, Lenox said, "Good. Excellent."

"But just a moment—how can I trust you? How can I be sure you're not involved?"

Lenox scribbled a few words on a piece of paper in his notebook and tore it out. "Here," he said, "take this to Inspector Jenkins at Scotland Yard. He'll tell you that I've been doing this for a long time."

Hallowell glanced at the paper, then folded it and put it in his pocket. "Tomorrow, then," he said. "Meet me here tomorrow at five in the afternoon."

"I shall."

"I may be late."

"I'll be here," said Lenox. He stood up. "You're doing the right thing. I can only promise you that. If you lose your job for any reason, because of this or not, you need only come to me, Hallowell."

CHAPTER FORTY-FIVE

After he left the Royal Oak, Lenox hailed a hansom cab and went to Hunt House. It was here, close to the river, where Dallington still lived with his parents. The house belonged to an old family with a relatively new dukedom; for centuries before their elevation the family had been a steady and well-respected line of local squires in Bedfordshire, but in the last hundred years they had gone from that prosperous station in England's landed gentry to the pinnacle of its nobility. Hunt House reflected that. It was quite modern, painted white with gold and green window frames, and every cut of stone and pane of glass sighed money.

They were an amusing family. The duchess was plain-spoken, pretty, well past fifty, and a close friend of Lady Jane's. The duke was a generous and entirely idle man. Both of them were continually at court, good friends to Victoria and once upon a time Prince Albert, who had been dead five years. Their heir was dull and industrious; their second son was vain and pious; and their third son was Lenox's apprentice.

Eager, quick-witted, and conscientious for the time being, the young lord had suddenly begun to seem indispensable to Lenox; a second set of eyes at the September Society during the meeting, what he had in mind for Dallington, might ultimately mean the difference between success and failure.

Lenox stepped out of his cab and rapped the door sharply. An eminently appropriate butler answered the door.

"How do you do, Mr. Lenox?" he said. "Please come in."

"Oh, I can't, thanks. I was only looking for the youngest of the brood."

"Lord John is not presently in, sir."

The respectful and cautious tone of these words made Lenox uneasy. "Do you know where he's gone?"

"I believe he stated an intention of visiting Claridge's, sir, with one or two friends."

Damn. "Thanks," said Lenox. "If he does return, hold him here for me, won't you?"

Lenox quickly hailed another cab and directed the driver to the hotel. Claridge's was an august establishment on Brook Street in Mayfair, about fifty years old, which the Queen had consecrated not long ago by calling on Empress Eugenie of France in her suite there. It also—and this was the cause of the butler's overly polite manner, perhaps, in referring to Dallington—housed a raucous bar full of slightly disreputable young aristocrats.

When he arrived at the terraced house, Lenox walked straight to the bar. Sure enough, Dallington was there, having a glass of champagne and unloosening his tie while he spoke with a florid, light-haired lad of about the same age. There was also an extremely pretty young woman with them. She wore a bright red dress and had a high, clear laugh that rang out across the room. Lenox went over to them.

"I'm sorry to interrupt, but might I have a word?" he said.

Dallington looked up blearily, then gave an excited start. "Oh, I say, Lenox! I say! Meet Solly Mayfair!"

Lenox shook hands and nodded at the woman, to whom he hadn't been introduced. "Nice to see you. Do you think I could have that word, Dallington?"

"About what? No secrets from Solly."

All three of them found this outlandishly funny.

"About the case, John."

"Quite right, Lenox, quite right—we *should* get a case of champagne. These bottles on their own seem so stingy. A case of champagne, a barrel of beer—that will set us to rights."

"Can you not be serious, for a moment?"

"I was never more serious in my life!" said the lad with a Falstaffian belch. "A case of champagne! A barrel of beer!"

Now Lenox realized that Dallington was too far-gone with drink to pay him any notice.

"Perhaps another time," he said. Nodding to Dallington's friends, he rapidly turned and left the bar, then the hotel.

It was a bitter disappointment. He wasn't exactly certain why. As he walked the short way home, however, he slowly realized how much this new attachment—friendship, even—had meant to him. A detective's work was so isolated, and while Lenox had come to accommodate the isolation, had agreed to it as a condition of the work he loved, the lad had seemed to offer a kind of professional companionship he hadn't known before. Even Jenkins, for instance, would grow gradually more conservative. He would begin to believe, if imperceptibly at first, that the Yard should be the sole authority over crime in London. The critical thing about Dallington was that in some significant way he was like Lenox. In his background. It had been gratifying to have an ally.

As he turned into Hampden Lane, Lenox decided to visit Lady Jane. With a dull thud of fear in his chest he realized that they might actually find themselves alone. When Kirk led him into the house a moment later, however, Lenox heard voices. When he came to the drawing room he stopped. It was the man he had seen at the door twice before, the tall, lean one who had both times worn a long gray coat. Now he stood as Lenox came into the room.

Lady Jane looked flustered, and sounded it, too. "Charles, how are you?" she said. "I'm so glad you've come. Won't you meet Michael Pierce? Mr. Pierce, this is Charles Lenox, my particular friend."

"How do you do, Mr. Lenox?" said the man, striding forward with his hand outstretched.

"I'm pleased to meet you," Lenox said. "Have I come at an inconvenient time, Jane?"

"I was just leaving, in fact," said Michael Pierce. "Good day, my Lady. Good day, Mr. Lenox. I'm pleased to have met you."

Lenox's mind was racing. He hadn't heard the name before. They had been sitting next to each other, not across from each other, which meant they were more than simply formal friends.

What followed was the first strained conversation of Lenox and Jane's long friendship. They weren't curt, precisely, but neither of them could find exactly what to say. At last they alit on the subject of his case.

"It's going well enough," he said.

"When will it be over?"

"Tomorrow, perhaps."

"That will be a relief."

Stiffly, he said, "Yes, it will. How is Annie, if I may ask?"

"Very well. Recovered, in fact."

"I found out something about the gun that did it."

"Did you?"

"Circumstantially it's linked to the September Society."

"How awful."

"Yes." It was horribly impolite, but he couldn't help himself from saying, in a strangled voice that sounded nothing like his own, "I hadn't met Mr. Pierce before."

"You wouldn't have. He's a friend of my brother's from school, only recently arrived in town from the colonies in Africa. He knows very few people."

Why did she still look so flustered?

"Oh, yes?"

Miserably, Lenox said, "Perhaps I ought to introduce him about."

"Yes, perhaps."

He stood. "Well, I had better go," he said. "I'll speak to you soon."

As he walked down the long hallway, and out again into the street, he thought that he had never felt unhappier in all the years of his life.

CHAPTER FORTY-SIX

D abney was sitting in a chair at the far end of the library, reading. When Lenox came in he marked his place in the book and laid it to the side.

"Hullo," he said. "Have you had a productive time out?"

Lenox again marveled at how Oxford had moderated his parents' Midlands accent. "Productive enough," he said. "We'll know it all by tomorrow evening, or I'd be very much surprised. I've arranged to infiltrate a meeting of the Society."

"Good," said Dabney with a firm nod. "How can I help?"

"I'm afraid you can't. I shall have to go alone."

"I'll come into the meeting with you."

"It won't be that easy."

"Have you convinced the Society that you're someone you're not? Or are you going to hide and observe from within the room?"

"I'm going to hide and observe, as you say. It's their annual meeting, the Society's most important evening of the year."

"Then I shall come and hide as well."

"I'm afraid it would be far too precarious. You might easily hinder me."

But Dabney was insistent. "See here, Mr. Lenox, you've been very kind to take me in, but I promised George that I would stick by him until his trouble was over, and though he's died I mean to keep that promise."

They wrangled for another moment over the question, and then Lenox relented. "If you must, then," he said. "I meant to ask a second man anyway, but he was unavailable."

"I'll be happy to follow your lead—just as long as I'm involved."

"Incidentally, perhaps you can help with something." Lenox pulled his small notebook from his pocket and flipped back to an early page in it. "I believe Payson left behind clues about his departure in his room. I'd like to run them past you to see if they make sense."

Dabney nodded amenably. "Fire away."

"I think your friend realized that he had very little time to leave his room, somehow. Perhaps an hour, but not longer. And he decided to do something bold: to kill the cat you two shared."

Dabney blanched. "Longshanks? Has Longshanks been killed?"

"Oh—yes. I'm sorry."

The lad waved it off. "It's no great loss in the end. Though I did love that cat."

"I don't think he died in vain, if it's any consolation. I think George killed Longshanks because

326

he needed a tangible, striking demonstration that he hadn't simply disappeared to a party in London or gotten waylaid some other way. Hence its double death, if you will: first by drugging, then by stabbing. He needed to signal—to me, to the police—that something strange had happened. His mother, as you may know, is rather high-strung, and perhaps even I would have attended her anxiety with less patience if there hadn't been this bizarre signpost. There's also the fact that the September Society's seal has a wildcat on it. So Longshanks served multiple purposes. Killing him was really a brilliant, even necessary solution."

Dabney nodded. "It sounds like George—he was fearfully clever. What was the poison that killed the cat?"

"Laudanum."

Dabney nodded again. "George had insomnia from time to time, particularly when he had heavy work. He used laudanum to sleep. That makes perfect sense."

Lenox's confidence rose with this confirmation. "I think the key to the scene in his room was the line of ash he left by the window. The window was just at hand, and the line of ash was scattered, as if it had just been disrupted. As fanciful as it sounds, I think he had—"

"To check whether somebody had been in the room while he was gone! He mentioned that to me once or twice, thought it clever—from some book he read, that's right."

Two for two, excellent. Lenox said, "Perfect. Dead on. It was left to set the scene; an artificial clue. Nobody actually disrupted the ash. It was his way of telling us that the room had been staged, and at the same time indicating that the room had probably been trespassed in his absence—"

"Which was why he had to leave clues rather than simply a letter," said Dabney.

"It was quick thinking. I have all the admiration in the world for the lad, I have to say. We know as well that he specifically sent down to the scout before he left, asking that his room remain undisturbed!"

"Did he?"

"What's puzzling, though, is the line of ash by your campsite in Christ Church Meadow. Why would he have wanted to draw attention to it? Wouldn't you have preferred us to think that it belonged to some tramp?"

"I remember him doing it—I smoke a pipe every so often, you see, my country ways—and he said he ought to, just in case somebody smart enough to figure it out came along."

"Did you ask what he meant?"

"No. I wish I had."

"It's even more peculiar because there was no indication that you were going to leave, was there, before he died?"

"No, we certainly meant to stay. George was playful, though. Who can say?" Both men thought silently for a moment. Then Dabney asked, "What's the next clue?"

"There are a number of clues relating to his father, which further research has subsequently borne out. A September Society card with pink and black pen marks on the back, meant to indicate the Payson crest; and of course the note underneath the cat, which read '12 Sflk 2,' his father's battalion, in a strange code called cross-tip."

"Yes," said Dabney. "It really does seem to hang together."

"Which means that I already *know* what happened. I simply haven't thought about it in the right way yet."

"What else is there?"

"The walking stick and the walking shoes."

"He loved that walking stick. It was his grandfather's."

"The shoes were muddied, as was the bottom of the stick. It was clear that he had just been on a long walk. But he left them both *in his armchair*. The stick, perhaps—but his shoes? I imagine he sat in that chair by the grate a good deal—"

"Yes," Dabney agreed.

"So it seems to me that he was drawing attention to them. But why? I think they were a memento of his long walks out past Christ Church Meadow to meet Geoffrey Canterbury. I think he intended them to reveal that he had been acting out of the ordinary."

"How do you mean?"

"One thing that everybody has said was that you'd be far more likely to find Payson in the pub than on a long walk."

"True," said Dabney with a fond laugh.

"So for the walking boots and the walking stick to have been so heavily used was out of the ordinary, and for him to put them on the armchair was doubly out of the ordinary. After all, why not just leave them by the door for the scout to clean?"

"But he met Canterbury—whoever that is—at the Jesus ball."

Lenox shook his head. "Only the night before he disappeared. It must have been urgent. I think Canterbury must have warned him he had to leave, or at least agreed on a signal that he ought to leave. For their earlier meetings they would have gone outside the city of Oxford, I should guess. A place where they both would have felt invisible, perhaps in a neighboring town, some public place."

After a gray morning it had become sunny and warm. During the lull in conversation Lenox looked out through the window and felt a sense of being closer than he had yet to the solution.

"Is that all of the clues?"

"No, there was one more."

"What?"

"On the rug in his sitting room—the rug that had once been his father's, bear in mind—was a small assembly of things. They were too far from the table by the window to have fallen there accidentally, I thought, and they were almost overly random. Too meticulous, like the line of cigar ash. I think they were another signal."

"What sort of objects?"

"A tomato, a bit of string, and a fountain pen."

Dabney scratched at the nape of his neck, where his hair was beginning to come in. "I remember that fountain pen."

"All three of them were—"

Lenox froze.

"Were?"

"Red," said Lenox softly, almost as if to himself. "Would you mind if I asked you a question?"

"Of course not."

"If you're not Bill Dabney, who are you?"

CHAPTER FORTY-SEVEN

There was a long, long pause.

Lenox was ambivalent about using guns in his work as a detective—although he loved to hunt—but now his mind kept drifting toward the small pistol in his desk drawer. This stranger was sitting between Lenox and the desk, but he still thought of making a run there. He had a notion of who this fake Dabney actually was, but at the moment he didn't feel especially confident about his notions. It had taken him long enough to figure out that Dabney was an impostor.

At last the young man said, more curiously than angrily, "How did you know?"

"It was a few things."

In fact it was three things, each of which had been slightly puzzling: the hair, the ash, and the voice.

"Do you know who I am, then?"

"A friend, I hope."

"I certainly mean no harm."

Lenox took a deep, measured breath. He felt the control of the situation was in his hands again, for some reason.

"Are you George Payson?" he asked.

"I am," said the dead man. He held out his hand. "It's nice to meet you, Mr. Lenox."

"Dabney, then? Dead?"

"Yes, Bill's dead." Payson's face remained impassive as he said this. Or perhaps it was a mask of impassivity. There seemed to be a kind of hysteria lurking behind it.

"Did you kill him?"

There was a long, almost frightening silence. Then Payson buried his head in his hands and started sobbing. It was then that Lenox knew he was safe.

"I did in a way. I might as well have," he said, choking back a sob. Looking up, he asked, "What gave me away?"

It had been the voice, in the end. What Lenox had at first mistaken for an Oxford polish in the lad's accent had in fact been the tones of a cosmopolitan and aristocratic young man. Then there was the puzzling nature of the second line of ash. As they had been discussing it, Lenox had noticed for the first time how genuinely out of key it was. Why would Payson have made the line of ash in the meadow *before* Dabney died, when he fully expected to stay there? The only solution was that he had left it as a clue *after* he had first realized the seriousness of his position—that is, after Dabney's death.

Then there was the hair. Shorn from the entire body, McConnell had said. Why? *Because*

George Payson's hair was red. It was too easily identifiable. And then, the decomposition of the body had made reliance upon the corpse's clothing and accessories for identification necessary . . .

Lenox explained this. Then he said, "You must have shaved Dabney's head and body after he died. That's when you would have seen that you were the real target, and that if you died the heat would subside a little bit."

"It was the hardest thing I ever had to do. Poor Dabs. He was the greatest, noblest friend you can imagine, Mr. Lenox. When I was pretending to be him last night, everything I said was absolutely true in a strange way. I did tell him he couldn't come, and he did insist on it. But I had to shave his body. Even knowing that it would nearly kill my mother—have you seen my mother? is she bearing up?—and that his parents would have false hope. But it felt as if I was desecrating him, somehow. It was awful."

"The decomposition?"

Payson looked at him glassily. "There are always foxes out in the meadow at night. I knew that . . . trusted in it." A tear dropped from his eye.

"Perhaps we had better go back to the beginning, then," said Lenox softly. "Or the middle, at any rate. How did Dabney die?"

"As I said I had. I went into town for food—

again as I said. I thought of it as an adventure, not anything we would get hurt over. I was scared, to be certain, but I was excited as well. At any rate. I went into town and came back with food, and I saw the man fleeing through the thicket. He looked behind him, but I could only just see his face."

"What did he look like?"

"In his forties, probably. He had graying hair, and he wore the kind of suit that always looks like a uniform, if you see what I mean. As if he were a waiter or a valet or something like that."

"What did you do?"

"I chased him, and then—well, you know what I did as well as I do myself, just as you know why I left the clues. I took his body into the middle of the meadow where there would be a great deal of foot traffic and left behind my little clues."

The lad sobbed again, trying to hold it back, and strangely enough the genuine sorrow that had convinced Lenox that Bill Dabney was innocent now did the same for George Payson. After the initial shock of realizing the lad was an impostor, Lenox could see the brilliance of what he had done. It was much safer at this moment to be Bill Dabney than George Payson, and how could he have known whether to trust Lenox? Stamp had, but Stamp also hadn't realized the full implications of Payson's position.

"Take me farther back. Why is this all happening? Who are these men? What did your father do to them? Who is Geoffrey Canterbury?"

With a deep breath to collect himself, Payson told his tale. "Most of those questions I can't answer, though some of them I can. That's one of the reasons I'm so anxious to go to this meeting tomorrow evening. I need to find out the truth myself.

"About two weeks ago I received a strange letter in the post from a man asking to meet me at a pub called the Crown in Didcot, a few miles away. The long walks, as you pointed out—I was counting on somebody thinking it was unusual of me to take a long walk when I put out the stick and the shoes. I do love that walking stick, by the way. My grandfather was a terrific chap.

"It was a cryptic and slightly mad letter, but I had to go for a plain enough reason. It made mention of my father, which I simply couldn't resist. My father died when I was so young, and people have always reacted so strangely to his name, that for me he holds a talismanic fascination. My shame, my pride—I'm not sure what he is. Perhaps it's the same way with all men and their fathers."

"What did the letter say specifically?"

"That the author of it—he called himself Canterbury, as you know, though he readily conceded that it was a false name—had known my father when they served together in India."

"You went to the meeting, then."

"Yes. The evening after I received the request."

"What did he look like?"

"Not really remarkable in any way. He had dark hair, a scar on his throat, and a military posture. As he had in the letter, he seemed slightly mad."

It was a dead-on description of Lysander except for madness, which might have been feigned. But why warn the lad? Was Lysander playing both sides against the middle? Did he have some old loyalty to James Payson?

"And what did he tell you?"

"He was very mysterious at first, but in the end it came out that he knew of a group called the September Society, a club of my father's peers from the army, all of whom were leading respectable, quiet lives, and who he said together were some of the most dangerous men in the country."

"What? How?" Lenox wondered whether this had been hyperbole or fact.

"He refused to say. All night long his refrain seemed to be 'I wish I could tell you that, young Mr. Payson, but I cannot. For your own sake and mine.' He must have said just those words six or seven times."

"Did he mention any names?"

"No, he didn't."

"Why did you believe him?"

Payson laughed wearily. "I didn't, not at first. I asked whether he was after money, perhaps. He only chuckled and took out an enormous pocket watch. It was from a London firm and had my father's name engraved on the back. Canterbury said that my father had asked him to keep it for me, but that he was only returning it now—had only returned now, in fact, from India—because of the threat of the Society. Because some anniversary was arriving, or something that I had done—something. It was vague."

Just so, Lenox thought. The pocket watch that the innkeeper who had identified Geoffrey Canterbury had noticed. "That might have been engraved last week, though."

Dabney shook his head. "I don't think so. It looked authentic, for one thing—you'll remember those old watches of the forties—and the inscription was well worn, nearly faded. I have it here."

He took it from his pocket and handed it to Lenox, who examined it closely.

"In addition to which," Payson went on, "Canterbury was simply plausible. He spoke familiarly of my father, the way my grandparents once did. Of his temper, of his winning manners when he was in a good mood, of his impetuousness. It didn't seem at all feigned to me. You may judge my judgment as you will, of course."

"I see. And," he said, handing the watch back,

"it does look authentic. How did you leave it with Canterbury?"

"He said he was going to go to London to look into matters more deeply and advised me to be ready to run at any moment. We agreed on a system of communication to arrange our meetings—"

"The empty letters you received?"

"Yes! How did you—? But yes, we settled on our next meeting every time we saw each other, and the empty letters indicated that the meeting was still on."

"How many times more did you meet?"

"Twice more, in different villages outside of Oxford. Until the night before I was forced to leave."

"That dance card," murmured Lenox. "You sent it down as a blind, with a separate note explaining that if he signed it Roland Light, your scout's name, it would appear incidental."

"Exactly. My, you really are omniscient."

"On the contrary, I'm as slow as the milk train."

"Canterbury wrote to me saying that he needed to see me urgently, and we agreed to meet at the Jesus ball. I was too nervous to dance or have anything like fun. We met, and he told me that I had to flee."

"Did he give a reason?"

"No, he didn't, but he seemed genuinely panicked."

"I see." Was it Lysander? *Why?* "Why did you meet with Hatch just before you left? At Shotter's?"

"Ah, there you've found one of the small secrets I was concealing, Mr. Lenox. I don't need anybody else hurt over me or my father."

(Was there bitterness in this last word? Hopes of some further knowledge of his missing parent dashed?)

"What do you mean?"

"Professor Hatch was the only person I told about Canterbury, except Dabs. I had been sitting with him one morning on the lawns and it had just burst out of me, in fact. Old Hatch was a brick about it, a real brick. He talked me through all of the possibilities. He encouraged me to talk about things—about feelings—that I never had before."

"And that morning?"

"I was in a panic. I had agreed to meet with him the night before, and I sent a note over suggesting Shotter's—a townie place, not many students or dons there, which I always rather liked. He met me, and I told him what I meant to do."

"Then you rushed back to your rooms, saw your mother . . . tell me, did you kill Longshanks?"

Payson shook his head. "He was dying. We had taken him, Dabs and I, out to one of the country vets round about Oxford, and he had cancer, poor chap. I loved that cat like a brother . . ."

"So you fed him laudanum?"

"He was in my lap the entire time, as trusting as he could be, the dear thing . . . you know, it's funny, but I feel near tears again. All of it's so bound up in my mind . . . my father, Dabney . . . this ridiculous cat." The lad covered his face.

"And you stabbed the cat with your father's letter opener, left a message beneath in public school cross-tip—and then you saw your mother in the courtyard?"

"Yes, precisely. I suppose she told you that. I put her off with some excuse. I know it seems cruel, but I knew she would set the alarms, and I needed people to know I was in danger—though what kind of danger I didn't really know."

"And Hatch brought you a parcel, later that day?"

"Yes—but how . . . yes, he did, down south of Christ Church Meadow. He came and said that if I was going to be obstinate I might as well have some help. The parcel had some food in it, a few other necessities, a bit like the packages one used to get in school, you know."

"Then it might be he who betrayed you."

"Never! He specifically said he'd keep our secret till the grave. Said a few cheery words, and then wished Bill and me good luck. Bill!"

Here Payson stifled a sob. Lenox looked past him toward the sunny streets, lost deep in thought.

CHAPTER FORTY-EIGHT

The two men spoke until nightfall, as Lenox gently pushed Payson to fill out his story with more detail. By the time they were done a part of the mystery was gone—the irrelevant part. All the clues Lenox had so ingeniously gathered and speculated about fit tidily into Payson's explanations.

But the larger question loomed. What was the nature of the history between Payson's father and his old battalion mates that it had such force twenty years into the future? That ostensibly reasonable men would kill for it?

As he went to sleep that evening Lenox felt a number of things. He was sorry for the loyal Bill Dabney and his parents; he was apprehensive about the Society's meeting; and in some small part of his mind he was relieved that it would all be over soon. It had been a strange and laborious case, doubled in anxiousness for him because Lady Jane was still so far from being his wife.

The next morning he wrote letters to McConnell and Jenkins. To the inspector he wrote a succinct summation of his plan, forgoing any mention of his young visitor, and asked him to be on hand somewhere outside in case either there was an arrest to be made or the plan collapsed. The note to McConnell was shorter and affectionate; in it Lenox proffered another adventure, gave the time and location where he could probably find Jenkins, and advised him not to come. *You are going to be a father,* Lenox wrote, and though he knew it to be beneath him felt once more a pang of jealousy, *and it's better that you give up being shot at or manhandled just for now.* He also wrote to Rosie Little, aching to tell her about George Payson, but bound to keep his secret—and hers, of course, for he hadn't mentioned Rosie to George.

Five o'clock approached rapidly. Lenox and Payson had lunch together and discussed their plan, agreeing to hide in separate parts of the September Society's main room so that if one were exposed the other might at least have a chance of remaining concealed. Lenox tried again to convince his young friend to stay behind, but Payson was grimly determined to participate. One way or the other, he said, he would see it through to the end. There was no backing out of it now.

Lenox's last act before they left was to write a note to Lady Annabelle, who after all had set him on this course. He told Mary, "Send this the moment I signal you to, please." It bore the tidings of her son's resurrection.

Finally, at a few minutes before five, the two set out in soft-soled shoes, charcoal gray suits, which were meant to look inconspicuous, though Payson's borrowed one was too large for him, and low-brimmed caps. At the Royal Oak, Hallowell was waiting for them at a front table. He looked extremely nervous.

"Not here," he said. "Wait a moment and then follow me out."

They regrouped in a low doorway in the alley-way outside.

"Who is this?" Hallowell asked.

"My assistant. He may prove indispensable."

"I agreed to hide you, Mr. Lenox. Two people simply won't work."

Payson piped up. "I'll find a place to hide. It's important."

Gradually they talked Hallowell around. With great reluctance he took them to the back gate of the Biblius Club's garden and unlatched the door.

"The Biblius will all be out tonight, as I mentioned to you once before, Mr. Lenox."

They went upstairs the back way, along the stairs that attached the kitchen to the two clubs' respective dining rooms. The September Society's dining room was small and comfortable without much decoration, a plain place.

The main room of the club was not.

It was a wide, long, high-ceilinged room, and

every surface in it was covered with artifacts of the Far East. There were ornate, painted clay pipes, old tin lamps, portraits of the Earl of Elgin, Lord Amherst, and a number of other British Viceroys of India, bolts of decorative cloth along every surface, old and battered service rifles (Lenox noted, thinking of Matte, the gun expert) hanging from the walls, and in one corner of the room a life-sized sculpture of a tiger with bared teeth. While Hallowell fretfully asked them where they meant to hide, Lenox and Payson took a short look at all of it. There was no question of the worth and quality of the objects. They had the usual value of imperial plunder.

It took no time at all to find two hiding places. Lenox meant to stay behind the thick, dark curtains in front of the window; Hallowell assured him that they would remain closed for the secretive meeting, and even if they were opened he would remain concealed. Payson chose a spot behind a massive wardrobe only five feet or so from where Lenox would hide. It was angled into a corner and had a triangle of space behind it that he could slide into. A clearly relieved Hallowell left them without much in the way of politeness, and Lenox and Payson, both armed, nervous, and bored, settled down for a long whispered conversation.

The hours passed agonizingly slowly. The edge of apprehension in the air gave the time an aura of adventure, but as the minutes crept by the feeling dissipated. At last they had been there two hours with only two to go; then suddenly there was only an hour to go, and their whispers grew hesitant and even softer; then there was half an hour to go before the meeting, and neither of them dared speak; and then, just as they both began to die a little, there was a footfall in the front hallway.

It was a thrilling, terrifying moment.

Lenox didn't recognize the man's face—he was just able to see the left half of the room—but he was obviously a member, of the right age, with the same military bearing Lysander had. Perhaps this was the enigmatic Theophilus Butler?

It took fifteen minutes for the rest of the members to arrive, first in ones and twos and then in a great flood. Lenox could hear himself breathing and tried desperately to quiet himself. While the majority of the men drank glasses of wine and traded stories, at the far end of the room, away from the windows, a smaller group was in deep conversation. Lenox guessed that these were to be the meeting's conductors. Among them he recognized only Maran.

Lysander wasn't anywhere to be seen.

In all there were twenty-two men present. Every one of them had the well-fed appearance of a contented middle age, far removed from the battlegrounds of the East. They scarcely looked dangerous—merely self-satisfied, lords of all they surveyed, a mood Lenox knew could be dangerous in itself. They looked like the kind of men who could justify any action to themselves, given a moment or two.

It was Maran who opened the meeting.

"Welcome back," he said. "You are all very welcome indeed. In a moment I'll turn this meeting over to Major Butler." He nodded at a doughy, narrow-eyed gentleman standing just behind him. "But first, please raise your glasses in a toast to the 12th Suffolk 2nd, in a toast to India, and in a toast to September."

The men drank each other's health, and then Butler stepped forward. Whether it was prejudice or not, Lenox didn't like the look of him.

"Gentlemen, how do you do?" His voice was startlingly high-pitched, with a cold maliciousness obvious in its slightly giddy, laughing tones. "This meeting finds us all in good moods. Our income is consistent, our plans move along smoothly, and Maran has done his work admirably."

A small ovation went up at this.

"There is only one situation of real concern to report on, as you are all aware."

A murmur of agreement and alarm moved around the room. "But our junior friend has handled it, hasn't he? All's set up just at this moment, isn't it?" A small man, tiny, wrinkled, and sun-baked, said this.

"Yes, it's all been smoothed over. But there's another aspect to the problem. A man we all once knew has indeed returned to London, and his problematic reappearance has only one solution. I trust that we all know what that solution is and remain in concord as to its execution."

"Hear, hear" went up the cry.

"We must find him and kill him."

Lenox's blood chilled. He understood very little of what Butler was saying, but here was tangible proof of what they had known from the start: that this Society was capable of murder.

"Yes, but where is he?" said a member from the side of the room.

"We know that he has left Oxford."

Returned to London? They were obviously talking about Canterbury—but did that mean that Canterbury wasn't Lysander? Where was Lysander?

"Where would he hide in London?"

Butler waved his hand. "The key is Dabney."

"No!" said several people at once, and several excited side conversations broke out.

"Can we end this farce?" said the man at the side of the room. "The solution to our problem is here with us, isn't it?"

Butler said mildly, "I thought it might not hurt to discuss our plans before that, but yes, as you wish." He turned to the door. "Friend, step in!" he shouted.

And with a sickening thud Lenox realized what had happened.

But our junior friend has handled it, hasn't he? All's set up just at this moment, isn't it?

Tomorrow, then. Meet me here tomorrow at five in the afternoon.

Can we end this farce? The solution to our problem is here with us, isn't it?

The man obviously had a brightness and quickness that were going to waste in his job. The perfect spy, in other words.

It was Hallowell.

"Oh, Lord," Lenox said softly, unable to help himself. He tried to signal out the window for Jenkins, but didn't know if it had worked.

"Come in, come in," Butler said genially. "Where did you say they were?"

Hallowell's voice was loud and clear, with none of the frightened quiver it had when he had left them to hide in the room. "Behind the curtain and the wardrobe respectively, Major."

"Thank you, Lance Corporal," said Butler. "Will you do the honors?"

"Dabney, run!" Lenox shouted.

His words were cut off as the bullet struck him.

CHAPTER FORTY-NINE

Lenox fell out from behind the curtain and into plain view, and although he was in pain he was conscious. It was obvious that there was some commotion at the door, a thudding. He saw Hallowell move the gun toward the wardrobe where Payson was concealed, and then saw somebody burst into the room and tackle the doorman.

It was Dallington.

Following on his heels were Jenkins and half a dozen police constables. Lenox reached futilely for his gun while the twenty-two members of the September Society raised their hands in bewilderment.

It only took a moment for Jenkins to calm the situation down, despite Butler's and Maran's repeated, slightly hysterical claims that Lenox had trespassed on private property and that he was a burglar. At the same time, Dallington rushed over to Lenox and kneeled beside him.

"Where did they get you?" he said. His eyes were rimmed red with a hangover, but he seemed alert and energetic.

"How did you get here?"

"Look, Lenox, I'm sorry about yesterday. I don't

even remember seeing you. A relapse. It won't happen again."

Lenox laughed wryly. The pain was starting to become more intense. "Don't mention it. How did you find us?"

"McConnell."

Just then Lenox saw McConnell rushing up, a look of deep concern on his face and his battered leather medical bag in his hand. "Charles, good God, you're shot! Where did they get you?"

"My chest, it went just between my chest and my left arm."

McConnell tore away the shirt and then breathed a sigh of relief. "Thank the Lord, Charles, only a grazing wound. Painful, but you'll survive it."

Dallington was everywhere, pointing out various members of the September Society, directing Jenkins and the constables, barking at Hallowell as he searched his pockets.

As McConnell went about bandaging the detective up, Payson began to come out, but Lenox motioned him to stay behind the cupboard. Jenkins came over and had a word: Everybody in the room would be taken as a witness, to begin with, except for Hallowell. He would be charged with attempted murder—and, if Lenox had anything to do with it, the murder of Bill Dabney. What had Payson said about the man he had seen running from Dabney's body? Dressed as if he were a valet or a waiter, graying hair. The description matched.

After the bandage had gone on securely, Lenox stood up and staggered to the couch, where he sat down heavily.

"We still have something to do," he told Jenkins, who had just come over as the members of the September Society filed out.

"What?"

"Canterbury. I know where he is."

"Where?"

"I don't want to say too much, in case I'm wrong."

But he knew he wasn't. There was a surprise left in the case yet, even after all this drama.

"I'll have to stop off and see my brother to get the address. George," Lenox went on, calling to Payson, "you had better come, too."

"George?" said Jenkins, and as Payson emerged from his hiding place an astonished Dallington said, "Payson! Good God!"

Payson said, "Is that you, Dallington? Haven't seen you since last fall. How did you come to be mixed up in this?"

"Gentlemen," said Lenox, "George Payson."

Briefly Lenox explained the past week of the lad's life.

"What a blow to Dabney's parents," said McConnell, grimacing.

Payson looked down at his feet. "I wish I could

have done it all differently," he said. It was the final hint of a reproach anyone made.

Questions all answered—Jenkins in particular had a few points he wanted cleared up—about fifteen minutes later Lenox, Jenkins, McConnell, Dallington, and Payson left. Jenkins had given his constables detailed instructions about the care of the prisoners and witnesses at the scene, and McConnell had checked on Lenox's wound and reluctantly pronounced the detective fit to move.

They took McConnell's carriage to Parliament, and Lenox dashed inside and had a word with Edmund. They came out a moment later together, and Edmund joined the miniature carnival. As they bumped along eastward, Lenox smiled inwardly. Only yesterday he had considered himself all alone in this endeavor, and now he was surrounded by friends and allies.

"I was stupid to trust Hallowell," Lenox said. "From the beginning he was so eager to speak with me. I assumed he was simply bored with his job, but the Society must have seen me before I saw them, so to speak—must have had their handyman out to meet me for precisely such a scenario."

"I wonder that you thought of it before he came in," Payson said.

"Still, not quickly enough. It wasn't a total loss, though, thanks to Dallington. We overheard them talking cold-bloodedly of murder. And if I'm not very much mistaken there are two serious financial crimes involved—one ancient and one ongoing—which we'll learn about shortly."

Pressed for more though he was, Lenox refused to say anything further in case he was mistaken. He had an idea of what had happened, but he knew the man calling himself Canterbury would be able to tell the story definitively.

If the West End part of London was unique in all the world, the height of cosmopolitan fashion, the East End was like the slums of Paris, of Cairo, of New York, of Vienna. There were the same narrow, darkened streets, the same low-lit pubs with their constant suggestion of imminent violence, the same ragpickers and children turning cartwheels for halfpence. They were coming into Gracechurch Street now, in the ward of Bishopsgate. Though it was violent and falling to pieces, Lenox had a peculiar affection for it and visited from time to time, for one reason: It was more or less the epicenter of the old Roman settlement of Londinium. The basilica, or public church (the biggest of its kind north of the Alps), and the forum had both run along it in those ancient days, and while they were gone Lenox could still picture them. At its pinnacle in the second century A.D., Londinium had been a civilized, fascinating, and cultured outpost of the empire. It was one of Lenox's favorite subjects within Roman history, combining as it did the remote and the familiar.

The carriage turned up Cannon Street and into Eastcheap. When they reached a low-slung red building with two torches blazing out front, Edmund nodded his head to his brother, and the carriage halted.

The ground floor inside the building was undivided, one large room with its roof held up by beams. In one part was a gin bar, where men and women flirted with each other and drank. In another was a curtained-off area where the same women could conduct their business. To the back of the room was a stairwell, which led to the rooms upstairs. At the center of it all, a wizened old woman with a monocle and a cat on her lap presided over the scene, collecting money from the girls, monitoring the bar for any arguments that might get out of hand, and barking commands to two large men who kept it all in order.

Lenox and Edmund went to her and had a whispered word. At first she shook her head furiously; then Lenox pointed to Jenkins, and the woman threw her hands up, as if conceding the point, and told them something.

The two brothers went back to the group.

"On the third floor. I'll lead, if you'll stick by my side, Jenkins. I doubt you'll have any cause to use your shackles, but it's not impossible. George, come up beside me, won't you? You've met Canterbury before, I believe."

There were two doors on the third floor. Lenox led the way to the right and knocked.

"Hullo?" There was no response. "Hullo? Canterbury? We've a large group here. George is here."

There was a shuffling in the room.

"I'm going to come in," said Lenox. "We don't mean you any harm, I promise."

Lenox turned the doorknob, and they all crowded around him to see inside. It was a large, drafty, out-of-sorts room with a bed, a desk, and a chair as its only adornments. A man—dark hair, average height, a military bearing, with a scar on his neck—sat in the chair. He was holding a revolver.

"Stand back!" he said. "Who—why, is that Charles Lenox?"

"It is."

"And Edmund? Good Lord! No wonder you found me here. My old haunt. Who have you brought, though?" The gun, which he had let fall to his lap, rose again.

"Please, please—the Society are all in police custody."

A great burden seemed to lift from Canterbury's face. He exhaled. "Thank God," he said. "It's over."

"Not yet." Lenox turned around. "George, come here, won't you?"

Payson came to the front. "Hullo, Mr. Canterbury," he said.

"No, George," said Lenox softly. "I'd like to introduce you to your father."

CHAPTER FIFTY

Lenox and Edmund's own father had been a good man, one who took care of his land, ruled judiciously over local disputes, served in Parliament for fifty years, and loved his wife and his two sons. When Lenox was young he had admired in his father the high seriousness of purpose, the goal of service to Queen and country, that had defined his public life. Now he wasn't sure that he didn't admire something else more: his father's good spirits, his cheerfulness, his ability to make things seem better. What had once almost seemed frivolous to Lenox, when he was young and serious himself, had now come to seem heroic, a putting of others before one's self. It was strange to him that his perception of his father went on changing even after the old man's death.

Greeted with his own father, Payson showed

the shock in his face. "How do you do?" he said feebly.

The father rose. "I didn't know whether or not to tell you, George," he said. "I had to make amends here first."

It was Dallington who said, "Perhaps we should withdraw."

So he, McConnell, Lenox, Edmund, and Jenkins went into the hallway for about ten minutes and studiously ignored the muffled voices through the door. At the end of that time the younger Payson came out, tears on his face, and invited them to come back into the room.

"How did you know?" he asked Lenox straight away.

"I had assumed for a long while that Geoffrey Canterbury was a man named John Lysander, a member of the September Society."

"Lysander!" spat out the elder Payson.

"It never quite added up. Why would he have been helping you? But there was the description to go on, and in particular the scar. Which I assume you'll tell us about, George? Why the two of you had identical scars? When Lady Annabelle came to me it was the first thing I remembered about you. To have forgotten it so promptly was shameful on my part, though in my defense I believed you to be dead . . . and then while you and I were hiding at that meeting, Payson, we heard Butler mention 'an old friend unexpectedly returned.' It was then that I remembered the scar, and combining that fact with the pocket watch . . . it simply seemed inevitable once I started to think about it."

"Hardly inevitable, I should have said."

"But why this sudden interest in the son of a long-dead man? They must have hoped to draw your father out by threatening you, killing you, whatever they planned to do. At any rate, I remembered that your father had once haunted this famous Eastcheap establishment, and guessed that if he were to lie low it would be here."

"Famous for it," said Edmund. "He was here night and day."

"Voluntarily then, involuntarily now," added James Payson. "This is the only place in London that I know inside and out, besides the Beefsteak Club." He laughed. "And that might have been conspicuous."

"I couldn't remember the address or the name, but Edmund did, and so here we are."

"And all extremely anxious to discover the origin of this entire horrible matter," said Jenkins.

The elder Payson sighed and lifted his eyes to the half-ring of men standing around him. His hand was in his son's.

Then he spoke. "It's a simple enough story," he said. "Or rather, two simple enough stories, one old, one new, the two of them intertwined. Any

Englishman who has left this island for the wider empire can tell you that terrible things are done in the name of the Queen, bless her. A little less than twenty years ago, just after you were born, George, and just between the Anglo-Sikh wars, I took part in one of those atrocities.

"My battalion and I were monitoring an area along the Sutlej Frontier in Punjab, and if I never lay eyes on it again it will be too soon. There were about thirty thousand troops there—it was our most important strategic position in India, you see, geographically, politically, and culturally—and we always got by far the best of the few little local skirmishes. We had won the first Anglo-Sikh war handily, and though the locals resented us we ruled with a firm hand. As a result, I and the other officers led an idle life there. Each of us had a small house and four or five native servants, and there was always a card game or a drink to be had in the officers' mess. Despite the heat, which none of us liked, it wasn't a bad kip.

"I was still pretty wild then, I'm afraid—Edmund and Charles remember me from Oxford—and my best friend in all of India was another like me, a man named Juniper. He wasn't in the army, though. He was an orphan, all alone in the world, with a few hundred pounds he had inherited, and when he came of age he set out for Lahore to make his fortune. The two of us drank together, hunted together, and even lived in the same house for some time together. They called us the twins, because there was some slight resemblance between us and because we were so inseparable.

"As you can gather, it wasn't too bad a life. I had a close friend, all the gin I wanted, some shooting, and a game of cards most evenings. But then one day I did something foolish.

"I was chappy enough with John Lysander at the time, and one evening the two of us and an official of the East India Company attached to our battalion—a lad named Simon Halloran, as green as he could be—decided to venture into the strictly Punjabi part of Lahore. An adventure, we figured. Well, at the first teahouse we stopped into we were kidnapped by (you'll scarcely credit this) a group of about ten boys, all of them armed to the teeth. They blindfolded us and led us out into the countryside. I've always had a keen enough sense of direction, and though they tried to turn us around and confuse us I knew which way we were going. Mark that—it comes back in a moment.

"Well, it was a hairy enough situation. The head of the village these boys belonged to searched us all over and eventually decided to send a message to the Queen by killing one of us. As you can no doubt guess, it was Halloran—nonmilitary, I suppose. He cut Halloran's throat right in front of our eyes, and for good measure gave Lysander and myself identical cuts, to mark us out as dangerous to his fellow tribesmen."

Payson's hand went to his throat.

"It raised a terrible ruckus back at camp, as goes without saying, and as I knew where this village was we received permission to go capture this headman who had decided to kill Halloran. Well, we did go back, and—well, the less we say of it, the better." His eyes looked ghostly as he said this. "We're not allowed to take back anything in this life, and we did what we did, you see.

"In the end it was three nonofficers who came across the village headman. My batman, Major Butler's batman, and a clever lance corporal named Hallowell. They came and fetched the officers—all of us bloody and exhausted, about twenty-five of us—and when we entered the tent we saw that somehow this small village had amassed an absolutely remarkable treasure. There were chests of rubies, bags of uncut diamonds, gold, silver, piles and piles of the stuff. Most spectacular of all was the largest, purest sapphire I've ever seen, perhaps the largest sapphire in the world. As large as a hawk's egg."

Softly, Lenox muttered, "September's birthstone."

The elder Payson turned to him. "Yes, that's right. Welcome to the little joke. This raid took place in September, and the name must have seemed inevitable. In any event, there was an instant unanimous decision. We would take it, never tell the army, and retire back to England rich men. All of us officers, and the three non-officers, too.

"But there was a problem. Another official of the East India Company, Halloran's boss. An older, white-haired fellow named Braithwaite, who stepped in straight away and claimed the money as the company's. From which he would receive a finder's fee, of course.

"One thing to understand about our battalion: We were the left behind. They were all like me, wild, angry, driven out of England by their behavior. A little pirate ship out in the desert. Well, it didn't take any time at all for them to decide to kill Braithwaite. Only two of us stood against it. Captain Larch and myself. Larch put his foot down; I simply said that I wouldn't be a part of it. Larch and Braithwaite died—victims of the battle, as it was later presented, both with their throats cut—and I lived. In fact, in official regiment history Larch and I are the only dead officers of our particular era . . .

"Fortunately Juniper and I had long planned to return to London on six months' leave, and almost immediately we left. I hoped it would all blow over—I think I saw both of you then, Charles and Edmund, and more importantly I saw you, George, beautiful infant that you were

—but when we returned, nothing was forgotten, and the next few weeks were the worst of my life. A dozen times I wished I had gone along with the plan. All of them would be rich, not a single one of them was speaking to me, and I knew that all of them doubted my staying silent.

"The blow fell pretty quickly. I was out hunting with Juniper, the only friend I had left for five thousand miles in any direction. We were in a growth of scrub about a mile away from the campsite, trying to track a flock of birds, when Hallowell ambushed us from about ten yards away. He shot Juniper dead on the spot and then fired at me. I wasn't hit, but I fell, hoping to fool him. And I did. Hallowell ran off. I listened to his footsteps receding . . ." He took a breath. "I often think about Juniper, all alone in the world as he was. His death wasn't worthy of him.

"I saw straight away that I had an opportunity to escape. I had never been that fond of the military, and now India was too hot to hold me. So I ran back to camp, careful to avoid notice, and grabbed my uniform and a few of my things—pictures from home and so forth, you can imagine—and went about the ugly, bloody job of changing Juniper into me."

"What about the scar?" McConnell asked.

"That was the catch, of course. But leave anything out in the scrub of India long enough and some animal will get interested. Juniper was

unrecognizable when they found him. To discourage any rumors—either of suicide or murder
—Lysander and Butler made up a story about me
getting shot over cards by a native. Preposterous,
of course, but they shouted it from the rooftops.
One thing they couldn't hide was the state of my
body."

"The third page of that report we saw, Thomas,"
said Lenox, looking up at his friend. "It must
have described the decomposition."

It was eerie for Lenox, to hear two tales so
similar from a father and son. Both had lost their
friends. Both had gone on the run. Both had
behaved cannily. And both had avoided death.
For now, anyway.

He shifted in his seat uncomfortably, the
wound in his chest still painful, and waited for
Payson to go on.

CHAPTER FIFTY-ONE

W here did you go?" asked Dallington curiously.

"China. I had a good deal of money because I
had just been paid six months' wages, and I
went to Shanghai and found work. It wasn't
long before I became pretty useful to a few
important gentlemen there—well, it's a story for

another time. I'm long since retired by now."

Here was the crucial question. "But then why return?" asked Lenox. "Why was the Society interested in your son when they knew you to be dead?"

"Wilson," said Payson.

"Wilson?"

"It was the worst luck you could possibly have. I had come back to England because I couldn't stand being away from George any longer. I thought I would find somewhere quiet to live, perhaps in northern Scotland, and watch my boy from afar. One day this summer I had to see him, and I went to Lincoln. And on High Street I saw Wilson, there with his son. It was only for a split second, but he knew it was me. I could see it in his eyes.

"Only Lysander and Hallowell had known— or thought they knew—Juniper to be alive, still. It must have been a right shock to old Wilson. So he ran off and told the Society."

"How do you know?" asked Jenkins.

"He wasn't a bad chap, Wilson. Certainly not the worst of them. He told them about me, but when they began to consider killing George, he found a way to pass George a note. I was living in Oxford by then, and with the help of Red Kelly, whom I had known long ago in my early days in the army, when our regiments had trained together—an old gambler and drinker, Red—"

"I was going to ask after him," said Lenox. "A friend of yours back then?"

"The most loyal friend I had. My private. When he was wounded I found him a job as a porter at Lincoln—not that I had had a glittering career there, but still, the Payson name carried some weight."

"Red! See, Lenox—I knew he knew something!" The young George Payson said this excitedly to Lenox. "He was the one who passed me the notes from Canterbury! How did he help you, Dad?"

"Passed Wilson's note addressed to you on to me. It warned you to leave Oxford. I knew then that he had told the Society, and that they had resolved on killing you to draw me out. I was dangerous to them. Still am, I suppose."

"And Wilson died for his troubles," said McConnell.

"Precisely," Lenox agreed.

"The rest is plain enough to you, I suppose. It became my only aim, my only concern in life, to save my son. But I didn't dare tell you who I was, George. I didn't want you to know I was still alive, in case they came after you with questions. The only way I could show you how I felt was that damned pocket watch."

"No, Dad, I loved it. It gave me hope while I was out there running."

As the father and son looked at each other,

tears brimming in the eyes of both, there was a strange silence in the room; perhaps the silence of sons thinking about their own fathers.

"At least you're both safe now," said Jenkins, with a great sigh.

Then a startling voice spoke from behind them in a tone full of hatred. "Are they? Can you be sure of that, Inspector?"

It was Lysander. And he had a gun.

Of course, thought Lenox. That's why I missed him at the meeting. He stayed back in case something precisely like this happened.

"Well, Lysander," he said. "You have us at your mercy."

But the detective spoke too hastily.

Lysander had seen all but one of them— McConnell, obscured by the door Lysander had opened, in one swift, athletic movement that made Lenox grateful for all the doctor's games of polo and golf, slammed the door into Lysander and pounced on the shocked man as he fell. The gun screamed into the surprised silence of the room and fired one harmless bullet into the wall.

After that it took a great deal of time to sort everything out, and by then the pain in Lenox's chest was more and more intense. McConnell gave him a solution in water from his medical kit, which helped slightly. Still, though, he decided that Jenkins could handle the questioning for that evening.

Just then, two constables came clattering up the stairs and into the room. Only one of them spoke, a small, strong-looking chap.

"Inspector Jenkins, sir, begging a moment of your time."

"Yes, Constable Roland?"

"During our search of the club's premises, we found something, sir." Here Roland paused.

"Well?"

"Lawrence and I have brought it—here you are, sir. Among a great lot of treasure hidden in the wall."

Here the constable, who had probably never seen more than twenty pounds put together in his life, pulled from his pocket a large, sparkling, pristine sapphire, of the darkest blue.

They had all heard James Payson refer to the stone; nevertheless, there was a sharp intake of breath across the room.

It was McConnell who spoke at last. "Not my area," he said softly, "and I wouldn't claim any special knowledge—but—but do you think I could hold it, for a moment, Constable? Thank you, thank you." He accepted it on his handkerchief. "My God, my God! It's four times the size of the Star of Bombay! Look at this rock! Insoluble, infusible, and above all perfectly faceted! My God!"

The whole room watched the doctor.

"There are only four truly precious stones," he

went on. "Emeralds, diamonds, and rubies—which are only red sapphires—and then these . . . it would be impossible to put a price on it! I don't think the headman of that village scavenged this, Mr. Payson . . . this must have come down through the generations. Look how perfectly it's cut! Why, there aren't a dozen people on this planet who can afford this, and only a handful more governments! Well, thank you for letting me see it," he said, handing the sapphire to Jenkins. "Thank you from the bottom of my heart."

Everybody in the room took turns examining it until finally Jenkins and the two constables bore it to a waiting brougham with a holy air. ("And you brought it to the heart of Eastcheap, you fathead?" said Jenkins.) Then the group sorted themselves out and arranged their departure.

What a strange matter it had been! Full of mistaken identity and misplaced trust. Even at this early stage Lenox could admit to himself that it had been one of his poorer efforts—marked by minor successes and major lapses. He couldn't blame himself entirely, though. He had been in love.

In the end it was Dallington who took him back to Hampden Lane. McConnell had freshly dressed his bandages and given him several packets of the pain solution, along with a promise to come by early the next morning, but he had been anxious to go home and check on Toto. They had finally settled on a name that both of them liked: Bella McConnell. It was a beautiful name, Lenox agreed—beautiful enough even to justify all the arguments that came before it.

In the carriage Dallington spoke quietly. "Will you make it through the night, then? Your wound, I mean."

"Oh, yes, I should say so. For which you deserve a great deal of the credit."

"I was pretty dashing, wasn't I?" said the young man with the first sign of his old grin. "Still, I'm sorry to have made it as close as it was."

As he climbed the stairs of his house, Lenox felt sore, relieved, and exhausted—but on the fringe of those feelings was a sort of affection as well. In this short, fraught time he had come to be truly fond of Dallington.

Graham still hadn't come home, and so in the front hallway it was Mary who exclaimed over his wound and took his overcoat. A cheerful constable named Addington was there as well and promised to stay the night. Lenox thanked him, asked Mary to find him some food, and then turned up the hallway toward the prospect of a nice smoke and some time alone in his library. It would be paradise, he thought.

But a different kind of paradise awaited him there. When Mary opened the doors Lenox saw that Lady Jane was sitting on the sofa, not even pretending to read.

"Oh, Charles!" she said, rising and rushing to his side. "Come sit next to me. Are you comfortable? Is it true what Addington says, you've been shot? Charles, how could you?"

Here she burst into unrestrained tears, which fell down her pale cheeks in little rivers. She clasped his hand tightly in hers. All the awkwardness of their last meeting was forgotten, and their old ease returned.

Laughing a little, Lenox said, "I'm awfully sorry. But it's not even bleeding any longer, look!"

She laughed, too, in a hiccupping way, her spent nerves spilling over, and dried her eyes with Lenox's handkerchief. In her plain pink dress and blue shawl, her hair falling in curls behind her ears, her large eyes bright and wet, she had never looked more beautiful to her friend. He wasn't sure what he saw precisely—simply some light that began in her and radiated out, which made her golden and lovely. Which made her Jane.

"What was it that happened, Charles?" she said.

"I was foolish enough to hide behind some curtains, and a bullet grazed me just here, between my left arm and my side. McConnell says it won't hurt for more than two or three days, though. More important, did you hear about little Bella?"

She laughed again, and finally her eyes were dry. Still, though, she hadn't let go of his hand. "I like it, don't you?"

"I think it's a perfect name," he agreed.

"Toto's so happy, too."

"And McConnell couldn't wait to find his way home this evening."

Then, suddenly, the conversation stopped. They were still looking into each other's eyes, but for the first time in their long friendship neither of them could say anything. At last Lenox said, "Michael Pierce, the man I met at your house, he was—"

"He asked me to marry him, Charles."

Lenox managed to say, "He seemed like a decent fellow when we met, though it wasn't for long. I would—"

"I said no, of course."

Their hands were still together, their eyes still met.

"Where have you been, Jane? What have you been doing, these past weeks? I feel as if my best friend were a ghost. What were you doing in the Seven Dials?" Preemptively, he added, "I saw you there accidentally, I promise."

"Of course I believe you, Charles. Of course." Hesitantly, gingerly, she went on. "As I told you, Michael is my brother's friend."

"Yes," he said, his heart racing.

"It's simple enough. He was at Eton with my

brother, and they became friends on the rugby pitch—but Michael was always wild, never a very good student. After his classmates went to university, he came to London and became a dilettante, a wastrel. He drank in low and high company alike. He even"—she shuddered—"he behaved badly. Until one night outside a public house in the Seven Dials, when a man named Peter Puddle tried to rob him at knifepoint. Michael was carrying a loaded blackjack and dealt him a blow to the head and—and killed him, Charles."

There was utter silence in the room.

"Michael's uncle, Lord Holdernesse, and my brother were the only two men who knew the secret. Lord Holdernesse arranged his transit to the colonies, and paid Peter Puddle's wife and children a weekly remittance and bought them a small house in the Dials. When he died, my brother began to pay the remittance and took me into his confidence; and for years now, three years I suppose, I've visited them one morning each week.

"At first they were sullenly respectful toward me—then friendlier—and finally a real friendship has sprung up between us. But then Michael returned, last month."

It was all so clear now, Lenox thought.

"He was rich, and wanted to make amends; and since he returned I've been visiting them not in my spare morning hours but nearly every day, trying to broker some kind of peace—to give Michael, whom my brother loves, some sort of redemption."

"You needn't say another word," Lenox answered, "and if I've been rude enough and unkind enough to question you, or make you feel accountable to me—I'm so sorry."

She sighed, tears standing in her eyes. "Then he came along with this absurd proposal of marriage, apparently persuaded of some affection between us that never existed. And of course I said no."

"Of course."

"But oh, Charles, no—don't you see—if he had been perfect, if he had been—"

Lenox, with a strange mixture of courage and happiness roiling in his heart, interrupted her, to say, "You know, for years I've been expecting somebody to come along and marry you. I knew it would be a duke or the Prime Minister or a bishop or somebody. I always look out my window and expect him to be strolling along to your house." He laughed. "And I would have accepted it with good grace, I hope. I knew you deserved the world. But for every moment that I've known you, Jane, for the entire time I've looked out through the window, I've loved you, too. Ardently, and without any anticipation of return. But while I have the courage to say it I must: You are the wisest person I know, and the most beautiful woman I know. And I love you from the bottom of my heart, and—and I want you to be my wife."

Different tears wet her eyes now, and a luminous smile was on her face.

"Will you?" he asked.

"Oh, of course, Charles," she said. "Of course I will."

She put her small hand on his shoulder and lifted her face to him, and they kissed.

CHAPTER FIFTY-TWO

The next few days were the happiest of Lenox's life.

He and Jane took long walks along the river, the sun arching high above, watery, warm, bright, leaves scattering at their feet, as they spoke: spoke again with the same ease and intimacy they always had, but in a way so sweetened by love, so strengthened by the acknowledgment of love, that it seemed the smallest word carried the entire freight of their emotions. They told a few friends, and together had several small dinner parties to announce their engagement. (The happiness of a dinner party! He could scarcely believe how becoming part of a couple changed the pleasures of that ritual.) Toto and McConnell, Dallington and the Duchess of Marchmain,

Cabot and Hilary, these old friends were constantly in and out of their houses, half as if they were already married. Lenox had a long conversation with Graham, a roundabout, reassuring conversation that ended with the two men pulling out a map and planning in great detail their tour of Morocco.

So the days passed, the weeks passed, each moment within them a small perfect crystal of happiness, undaunted by what might come next—the happiness of those living entirely in the present.

A month later, it was truly autumn. Along their little slip of London, leaves were falling at any breeze and the glow of fireplaces shone in every window, while above the high houses birds fell and rose on the cooler drifts of air. There was that note of melancholy in the air that comes briefly when at last summer is really over—when there will be no more exotically warm days interspersed among the colder ones—when finally people pull their collars up against the wind and children submit to heavy sweaters. A pink-cheeked, nightfall time of year, when the light was always diminishing.

The "Oxford and India Scandal," as one paper had taken to calling the Payson case, had for some weeks been the talk of London. At dinner parties people had discussed the strange reappearance of the fearful James Payson and decried his decision to retreat to Scotland with his son; rumors that he was much changed, mellow even, were instantly dismissed. People's hearts lifted when they spoke of Lady Annabelle and fell when the conversation turned to young Bill Dabney, whom the press had cast as the heroic figure in the story, the loyal and unquestioning young Englishman who had laid down his life for friendship. In England there is always a nostalgia for Oxford and Cambridge, almost especially among people who never went there, and so it was Dabney who captured people's hearts. At the funeral, which Lenox and Lady Jane attended, it had been hard to witness his parents' deep and silent midcountry sorrow.

There was one certain memorial for him. The multitude of gems, gold pieces, semiprecious stones, and silver dishes that had lain in the dusty walls of the September Society, and above all the great sapphire that had lain with them, had reverted to the East India Company. Under the strength of popular demand, they had sold the sapphire in an instantly famous auction (to participate required a letter from one's bankers attesting to savings of at least a hundred thousand pounds sterling) to an obscure German count, and donated the proceeds of the sale to Lincoln College, where among other things a seat in classics would be founded in Bill Dabney's name. His father had written the bequest: "To be given to lads of great spirit and loyalty, who possess both the gift of friendship and the dignity of greatness."

Meanwhile the villains of the September Society had long turned against each other, and eventually the greatest offenders were brought to trial. Maran had resigned instantly from Parliament, and the full implications of his corruption were only slowly coming to light. His malfeasance had been at once of a unique and utterly mundane kind: One moment he would be diverting sums to obscure military manufacturers that turned out to be hastily assembled fronts of fellow September Society members, who kicked back to Maran; the next he would be doing something as simple as finding a sinecure in government for the underqualified nephew or cousin of a fellow veteran. These various stratagems to defraud Her Majesty had only begun to be parsed, and it was clear that at least an indirect accomplishment of Lenox's and Goodson's had been to save the country a great deal of money and scandal. In fact, the discovery had put back into broad public favor Lord Russell's reform bill, which called for among other things greater transparency in government spending—and which Lenox had only recently been discussing in that lunch in Parliament with Russell himself.

Lenox had received a note of congratulations

from the Prince of Wales and gone to see His Highness, but turned down the majority of other invitations in favor of nights in with Jane, Toto, and Thomas, the occasional drink with James Hilary or Lord Cabot, and his books—and one celebratory cup of champagne with a newly engaged couple: George Payson and Rosie Little. She had flown to London against her father's wishes when she learned that he was alive and, with more courage than Lenox had suspected of her, laid the truth before Payson. In turn he had confessed that when he had flirted with her at the dances, his intentions had been more serious than she realized. Despite the ire of their parents (Lady Annabelle's moderated by her overwhelming happiness), they were as happy as any people in the world, and determined to be happy their whole lives long. Rosie, for one, viewed Lenox as her closest friend, and it appeared that soon enough he would be godfather to two new children.

And so the case passed from one stage of notoriety to a lower one; and so it passed out of the common conversations of the day, and things were returned to normal.

There had been one black moment: a letter of congratulations from George Barnard, the powerful, rich government official, onetime courter of Lady Jane, and, Lenox knew for certain, criminal mastermind. There was still work to do there—

but he was too happy, for those few days, to contemplate it just yet.

On an afternoon just after the height of the scandal's celebrity, Lenox and Lady Jane were in his library, having lunch. She was telling a story animatedly and laughing when there was a knock at the door outside. Graham, restored to his front hallway at last, answered it. A moment later he appeared with three visitors in tow.

"Sir Edmund Lenox, Mr. Hilary, Mr. Brick," he said, leading them in.

"Thanks," said Lenox and rose to shake their hands. "How do you do, Mr. Brick? I don't believe we've met since we had lunch in Parliament. James, Edmund, how are you? All three of you know Jane, of course."

"Hello, Charles," said Edmund. "Hello, Jane."

"And congratulations, to both of you," added Brick.

"I'll add mine once more, too, just for good measure," said Hilary pleasantly—a Bingley personified, Toto always said. "The springtime, I hear?"

"Yes, that's right," said Lady Jane. "We're awfully happy."

Looking at them, it was plain this was true. The pink in her pale cheeks was a sign of her high spirits. As for Lenox, he seemed to stand a little higher. He had already abandoned most of his bachelor ways with an ease that had surprised him.

"Sorry to barge in, Charles," Edmund said when they were all sitting. "I know you and I were meant to have supper tonight, but as it turns out I'll be in the House. Brick, Hilary, will you speak? I told you a thousand times I didn't want to come."

"Didn't want to come?" said Lenox. "Why on earth not?"

It was Brick who spoke. "He feared the whispers of nepotism. But we're here on the strength of my word—mine, Hilary's, half a dozen other men."

"Look here—what's this about?"

Hilary spoke up, beaming. "We'd like you to run for Parliament, Charles."

"Parliament?"

"There's a by-election soon outside Durham—"

"In Stirrington?" said Lenox.

Brick spoke to Edmund. "There you are," he said. "I thought as much after that lunch—your brother knows politics."

"At Stirrington," Hilary went on. "It wouldn't cost you above eight hundred pounds—a good deal of money, of course, but that's your lookout—and though you'd only be in for eight months or so, when the regular elections came back around you would be excellently situated."

"The Member there is Stoke," said Brick, "and

he's never done a single useful thing in his life, but his first will be to throw his weight behind you pretty heartily. The Stoke name still means something there, so that will be a help to you."

"Parliament?" said Lenox, slightly in shock.

"Yes," said Edmund grumpily. "Don't sit there gaping at us, won't you?"

Lady Jane held Lenox's hand, looking at him. "You ought to, Charles. You've always wanted to."

"Why me?" Lenox asked.

Brick spoke. "You gained my attention when we dined together, as I only just said. Hilary speaks very highly of your acumen—says he often comes to you for advice when the cacophony of voices becomes too jarring."

"Not often," said Lenox. "Certainly not often."

"Lord Cabot specifically mentioned you to me. Lord Russell put in a good word. And the press about this Payson matter hasn't hurt."

Lenox sat looking at three of the most powerful five men in the party he had always pledged allegiance to, three men offering him what had always been his dream, to do the work his father had done, his grandfather had done, that Pitt and Burke and Palmerston and Peel had done—he looked at them and said, "No."

"No!" said Edmund, now truly roused.

"I have to speak to Jane about it," said Lenox.

"I'm right here, telling you that you ought to

say yes!" said Lady Jane, her hand on his forearm.

He looked at her doubtfully. "Do you mean it?"

"Do I mean it? Of course I do! It's where you belong, Charles."

This was why he loved her: because a thousand times he had said, "This is where I belong, Parliament," to himself, but never to another soul.

He looked at the three men. "Then I accept, of course. It shall be my honor."

"Capital!" said Brick.

The three men crowded around him and shook hands.

"You and I can talk about strategy," said Hilary, who had a prominent voice within the Liberal Party on matters electoral. "You'll have to visit Stirrington soon. Have you ever been?"

"No."

"No matter. There's an excellent election agent there, Talmadge. We'll wire him with your name and background straight away."

"It will play well that you've worked on so many high-profile cases," said Brick.

"How about a meeting this afternoon, Charles?" said Hilary, looking in his pocket diary. "Say, four o'clock?"

"Of course. Where?"

"Oh, in the Members' bar. You'll have to get used to it, won't you?" Hilary said this slyly and then stood, checking his watch and suddenly looking preoccupied. "We'll speak then—and have a celebratory glass of champagne!"

Hilary and Brick shook Lenox's hand and congratulated him, then tipped their hats to Lady Jane and walked out. Edmund said he would stay behind for a moment.

"Well, Charles, and are you pleased?" he said when they were gone.

"Dazzled, more like. I have to thank you."

"On the contrary, it was Brick's idea, and then Hilary's, though of course when they mentioned it I enthusiastically recommended you."

"I still owe you my thanks, then."

Jane said, "Your father would have been so proud!"

"He was awfully proud of you, Edmund, when you took your seat."

"Yes, but I think Jane is right—he would have loved to see the day when we sat side by side on the benches of Parliament."

"Don't be too hasty, either of you," said Lenox, though with a smile on his face.

"Well, well," said Edmund, standing. "After you see Hilary, stop in with me, won't you?"

"Yes, of course," said Lenox.

"Then I'll go."

Edmund said good-bye and walked out into the chill evening, putting his hat on as he went. In the street he thought of something else he wanted to tell his brother, and turned back toward the house—but through the window of the library he saw Lenox and Lady Jane speaking excitedly, and then saw them embrace. So he reminded himself to mention it later and stepped into his carriage, a comprehending smile on his face, off again to work, as above him rivers of autumn pink and purple ran across the heavens.

Center Point Publishing

600 Brooks Road • PO Box 1
Thorndike ME 04986-0001 USA

(207) 568-3717

US & Canada:
1 800 929-9108
www.centerpointlargeprint.com